COMING S[KU-372-391]

DEADLY CONTEMPLATION
TOUGH JUSTICE

DEADLY CONTEMPLATION
UNRAVELLED REVENGE

To: Cathy.

Thank for your support

15/09/2014

DEADLY CONTEMPLATION

ENCOURAGED DECEPTION

G.K. TAYLOR

Visit: www.gktaylor.co.uk

ACKNOWLEDGMENTS

First of all, I would like to say thank you to my children. All of those missed bedtime stories were not in vain! My family have all been understanding and supportive.

A special thanks to Belinda for your ideas. Without it, who knows how far I would have gone.

Thanks to my 'editor/sister in laws' Tanya and Parisse for your 'critical analysis'

Thanks also to my Aunt Patricia, and husband Carl. You have always pushed me to be the best I can be.

And thank you to my friend Dexter for offering to buy the first copy of this book. This means a lot; it shows that you believe in me.

Last but not least, my dad, who has been my role model throughout my life.

A big inspiration comes from up and coming entrepreneur Dwayne Patrick. I wish him all the success with his new children's book "I Can".
Because I did.

CHAPTER 1

She slept long and deep. The shadowy reflection on the wall revealed a six foot tall, medium built man. He was standing over her with a huge knife in his hand. He moved closer and closer towards her chest, leaning forward with one hand reaching for her mouth. He then poked the knife into her heart; twisting it as if he was wrenching the gut of an orange. Blood gashed from the wound and splattered all over his face. She didn't have a chance to scream as he covered her mouth with his big strong hand. He then walked out of the room with a smile. THE END.

"Ahhhh. Is that how it ends?" Paul exclaimed looking at Sophia, before standing up from his seat and attempting to leave.

Other people in the cinema were doing the same from the front row. Paul and Sophia were sitting in the middle and had to wait a few minutes before they could leave after that long and terrifying film. Paul joked with her about how scared she was.

"I shall take a bite," he said as he nibbled on her neck with a wolf like sound.

She wasn't too impressed by his gesture and looked scared—her eyes popped wide open with a chilly, panicked smile. It was about fifteen degrees inside, and a little nippier outside, so Sophia moved closer towards Paul, shaking and looking for warmth. Still shivering Sophia raised her head and looked at Paul wondering how she was going to survive when she got outside. She remembered the argument they'd had about her not wrapping up warmly enough. She looked pitiful so Paul wrapped his dark brown leather jacket around her. As he did so she lifted her head to thank him.

There was a stain on her dress from the Pepsi she'd been drinking when she'd reacted in fear to one of the scenes. Popcorn was stuck to it too and she desperately tried to dust them off before leaving the foyer as Paul's jacket wasn't long enough to hide it. To top it off her dark velvet boots, zipped halfway up, were also packed with popcorn and Paul attempted to help by shovelling them out with his bare hands. She realised they must have fallen in when she'd gripped tight to the seat and slumped backwards, tipping the popcorn off her lap and into the boots.

On top of the frightening scenes, Paul's constant teasing had not helped. Before they went outside he reassured her he would stop joking around and helped her fix her dress as he knew it was partially his fault.

Paul did not drive, so they had to wait for a bus in Stratford. It was getting late, cold and dark. The memory of the film was still vivid in Sophia's mind. Paul was still thinking of having another go at frightening her, as he found it very funny, but remembered his promise. The bus came at about 11:20 P.M. and they got on. Putting his arms around her shoulder, he reassured her that she was safe and protected.

"Did you have a good time tonight?" he asked, while cuddling her tightly to show her how secure she was in his arms, while staring into her eyes.

She whispered, still frightened, "Oh, yes."

They got off the bus close to midnight, with five minutes to walk home. The sound of stray cats moaning in the darkness and the creepy sounds of the wind mixed with momentary silences, created a scary experience on their way home. The walk towards the house along the dark alleyway mirrored some scenes of the movie and scared even Paul. But being a man, he kept his composure and smiled to hide his fears. Sophia watched him out of the corner of her eyes, wondering why he was smiling.

"Have you got your keys?" he asked, as they approached the flat, desperate to get inside.

"Yes," she replied, as she reached in her handbag, scuffled around and handed them over. When they finally got inside she exhaled in relief to be in the comfort of her home. She yawned as she headed towards the bathroom and put on her pyjamas.

"I'm too tired," yawned Sophia, "even to talk tonight. I don't know about you, but I'm going straight to my bed."

"Me too." He got into his night clothes and went straight to bed.

Saturday morning, the day after, Sophia was still asleep. The sun shone brightly through the windows. The blinds were drawn and Paul was downstairs in the kitchen. He took up a knife. He held it in his hand as he thought about how fed up he was with their arguments. The kettle sounded when it boiled and the toaster popped. He poured out hot water into the tea cups, then slid over towards the fridge and took out Sophia's favourite peach flavoured jam for the toast.

Sophia was still in bed in a deep sleep. She twisted and turned and ended up on the right hand side of the bed as she subconsciously fixed her pillow for cosiness. It was now 8 A.M. and she was still drained and exhausted; even the sun shining brightly through the window directly in her face did not wake her. She intuitively felt for Paul on the bed, as she rolled further towards the right, closer to the edge of the bed. She felt his pillow, which was enough to convince her he was still there.

"I love you," she muttered half asleep in her morning voice, not realising he was downstairs in the kitchen.

Meanwhile Paul added Sophia's favourite tea to her cup and made herbal tea for himself. Yesterday's newspaper lay next to the bread pan and Paul spotted the headline: "A man stabbed his wife in her sleep."

"I bet they were arguing a lot," he muttered joking under his breath. "I'm fed up of arguing with Sophia. I hope things will change for the better," he thought, while looking at the knife. It was next to the cups and while he poured out hot water to make her tea he decided to take it with him upstairs. He looked on top of the fridge and took down the two trays. He loaded the first one with her breakfast and realised it would be difficult to carry two trays at once so he decided to make two trips. He silently went upstairs. He got into the room. Sophia was still asleep. He rested the tray on the bedside table. He tiptoed back downstairs so he wouldn't wake her up. He wanted to surprise her. Paul picked up the other tray in one hand and placed his breakfast on it, holding the knife and a carton of orange juice in the other hand.

As he quietly opened the door in the room, Sophia turned, groaned, and stretched as if she was about to wake up, however her eyes remained closed. He rested his tray on his side of the bedside table. Their bed was designed with two wings that could be used as a bedside table, so he knew they had enough room to have breakfast in bed, without resting the food on the bed itself. Paul moved closer to her. He watched her for any sign of stirring. Behind him was the knife. He moved a little closer. He bent forward in an arched position towards her and kissed her on the lips. She opened her eyes.

"Paul," she uttered.

"Yes" he answered with a serious face staring at her.

"Breakfast in bed?" she asked looking at the trays. "What a surprise!"

"Sure, well spotted. I also set you a bath and your toothbrush is ready and waiting with water in the basin," he said.

"Oh, thanks hun. You are so sweet," she replied. "Let me go and brush my teeth." She checked her tray to see if he had brought up everything she needed for breakfast. She saw the jam, toast, orange juice and her tea. "There's something I don't see on the tray that is needed to complete the whole breakfast in bed gesture," she smiled.

"And what is that may I ask madam?" he laughed.

"The knife to spread the jam on my toast," she smiled again, looking innocent. "It was a good try, but incomplete."

"Taddaaa, here it is," smiled Paul, as he took the dinner knife he had from behind his back.

She didn't know why he had kept the knife separate, but she knew he was always joking, so she though it was one of his gimmicks.

Five minutes later she returned after freshening up. Paul looked at her face smiling. He gave her a towel to wipe away the toothpaste residue left on her face. She took it in frustration with a look that said, "What are you saying?" But she sat down quietly and started eating.

"What time did you get up?" she asked, munching with her mouth full.

"6:45 A.M."

"Really?" she said, "that was early. Just to do this all this for me, ermm, I must be special."

"You are, my love, you are," he replied. "Did you see yesterday's papers? A man murdered his wife in her sleep."

"What has this country, or the world, gone to," she uttered, a few minutes later after she swallowed her last pieces of toast. "Too much deception going on these days."

"Well, no deception in this house," he assured her. "Any deception would be to get some of that sexy thing you have going on there," he smiled as he hugged her tightly in anticipation of her giving in.

"What thing?" she smiled pretending she didn't understand but knowing full well what he was talking about.

"And, I'm in that mood," he said.

"Let's watch some TV," she suggested as she attempted to change the subject. "I'm too tired for that. On a different note, when are we going to talk about having children?" Paul turned and looked at her. She stared into his eyes, waiting for an answer.

"We fight too much, let's address that issue first," he said. Paul thought this was a distraction, but she was serious. He moved his head around the room scanning to see what else he could find to occupy his mind. He sensed a tension coming on. He spotted his book.

Paul reached for his book in disappointment as he realised that he wasn't going to get what he had worked so hard for. Sophia watched TV. She rested her head on his legs, while she laid cross-ways on the bed with her legs hanging off the side. He raised his hand to get her attention to indicate the volume was too high and he wasn't able to concentrate on his book.

"The TV volume is too high, can you turn it down please?" he whispered while still looking at his book. She didn't respond so he reached for the remote and decreased the volume.

Sophia thought it was too low and couldn't hear what was being said so she increased the volume even higher than it was before.

"Why did you just do that?" he asked. "I need to finish this book and I can't concentrate while the TV is so high."

"And I need to hear what's going on."

"But I reduced it to an acceptable level," Paul said

aloud but thought to himself she was being selfish. He wanted sex and she knew that, but she wanted his attention instead. They repeatedly adjusted the volume until they reached a stalemate. The tension was building up.

"Who will start the argument first?" thought Paul. He kept his composure.

She kept hers, while looking at him out of the corner of her eyes.

He couldn't keep it in any longer, so he burst out into a rage. "YOU ARE SO SELFISH, DO YOU KNOW THAT?"

She ignored him.

He didn't like to be ignored, so he tried again. "Did you hear what I just said?"

"Yes, I heard," she replied, "but I'm not going continue to entertain your rubbish, as I have done in the past."

"To ignore someone, when they are talking to you, is also rude."

"I know, but what's the point? What better way to keep the peace, than to do just that."

"So, if you think by doing that, you are keeping the peace, think again," he replied. He sighed and tried to read his book again but he was frustrated and the sound from the TV was still bothering him. He wanted to spite her so he put the book down and took up his trousers. He got dressed, slipped on his shoes and walked towards the door. He knew this would upset her. "Payback time," he thought.

"Where are you going?" she asked as he was about to take the first step down the stairs.

He ignored her for a moment. "Now you know what it feels like to be ignored by someone," he said as he carried on downstairs.

She heard the door slam and knew he had gone outside. This was normal and it didn't bother her so she continued to enjoy her programme.

CHAPTER 2

The following evening thoughts of past happiness were going through Martin's mind. His wife, Susan, was tidying up when she saw his pensive face. He was thinking about his younger brother Paul and how he had played with him in the garden when they were young. At the time Paul was twelve and he was eighteen. Martin looked on the table and spotted his favourite mug that was similar to the one Paul had. The difference was that Paul had Donald Duck engraved on his and he had Mickey Mouse; they'd been given them as Christmas presents. Next to the mug was a family photograph framed in a beech wood, antique photo frame. In the photograph he was standing next to Paul, who was wearing a light blue shirt buttoned to his neck and brown, 70s style trousers. Both their shoes were traditional Clarks, with stitched nylon on the front and back that was the style at the time. Behind Paul was ten-year-old Sophia; she was a family friend, and lived next door. She would play with him, although not all of his family knew her parents, as her mum would normally stay indoors, and they had never seen her father. Her mum would allow Sophia to play outside. The lady that visited frequently would normally take her out to play. The family wondered if it was her aunt, as they look alike.

"I didn't think my brother would have grown up to love her," Martin thought to himself contemplating the relationship Paul now had with Sophia. "She was fat back then but beautiful at the same time." He was always protective of his younger brother, but believed it was wrong to fight or hurt anyone as they did, although he would, if he had to.

"Dinner is ready hun," Susan called.

Martin snapped out of his memories. "Sure," he replied, while he picked up his knife and fork ready to pounce on his favourite meal.

"You were miles away hun. Ermm, are you OK?" she asked.

"Yeah. I was just thinking about Paul."

"He is OK, he is a big boy now."

As he was about to eat, the phone rang-it was Paul.

"Martin," said Paul, "we are fighting again."

Martin advised his brother to go out for a walk and cool off as he thought this would help the situation. The call ended. As he made his second attempt to eat his dinner the phone rang again. This time it was Sophia.

"Can I speak to Martin please?" she asked Susan. She was breathing heavily, in rage, but fearful of Paul walking out so late at night as she believed it was dangerous out there. "Can you believe it, we were having a discussion and he just left. He'd been doing this quite a lot recently," said Sophia when Martin came on the phone.

"Really?" replied Martin. "Well, I told him to go for a walk, as I think it's best that he does that to calm down."

"When he comes back in I know he'll either threaten to leave me or hold me down on the bed, jokingly putting the pillow over my head as if threatening to suffocate me, but he won't come to any sort of resolution about the argument we've just had. He will totally ignore everything and act as if nothing happened."

"He is only playing. That is love. Just ignore him," assured Martin. "Take it from a veteran and put on some sexy lingerie for him. This will prevent further arguments."

Susan smiled at his advice, as she poured out his drink. She was interested to hear what was being said, she moved her body closer to Martin eavesdropping. Not hearing Sophia's response from the audible ear piece from the phone, Susan thought she was listening to Martin's advice, and taking it well. Susan moved her body back to her original position, and reached for her glasses. Her intention was to read the paper she wanted to read earlier. She picked it up, while Martin was still on the phone.

The next day Paul called Martin, happiness resonating in his voice. "What did you say to her last night?" he asked Martin.

"Why, were you fighting again?" Martin asked.

"No," Paul replied, "it's the opposite actually."

Martin smiled thinking that his counselling job had paid off. When he had finished on the phone he decided he needed to get something in Lewisham. When he was on the high street he spotted one of his younger brothers Robert. "Hi," he said, as he got closer to him. "Where are you going?"

"I'm off today, so I'm going to do some shopping," replied Robert, who had a dark brown shopping bag in his hand. In it were shoes; one of his favourite brands.

"What is in the bag?" asked Martin, as he tried to peek inside.

"Well, have a look!!" Robert replied joyfully handing the shoes to him.

"Ah," said Martin, "they don't make them as they used to now-a-days. Remember the ones we use to wear? They don't make them that strong anymore."

"I know," replied Robert.

"Anyway, I have to run," said Martin while walking away.

"Have you heard from Paul recently?" shouted Robert.

"Yes, they are at it again," answered Martin, as he walked away, narrowly missing a passer-by who almost knocked him over as he was not paying attention to where he was going and chatting to his friends.

"Youngsters," moaned Robert, as he smiled and said, "later."

"Bye," replied Martin.

Martin got to the shopping centre. He window shopped for a while. His main intention was to buy a pair of the latest Clarks that had come out a month ago. When he went into the store he searched for the shoes on the shelves but was unable to find what he was looking for.

"Excuse me," said Martin to the store assistant. "I'm looking for the latest pair of shoes that came out a month ago."

"Oh, I think know the ones you are talking about," replied the store assistant. "I'm sorry, but they have been sold out."

Martin sighed in disappointment. "Are you sure?" he asked.

The conversation was heard by the store manager who had spotted Martin, one of his favourite customers. He stopped to enquire, "Are you OK Martin?"

The store assistant didn't know that the manager knew him by name. "He was looking for the latest design, but I told him we have sold them out," pointed out the store assistant.

"We have it in stock," replied the manager.

"But—but the four we have are reserved for regular customers," suggested the store assistant. The look on her manager's face was clear to her that he was not prepared to let Martin leave without a pair.

"Martin is one of our most regular customers," replied the manager.

By this time Martin was smiling, as he was happy to be treated this special by the manager. The store assistant had just started working there so she had never met him before, but she went and got the shoes for him. He paid, said his goodbyes and left the store. As he walked away he saw the store manager giving the store assistant a telling off. He had told her to always bring to his attention anyone who asked to buy Deserts. She wasn't happy because she'd spotted another brand of shoes on Martin's feet and didn't think Clarks was his favourite brand or that he was a frequent customer. The two customers, who came in a few minutes after her manager started telling her off, looked and smiled. They recently had a bad experience with her, when she refused to serve them because of their rude behaviour. One of them turned and looked at her with a smirk on her face. The other glanced out of the corner of his eye, while picking up one of the latest pairs of Darby Desert; not the one Martin wanted and showed it to his friend. They bought it and left the shop smiling.

CHAPTER 3

The peace and tranquil atmosphere had set the mood for a quiet discussion at Robert's house. The TV was on but on low volume. Both Robert and his sister Jessica glanced at it from time to time. When Robert saw the news was about to start he turned to face the TV, clutching the remote to increase the volume. Robert and Jessica were sitting in the front room sipping from cups of tea. One of the first news reports was about a husband that killed his estranged wife.

The light in the room was bright thanks to a hundred watt florescent bulb Robert had bought recently from the corner shop. The shop keeper thought Robert was going to have a party before he reassured him it was for this front room. A metre away from them was Mark, Robert's son, sitting around his computer desk revising for his law exams. He needed the bright light for his exam revision. This was his final year at university; he had done well in both his first and second year passing all his modules with first class grades.

The conversation paused for a moment, while Robert stared in silence. He was contemplating how devoted his brother Martin was to the church. His dog Lassie broke the silence when she came storming into the room and crashed into the table, knocking over his drink. Robert went down on his knees and cleaned the mess up before it stained his precious carpet. Jessica had to grab a hold of her drink to save it from toppling over.

"Have you heard from Paul recently?" asked Jessica.

"Not really, I heard he is very happy with his girlfriend," replied Robert

"One of her friends in the church told me that she can be devious," warned Jessica.

"Don't be silly, that girl would not hurt a fly," replied Robert.

"If she ever hurts my brother, I will kill her," thought Jessica.

They continued the conversation for another half an hour, until it was time for Jessica to go. She then called a cab, and left Robert still cleaning up the mess made by his dog.

Two weeks later, a worried Jessica rang Paul to find out how he was doing as she hadn't spoken to him in a while. She was at work and the noise from the photocopier, phones and conversing staff made it difficult for her to concentrate and hear everything he said. But she heard enough to believe that he was doing fine. Her boss was watching her from across the hallway, wondering whether her call was work related, or not. She smiled at him as he cleaned his glasses, then buried his head back into his paperwork, still glancing up at her from time to time. His secretary was standing beside him and attempted to whisper something of importance to him. As he was now distracted, Jessica decided to close her office door for privacy. After she had done so, her mobile went off. She looked at the screen and saw it was Martin. She reduced the volume on her radio and a song by Barry White, and answered the call.

Martin wanted to know if she was going church the following Sunday. As Martin was a Seventh Day Adventist, he wanted to see her on the Sunday, as he worked Monday to Thursday, and was off Friday to Sunday. He wanted to talk to her about the house they'd inherited from their parents. As she was the oldest and the main trustee of the property, he wanted to see if he could put in an offer to purchase the house for himself. But Jessica could see her boss coming towards her office, so she told him that she would call him back. Her boss came into the room pretending to be looking for an important file. He leaned over to see if he could make out any numbers on her mobile phone left idle on her desk. He was the type of boss that checked everything, even when the situation had no relevance to him. His glasses fell off, hitting the table, and ricocheted into her bin. Not able to ascertain anything, he picked up his glasses and went back to his desk, pretending he had left it somewhere else.

Jessica went to see Martin that same evening where they

continued the conversation at his house. Susan was out, so it was the perfect time to have a private conversation. Martin wanted to settle in the U.S. where the house was, but needed financial help to purchase it. Jessica, a chartered accountant, earned the most in the family and agreed to partner with him for both to own the full share of the property. She contemplated asking about Paul, but before she could mention it, he said, "I heard from Paul a few weeks ago." Instantly she looked up.

Really!" she replied. "How is he doing?" she asked, but continued before he could answer. "I rang him earlier too and he sounded OK. I was with Robert on Sunday, and his dog spilled his drink on his precious carpet, you know how he treasures his carpets. You should have seen how he got down on his knees to clean it!"

"Well, everyone treasures something in life," said Martin. "You, your house, for me my God, and my car for me, and Robert his Clarks, and carpets, and for us," said Martin, they both shouted, "our little brother Paul."

"You have left something out," she said, looking at him with a smile; her mouth opened wide waiting for him to tell her.

"What is that?" he asked.

"Your wife!" Martin smiled and assured Jessica that Susan was in a different category. Changing the subject Jessica spotted the family photo; the one Sophia is on when she was ten.

"There is something about his girlfriend I don't trust. She also resembles someone I know," said Jessica.

"Leave them alone, they are young lovers," replied Martin.

"Yes, I suppose," murmured Jessica. "Anyway, I will

let you know if I will be around on Sunday, which is—"
she paused for a moment quietly, looking at the picture
on his table, next to his Mickey Mouse mug, "five days
from now, isn't it?"

Martin replied, "Yes, it is."

"So see you later then, Martin."

"Bye, sis."

Meanwhile, that very same Tuesday night, Paul was
having a quiet time with Sophia. He was only wearing
boxer shorts and she was wearing a range of Ann
Summers lingerie. She was in the middle of the bed while
he sat on the left edge with his back facing the TV and
smiling at her. His drink was on the left wing of the bed.
She seductively called him to come closer but he
reluctantly refused, still smiling. Her lingerie was see
through and her bed slippers were scattered across the
room as she'd run to hop into bed before he came out
the shower, remembering Martin's advice. He then
heeded to feminist pressure, and climbed in next to her.
He was playing rough to the point where the bed was
now only half covered by the fitted sheet. She thought to
herself he was so rough he was going to rape her as he
was aggressive in trying to overpower her on the bed.

As she loved a bit of playing before romance, she
thought it would be a good idea to reverse the situation,
so she pushed him hard over onto his back and pinned
down both his arms with her legs and sat on his chest
close to his face. She then started to kiss him, as she
released his arms sliding her legs on top of him until they

were evenly face to face. They kissed passionately, and stroked each other's bodies. He then rolled her over and started to make love to her. The moans and groans of her passion were heard by the neighbours. One of her fists was clenched, while the other gripped on to the bed rail as it rattled against the wall. He was bursting with passion and whispered her name fervently. Half an hour later they both went downstairs to get a drink to cool off.

She shouted, "Round two," and ran back upstairs.

"Oh, yes," he replied, as he chased after her.

CHAPTER 4

It was raining, cold and dark. Thunder could be heard and lightning illuminated the streets outside Robert's house. The sound of the wind rattled the windows, battering it as if it was being repaired by workmen. Creepy sounds came from the swinging antenna on top of the chimney. Droplets pounded the windows like hailstones. The BBC ten o'clock news had just started while Robert was having a cup of tea, and a few oat biscuits sat next to him on a tray.

One of the stories was about a high profile celebrity accused of rape. While reports of rape were on the increase in the UK, he silently thought to himself that women were sometimes to be blamed for their actions, especially if they were drunk and consenting. The report explained that binge drinking was also on the increase and it was costing the NHS a fortune. In this case the man had been accused of rape but later cleared due to drunken consent that the courts accepted. A BBC reporter caught up with the man near his home and started to interview him.

Robert moved closer towards the TV focusing directly on what was being said. A flash of lightening and peel of thunder frightened him and he jumped in the chair, putting his hand on his chest to feel his pounding heart. It distracted him for a little while, and diverted his attention towards the windows. The power surge from the lightning affected the TV a little bit, but it was not enough to deter his concentration and he knew his surge protector would protect it. The man was still being interviewed and categorically denied raping anyone to the reporter, "Without their consent," he said before approaching his front door.

The next story was about theft also increasing. While Robert was reaching for the remote to switch over to his favourite series of CSI, he heard the doorbell ring. "Who could this be, at this time?" he wondered and waited silently for a second ring but heard nothing. He got up from his chair to investigate searching for the light switch in the dark. Another lightning flash illuminated the passageway and he found the light switch and flipped it. On his way to the door, he almost tripped over his own slippers, left idly by in the passageway. He looked through the peephole and saw a man walking away from the house. The man looked familiar, so he braved it and open the door.

"Excuse me, did you just press this buzzer?" he shouted.

"Yes," the man bravely replied.

As the man came closer Robert recognised it was his

brother Chris, whom he hadn't seen for five years.

"Chris, is that you?" he excitedly asked.

"Yes, it's me alright."

"We haven't seen or heard from you in ages," said Robert. "Where have you been? Come in out of the rain." He rushed his brother inside while the wind blew rain drops in his face.

Robert looked him up and down from head to toe. He hadn't seen him for a long time and wanted to see how much his appearance had changed. He observed his bald head and white t-shirt, with the message, "Rape is wrong, but accusation is even worse." Chris' strange appearance shocked Robert.

On his face were dark glasses that were wet from the rain. Attached to the arm was a string to prevent them from falling to the ground as the arm was wide and worn out. It was barely visible hidden through his bearded face, while tucked behind his ears.

Chris remembered putting them on and how they had fallen off his face, so he tightened the string as he thought his behaviour was similar to that of an old man protecting his glasses. He also knew that he had to protect his identity now he was back in town. His ash grey jeans and Nike trainers were similar to Robert's and caught his brother's attention. Around his neck was a chain with a crucifix pendant hitched to it. Robert laughed at him for wearing dark glasses at night. He took them off as he entered the house; he knew Robert was just taking the mickey and ignored him. Chris had just come back from the States after being accused of attempted murder. It was self defence and he was found not guilty by the court. He told Robert about the case that night. Robert knew his brother had a bad temper and that he got upset very easily sometimes.

Robert also knew that Chris had dumped the girl he was lodging with who he had been seeing briefly in the States after she had accused him of rape – he'd been told this by a friend. He had never cheated on his long term relationship of 15 years and he'd been accused after a one night stand with the girl in the States. The girl he lodged with there was not willing to accept that it was just that. Chris had always been seen as loner by his family as he kept his personal life a secret, but he did visit them from time to time. As the conversation developed, Chris told his brother bits of his story of living in the States.

"How is everyone doing? Where is my little brother Paul?" he asked, while placing his trainers on the radiator to dry.

"Fine," replied Robert.

They chatted until late that night, before they went off to sleep.

The next day, Robert was downstairs in the kitchen before Chris got up at about 8:30 A.M. and joined him. Robert was sitting around the table reading his morning newspaper and spreading his toast with his favourite strawberry jam. The kettle had just boiled and was still cooling down. Chris thought a fuse had blown in the fuse box in the kitchen.

Chris looked over his brother's shoulder and saw the headline: "Hit man hired to murder business man." He then looked at the table, which was when Robert offered him his breakfast. While they sat around the table silently, the quiet atmosphere was disturbed by a phone call from

Paul. Robert answered it and his face took on a frantic look and he shouted, "What!!" Chris looked on attentively to hear what was being said. He heard Robert telling Paul that his brother Chris was here.

Chris smiled and said, "Tell him I will come and see him soon."

The phone call ended and Chris anxiously waited to hear what it was all about. Robert explained that Paul had broken up with his girlfriend Sophia.

Chris showed no emotion, but asked, "When did this happen?"

"Last night," he replied, "I saw it coming."

"Really, why?"

"They were too close, ermm, and fought all the time," he said looking Chris in the eye as if he was suggesting he had always known the relationship wouldn't work.

Chris was not bothered either way, so they continued the conversation.

12 P.M. that same day, Paul showed up at his sister's work place and broke the news to her. As Paul entered her office, her boss' secretary went over to him and whispered something, as she normally did when Jessica had visitors. Her boss smiled and stared back at Jessica as if he was saying, "OK, it's time to get back to work now."

"They must be having an affair," thought Jessica.

Paul closed the door behind him. He asked her if he could crash with her at her house until he had sorted himself out. She gladly offered him the spare room, while she tried to send an email to a client, focusing on Paul and the email at the same time.

"When can I move in?" he asked.

"Hang on," she replied, as she clicked the send button and watched it being delivered. "Tonight, of course," she answered now she was able to concentrate on the conversation. She checked her watch and saw that it was 12:30 P.M. "I am going for lunch now, would you like to join me?"

"Sure," he replied.

Jessica gathered her things and took her office keys, which were hanging on the key holder next to the coat hanger. As they walked through the corridor, the boss' secretary smiled at Paul. He smiled back, looking at her bottom, almost knocking over the chairs near the stairs where visitors sat.

The secretary thought to herself, "He looked really handsome."

Paul contemplated asking her out but realised it was too soon to date after breaking up with Sophia. Nevertheless, he thought, "She looked really sexy."

Jessica knew what he was thinking, and muttered under her breath, "Keep your eyes off," as they exited down the stairs.

"I wonder if this girl is a slag. Every client that comes in, she would smile and flirted with them," thought Jessica, as she continued down the stairs. "Maybe I'm just jealous; it is her job to greet visitors when they are here to see the boss. She is really attractive—I must stop this," continued Jessica in her head. She remembered an ex member of staff who knew the secretary well, saying that she was the opposite of what she thought of her, and that she had self-respect. Jessica was still not convinced. She took it upon herself to try and find out more about her work colleague. She would occasionally invite her out to lunch.

Two months later, Paul got the secretary's number from Jessica. She was reluctant to pass it on as she believed the boss may be sleeping with her and didn't want her brother to be getting involved. The few times she'd been out to lunch with her boss's secretary revealed nothing. She would not divulge any information about herself unless she is confident that she could trust the person. She clearly didn't trust Jessica. Not that much it appeared.

Later that day the secretary's phone rang for a couple of minutes. She normally refused to answer anonymous calls but she eventually answered it.

"Hello, who is this?" she asked.

"It's me, Paul," he replied.

"Paul, from where?"

"I got your number from Jessica, my sister," he explained.

"Oh, it's you," she realised as she filed documents and smiled.

"I'm sorry to have called you like this, but is it possible to meet one day?"

"Maybe," she replied, in a seductive voice.

"I'm sorry, but I cannot remember your name," he enquired.

"My name? It's Jade," she answered.

"Nice to meet you Jade," he responded.

"Same here, look! I have to go now," rushed Jade.

"OK, save my number and we will talk again soon, bye."

CHAPTER 5

When Paul showed up at Jessica's office at lunchtime, he brought a bunch of flowers with him. He rang the bell, and waited for the receptionist to let him in.

"Morning, can I leave these for Jade please?" he asked.

"Who should I say it's from?" asked the receptionist, as she took them from him.

"Don't worry, it's got a note attached to it," he said, as he whisked outside the door in a hurry.

Jessica looked from her office, and saw the flowers being delivered to Jade. She wondered who could have sent them to her. Jade's boss looked a bit jealous, as she read the note, blushed and smiled.

"Ermm, who-who are they from?" asked her boss, stretching his neck and trying desperately to see what was written on the card. Without his glasses, he couldn't see anything, so he had to rely on her response.

"A secret admirer," smiled Jade.

Jessica popped over to satisfy her curiosity. This was not the first time she had sought to find out information on Jade and the memory of that moment was still fresh in her mind. Nevertheless she decided to try again. "This person is interested, it seems," she said to Jade as she fished around to get answers.

Jade knew what she was doing but she could still vividly recall Jessica prying into her affairs in the past, especially during their lunch trips. It was the battle of the minds which no one was going to win. It was obvious that both were playing mind games. "Wouldn't you like to know," smiled Jade, as she expanded the suspense even further and happily went to the kitchen to search for a vase. Under the cupboard she found one that had been used for the previous year's Christmas party. She filled it with water and placed her dozen red roses in there.

Her boss followed her into the kitchen, pretending to be searching for milk in the refrigerator to make a cup of tea. This time he was armed with his glasses. He remembered how close he was to identifying the note on the card. Behind him was Jessica who wanted to see what was going on. She knew that their boss was just being nosy, by pretending to search for milk, and she was doing the same. Jade had become the centre of attention, but she was aware of it and playing hardball. Jade hid the card from both of them. She was assertive and smiled for the rest of the day. In her mind she contemplated calling him to thank him for the gift, but she wanted to do it after work, as she didn't want more attention from the prying ears and eyes. Four o'clock came and there was an hour to go before the close of business but her feeling of anxiety made it difficult to wait. She succumbed to her desire, and went to the toilet, called and thanked him. During that conversation, he asked to take her out for lunch the next day. She knew she wasn't going to let the offer pass, so she willingly accepted.

The next day they met up for lunch. They knew that it was best to have lunch some distance away to keep the suspicion of her colleagues at bay and avoid staff seeing them together. She observed the white t-shirt he was wearing titled: "Deception and love don't mix." She wondered why he would wear something like that on a first date and realised he wanted her to get the message loud and clear. It was almost a turn off for her, but the flowers saved the day. She was however impressed by his taste in clothes and style. She examined his True Religion jeans that were ripped in the style of the day. He also wore the latest Desert Clarks, although they had almost got wet as he narrowly missed a puddle as they were making their way towards the restaurant.

For Paul, Jade's beautiful pink dress with white lace edges, reminded him of a similar one he bought some time ago for Sophia. And the sight of her velvet laced boots taunted him as they brought back memories of the night of the cinema with Sophia. It wasn't the film that freaked him out this time, but memories of her that were sunk in his heart. Some of these were good and some were bad and he checked himself wondering if he missed her. He looked again at her shoes and spotted a slight difference; although they were similar to the ones Sophia wore, Jade had lace on hers matching her dress. As they got to the restaurant, he opened the door for her, and she smiled and thanked him for being such a gentleman. They sat at their reserved table and were approached by a waiter.

"The lady orders first," he said.

The table was decorated with candles, flowers, and a card. She was taken aback as she realised he must have organised it beforehand. She didn't want to show too much emotion on her first date even though she was bursting with it and it was hard to contain. She felt as if he were hitting the right buttons. The waiter proceeded with their orders while they sipped red wine.

"What is so special about me?" she asked.

"Well, it's your as ... sorry, your beautiful smile," he answered. He remembered looking at her bottom when he visited Jessica at work.

"Tell me about yourself," she enquired.

"Well, I'm single, poor, greedy, and love fat women," he said knowing she was slim built.

"And?" she pushed.

"I am also interested in secretaries, and mixed race girls. I'm joking," he laughed. "I'm honest, friendly, hardworking, and hate deception. I've lost my job recently, and I'm qualified as an electrician. I also know how to fix computers. What about you?"

"I'm a qualified PA, working for ten years, I'm a bit older than you, and I don't like short men."

As Paul was shorter than her, he wondered if he had a chance after hearing that statement. But just as he'd joked with her earlier, it became apparent she was doing the same. He decided not to let her comments bother him. His intention was to win her although he realised he hadn't had to work so hard with Sophia as they had grown up together.

But they'd got this far and he told himself that it was

looking positive. The conversation continued for 45 minutes before he walked her back to her work. As they approached the building, they were spotted by Jessica, who was just coming back from her lunch break. Piecing the puzzle together, Jessica realised the flowers had come from Paul. Jade also had the same look on her face as when she had received them.

"Hi Jessica," said a frightened Jade.

"Hi. Where are you guys, coming from? Ah, you went on a date? That is why you are dressed so elegantly today, Jade," smiled Jessica. She had never seen her brother looking so happy. His encounter with Sophia hadn't lasted that long, although they'd know each other a long time and from what she heard it had never been that happy. This didn't change her perception of Jade, as she still believed she was secretly going out with the boss, but she was also happy to see Paul smile again.

That same evening, Paul and Jessica had dinner. Jessica questioned Paul about Sophia to see if Paul had gotten over her. Jade and Paul had been secretly corresponding, and seeing each other for a few months, but the memories of Sophia was still vivid in his mind.

As he moved towards the TV his wallet fell out on the floor. He went to pick it up, but he was distracted by a photo of the family on the TV stand. In the picture everyone was conversing except for Chris. Paul pointed this out to Jessica to see if she could tell him why. She explained how Chris had always been the quiet one in the family. His wallet was still on the floor so Jessica bent to pick it up. A photo of Sophia fell from it and she was convinced that he had not gotten over her. Looking at her little brother, she remembered when he was born.

The Reynolds family was a close knit family; Mr and Mrs Reynolds and their five children. Mr Reynolds died four years before his wife, leaving Jessica (the eldest) feeling that she needed to protect her younger siblings, especially Paul – the baby of the bunch. Born premature, Paul was very much loved and cherished by both his parents and siblings, who consider him lucky.

"Look at him, he is going to survive," said Mrs Reynolds.

"Yes, he will," responded her husband, as he walked over to the incubator to watch his son breathing. Born two months early, Paul was wired up from head to toe. The ventilator placed in his mouth drew his father's attention to his inconsistent breathing. The various heavy wires and tubes were also a cause for concern to his father; who thought they looked really uncomfortable for someone so delicate.

As if reading his mind, a neonatal nurse appeared to fix the baby's ECG, blood monitor and feeding tube. After taking note of the various readings, she advised them that all was well and suggested that they get some sleep, as they hadn't left the baby's side since his delivery to the unit.

"I'll be back tomorrow son," said Mrs Reynolds, her voice breaking as she tried to stop the tears that had been welling up from falling. Her husband reached into his pocket, and pulled out a handkerchief. Struggling to control his own emotions, he extended his right arm whilst moving towards her. After she'd dried her eyes, He then moved even closer, and cuddled her.

Jessica, Martin, Robert and Chris the youngest of the

group, looked helpless at their parents in distress.

"You must protect this lucky boy, as he grows," said Mrs Reynolds as she wiped her tears for the third time. They all nodded. Chris looked on in oblivion as he tried to comprehend what his mother had just said.

Jessica continued to look back, while Paul went to the kitchen. She remembered one of her favourite doll. Jessica rubbed her fingers on the front of the photo, almost in tears. She saw herself in her church dress. The hospital visit was the Saturday, as she remembered the next day.

It was Sunday morning. The Reynolds were getting ready for church. Jessica was always playing with her dolls. She would do this every day before leaving the house. Martin; as always was reading his bible. This was a pleasing sight for his parents to see at least one of their children following their example. Robert climbed over Martin who was blocking the doorway; as he wanted to make his way towards the shoe stand. He stretched his arm towards the top shelf of the shoe stand trying to grab a hold of his pair. He was much shorter than the stand. In a corner where he'd kept his things, were four pairs of his own shoes, and he wanted to make it his fifth. Mrs Reynolds didn't know why he was gathering his shoes, as she watched his every move. "Look at him, he is going to be the most organised of them," whispered Mrs Reynolds to her husband, as she ran the iron over Robert's trousers. She then looked over in the far right corner of the room, and spotted Chris. His father also observed him; who sat by himself playing. He was playing with his soldier toys, and water gun. "He is such a loner," whispered Mrs

Reynolds, while Mr Reynolds nodded in agreement, and smiled.

"Come on boys, it's time to go," said Mr Reynolds in his deep voice. Everyone moved instantly, as they feared him. Chris was still playing with his toys. "Did you hear what I said boy."

"Yes, dad," said Chris, but still not moving. He moved five minutes later. Mr Reynolds knew that Chris was the child that was going to be tough to handle. But he would not allow any of his sons to be unruly.

Jessica thought Jade was the better option for Paul when she compared the two. She wasn't a fan of Sophia and believed she was devious and would stop at nothing to get her way. Paul however, believed that there was a future with Sophia, but questioned whether he would have been happy living with her as husband and wife. This same thought came to his mind as he saw Sophia's picture on the floor. His behaviour towards the picture was such that it gave the impression that she meant nothing to him anymore, and he had forgotten that it was in his wallet.

"Jade or Sophia?" laughed Jessica.

"Neither," smiled Paul.

"Well, it's been seven months," she said.

"Can we watch TV?" asked Paul, as he tried to change the subject, and picked up the remote next to his tea. He quickly switched the TV on and started to scan the channels.

Jessica wasn't going to let him off so lightly. She smiled as she thought to herself, "You think I believe you have gotten over Sophia, well let's see what happens

41

when we watch Sophia's favourite soap." She wanted to see how far she could push him to reveal more so she suggested they watch one of the programs Sophia liked.

"Why, would you want to watch that, it's boring," answered Paul, rejecting her suggestion. He remembered what one of his friends had taught him; to take the heat off yourself you have to reverse the question.

They both were playing games; Jessica was searching while Paul was hiding his feelings. He tried everything. He realised that she was very persistent, so he planned an escape strategy. He went to get something to eat. While he was heading towards the kitchen, he saw a handwritten note on the table in the sitting room. He didn't want to pry as he respected his sister's privacy, but couldn't help but notice that it was from a man he thought he saw called, Waitie. He also spotted the word *love* and *forgiven*. He paused for a while to read it and saw the words, *Tina was a mistake*. He couldn't make much of it, so he carried on to the kitchen and grabbed himself a snack. He stayed in the kitchen for a little while to avoid the questions. He also didn't want to question her, so he quietly sat back down where he was sitting, staring at the same photograph he saw earlier next to the TV.

Changing the subject, he asked, "Have you recently broken up with anyone?"

"Not really," she replied. "Why do you ask?"

"Nothing really, I just wondered if you can relate to my situation."

"You mean Sophia or Jade?" smiled Jessica.

"Not again," he thought. "Both," he replied. "Have you ever been betrayed, or deceived?"

"Well, I knew a guy once, and he lied to me; it's

history now," she responded. Waitie came to her mind as she responded, but she tried to dismiss it in her head. She knew it was hard to forget history but she thought it should be easy for Paul as she wasn't a fan of Sophia.

Telepathically, it was Waitie, he had in his mind that deceived her, and it was on her mind.

The letter was on Paul's mind as he tried to work out a link. He wanted to know more about his big sister. He thought of speaking to Martin, as he knew they were close, and he might have shared the letter with him. But he didn't know how to approach Martin. So he contemplated talking about his relationship with Sophia, as he believed that might lead to an openness between them.

"You are very secretive, sis," he said.

"Am I? I share almost everything with your brother, Martin, maybe not you," joked Jessica.

"Really! Why not me?" asked Paul. "Has he ever done anything to protect you while you were growing up?"

"Well, he knocked out a guy for me once," laughed Jessica, "the guy was stalking me, and he was warned by Martin, but he didn't listen," she continued, folding up her ironed clothes. She also hung some of Paul's in his wardrobe.

"Martin? He wouldn't hurt a fly," smiled Paul, as she handed him the rest of his trousers.

"Well he hurt that guy, I thought he was going to kill him," said Jessica, picking up the clothes basket, and switching off the iron. "Can you pack away the ironing board for me please?"

"Sure, where should it go?"

"In the cupboard in the wash room," she said and

they carried on the conversation. "The guy never looked at me again, even on the day we were moving out of the area."

Paul ended the conversation because he needed to make plans for his trip to Lewisham.

CHAPTER 6

Three years later Paul saw Sophia in the Lewisham shopping mall.

He walked over to her and said, "Hi."

"Hi," she replied.

"How are you keeping?" he asked, feeling sorry for her, and wanting to give her a cuddle.

She wanted the same, but refused to be seen as weak, so she pretended to be over him. "I'm OK," she responded brightly. But in her mind, she thought, "You are the reason for all my failed relationships; you will pay one day, although I still love you." Instead she said aloud, "I have to go now," and pretended she didn't have time to chat. Deep down she was suffering and she walked off wondering if she had just destroyed her only chance of rekindling their relationship.

"OK, take care."

The sound of *take care* rang in her ears. No one saw

the tears except an old lady passing by. Sophia turned her head and looked at one of the stores. She saw Paul's reflection as he watched her walk away. Her heart sank. She desperately wanted to go back, but her pride kept her from doing so. He watched her as she disappeared around the corner, then he turned the other way and carried on walking.

She went back to the flat in Stratford. On her way back, she stopped at her mum's, Tina.

"You don't look OK," said Tina, observing her daughter.

"I'm keeping fine, Mum," Sophia replied.

"Really, or maybe you are suffering in silence?" Tina enquired.

"Mum, it has been three years, it is enough time for anyone to get over anyone," she assured her mum, dusting and adjusting the furniture.

She did this all the time, and her mum hated it. She placed the cushion on the sofa in a diamond shape, while her mum fixed it back to its squared shape. Her mum had told her before not to come to her house and give it a makeover. Set in her ways, Sophia ignored her. She looked towards the kitchen to see if there were dishes to be done, but knowing who she was, her mum was prepared. It was not that her help wasn't appreciated, but Tina liked her place to look a certain way. Tina was baffled by her willingness to tidy up. It had been a task to get her to tidy her room when she was younger, and in her teenage years, especially when she was playing, or talking to Paul. She remembered on one occasion she'd called her in to tidy her room and Sophia had cried all day because she didn't want to do it. But Tina hadn't let her off and persisted that she had to tidy her room whether she wanted to or not.

Meanwhile, back at her own flat, Sophia sat in silence for two hours, contemplating revenge. She believed Paul had ruined her life. The sight of him had brought back mixed memories. She knew she had never fully gotten over him, although she tried to paint a different picture to her mum. She called a friend and they decided to meet up.

Before setting out she took a bath. She lit four candles on the edges of each corner of the bath. The candles were situated where her feet was pointing; there were two red ones which had burnt down quicker than the pink ones at her shoulders. She leaned back in a relaxing position and the aroma of the candles provided a relaxing atmosphere. A few minutes later in the dark, she started to cry. She looked up to see if it was possible to still see her reflection in the dark. She didn't want to see her own face. She didn't like being weak, but losing Paul had tested her. She realised it was not possible to reach the drawer, given her position in the bath, unless she stood up. As she got up she hid her face from the mirror. She felt in the drawer for the pills she took for a bladder infection as she'd missed taking the day's dose. She didn't know how vulnerable she was with a bottle of pills in her hand. On top of the drawer was a large kitchen knife which caught her eyes. She and Paul had put it there for security. She took the knife in one hand, the pills in the other. She was crying.

She poked the knife into the stuffed teddy next to her on the toilet seat; Paul had given it to her as a birthday present. She wondered if she could really do that in real life. She felt bitter and angry. She got back in the bath leaving the knife stuck in the teddy. The pills were in her right hand. She felt sleepy after she'd soaked for about twenty minutes and decided it was time for bed. She believed a good night's sleep would rid her of all her negative thoughts. She got out of the bath and prepared for bed. Her mind was so consumed with thoughts she forgot where she had left the pills. She searched in the dark for them but couldn't find them and decided to give up looking and go to sleep. She knew they weren't sleeping pills, but anything to rid her mind of memories of Paul would be justified. She was happy she wasn't able to locate them in that state of mind as killing herself went against her principles. As she made her way out of the bathroom, releasing the water from the bath, she thought of switching off her phone, as she didn't want to be disturbed. But little did she know she was about to be surprised by a strange man at the door.

When the doorbell rang she rushed to get dressed. She went to the door and looked to see who it was. "Who is it?" she shouted, as she held the knife behind her.

"Sorry, for the late visit, but I'm here to check on your boiler," replied the stranger. "My name is, just called me "Wa, never mind," as the stranger attempted to give his name, but drew it back. He placed his tool box on the floor, and stood up. He held on to his ID; holding up for visibility. When he heard the rattling of chains from the door he released it, which swung and settled behind his tie.

At this time, the door was slightly opened but hinged on the security chain. She refused to let anyone in at that time. She was suspicious but the stranger had familiar features about him and could have passed as her brother. The stranger looked her in the eyes as if he'd seen her before. She looked at him in that same way. Sophia was curious.

"Are we related?" she asked, as she looked him up and down.

"I don't think so," he replied, "I will come back tomorrow." Around his neck, was his ID. She only got a glimpse of it and made out the name *W..ty* as it was hidden by his tie. She spotted the council logo which was enough to convince her but she wanted to know if he was contracted by another company.

"What is the name of your company?" she enquired.

"I'm from the local council," he replied.

I know, but do you work for a contracting company?" The stranger refused to go into any details.

"Don't worry, I understand it's late, I will come back tomorrow," he replied, and ignored her specific question. While he was walking away, he kept on looking back, and shaking his head, as if he wanted to say more or felt sorry for her. Sophia knew there was something about the stranger, but she couldn't put her finger on it. She decided to investigate. By this time, she had cancelled the meeting with her friend until the following day due to lateness, and her strange encounter. She went back to her room, and settled herself down on the bed. She wondered where to start, before she'd fallen off to sleep.

The next day, she decided to ring her mum to enquire if she had a brother that she knew nothing about. She was perplexed by the thought of a man showing up late at night that looked like her. "I wonder if he was my brother? There's only one way to find out," she said to herself.

When Sophia asked her mum, Tina waited for a while in disbelief before replying, as she was taken back by the question. She was knitting a jumper for next winter and as her arms shook in panic, so too did the red, blue and green thread. She had to assure Sophia that she had no brother, but she was bewildered, perturbed and reticent to respond and the look of guilt and concealment was vivid on her face. She was happy Sophia wasn't there in person as her face would have given her away.

"Mum, are you telling me the truth?"

"Yes, I am," grunted Tina.

"Then, why did you pause for a while, before answering the question?" she continued, thinking her mum was hiding something. Tina turned to other side of the chair and crossed her legs. She moved the phone from the left ear to the right.

"I was just wondering, where this question is coming from. You have never asked me this before," replied Tina.

"Sorry, Mum, some parents have hidden siblings from their other children before. I'm not saying that you have, but I just wondered. Anyway, I have to go Mum, I will call you again later," rushed Sophia, as she said her goodbyes.

"Bye hun," replied Tina.

Tina stopped knitting and went for a drink in the kitchen. She remembered the son she had only met briefly and the conversation with the nurse when she was told he died at the hospital after she gave birth. She pondered over this as she sat quietly on the sofa. The memory of a story on the radio recently was also vivid in her mind and thoughts of her son's death came back to haunt her. She had tried for years to bury them, but felt guilty, as if she blamed herself for his death. She switched on the radio, and heard the same report again of how police had interviewed nurses from an East London hospital on the alleged suspicion of child abduction in the 1980s. They believed that they'd made a breakthrough in the case. She thought hearing the report would only exacerbate the situation. Ironically, it gave her hope. She knew the challenge for her would be breaking the news to Sophia, given that she had lied to her.

When Tina heard the story on the radio, she knew that there was hope, of her son being alive. She remembered how the news of his death had devastated her. Initially it hadn't as she was too weak and tired after the labour. A bright light was shone in her face and she heard sounds coming from her bedside that concerned her. She thought she was in the operating theatre. Her tired body couldn't move not even to turn her head to identify who was there. She increased the volume on the radio, which took her back to reality. She remembered Sophia's dad telling her not to do any lifting when she was pregnant with their son. She started feeling guilty as if it was her fault her baby son had died. The conflicting memories of uncertainty plagued her mind as tears flowed down her cheeks, as she tried desperately to console herself.

She remembered saying to Sophia's dad, "You only love that woman, not us - just go." She rushed to the kitchen again, opened the drawer where the cutlery was stored, and pulled out a knife. She slowly walked towards the back room. She rested it on the table next to a loaf of bread she had wanted to use for her sandwich, before being disturbed by Sophia's phone call. She took up the knife and buttered her bread for the sandwich. Finishing her lunch took her mind off things for a while. She was also distracted by the antique show that was being aired on TV at the time.

In the meantime, Sophia waited for the return visit from the mysterious council worker. She knew he had to be more than just a plumber hired to repair the boiler. She spent the whole morning waiting for him, wondering if he was a relative and someone was hiding something from her. When he didn't show up, which raised alarm bells, she became suspicious and set up an appointment to visit the police station. Before going to the station she wanted to talk the matter over with a friend and confront her mum again, this time face to face. The prime suspect was her mum. Sophia decided to probe more into the matter, so she invited her mum over that evening. While she was waiting for her mum, she looked through her window and saw a man that looked similar to the one that had visited her last night. The stranger walked passed the house twice.

She decided to investigate, wondering if he had missed the address as it had been quite late when he came last night. By the time she got to the window closest to the door the man had disappeared. She rushed to open the door. She looked left and right, but he was nowhere to be found. Her friend dropped by afterwards and they spoke for twenty minutes. She didn't want to entertain him for long as she knew her mother was coming around and she didn't want her to see him, so he left shortly after their conversation. Sophia's mum had never met this man. He had barely walked ten metres from the house, when she spotted her mum coming. The narrow pathway meant they would pass within a close proximity of each other, but her mum's head was held straight and she didn't realise he was coming from Sophia's house. All she knew was that she'd walked pass a stranger. He himself didn't know it was Sophia's mum. It appeared that Sophia didn't want her friend to know or met her mum. Tina came in and sat next to Sophia's computer. On the computer desk, was a book titled, *The brother I never met*. She was uneasy again and thought she had put it there deliberately. She had no intention of telling her about her brother until she had learnt the truth; then there would be no reason for holding it back from her.

"Mum, can I get you a drink?"

"Yes please."

"What would you prefer Mum?"

"Well, something strong."

"Here's a beer," she offered.

"Thanks."

"Mum, I want to know about my dad."

"What about him?"

"First of all, do you know where he is?" Sophia asked.

"No," she replied.

"Do you know if he had any other children?"

"Not that I'm aware of. All I know for sure is that he is a dangerous man," she replied.

"Why do you say that Mum?"

"I saw him with a gun once, this was years back," she replied. She wanted to paint a bad image of him so Sophia would not delve too much into knowing him as she had had bad experiences in the relationship. But Sophia was not put off by her response; instead she wanted to know more.

"A gun?"

"Yes, a gun."

"Why did you guys break up?" asked Sophia.

"He was in love with another woman," she said, sobbing slightly.

"Why are you crying Mum?" asked Sophia, as she handed her mum a handkerchief.

"This brings back painful memories."

"Do I know this person?" asked Sophia.

"Well, yes, but I don't want to get into that now," replied Tina, as she assured Sophia that her dad loved her very much and would die to protect her. Sophia looked confused. "How can someone love their child so much to the point they would die for them, but yet don't visit them? That doesn't make sense to me," thought Sophia. Tina changed the subject, and continued the conversation. She stayed for another hour before rushing to get a bus to go into to Stratford centre.

That same evening she told her mum that she would be going to the police station, but she didn't say when or why. Her mum thought she was going to report her dad to the police.

"Don't do anything stupid," said Tina.

"No, Mum, I just need to pay someone back, nothing to worry about," she assured her.

Tina was worried but she didn't pry as she trusted her

daughter not to do anything stupid.

CHAPTER 7

A few days later, Susan was visiting the East End of London to do some shopping. She was going past the police station when she spotted Sophia emerging from the front door. Susan's first impression was she was visiting a friend or a family member. Sophia was shocked to see Susan, but didn't say anything. And even if she did, Susan wouldn't have heard, because the sound of sirens from the police cars rushing out of the station on emergency calls would have drowned out her voice.

Susan had actually stopped outside the police station as she had lost her bearings on the way to the shops. She was just about to ask a police officer on the steps outside for help, when she suddenly worked out where she was. The officer had turned towards her but realised she no longer needed his assistance. It was then Susan spotted Sophia. Afterwards she continued on her way to the shops.

"Not again, two in one week," though Sophia, after she realised Susan had spotted her. "I saw Jessica recently, and now Susan. I'm not going to say hello," thought Sophia. She remembered seeing Jessica recently, as visible as she was seeing Susan. Unlike Jessica's sighting, there was no bus to escape.

Sophia believed that Paul shouldn't have left her because of their silly arguments. She also thought there was more to it than just simply arguments between them. She knew she wasn't Jessica's favourite sister-in law. Her memory was cased back to that moment she saw Jessica. She saw her and Jade walking on the high street near her workplace, and felt that one day she would encourage Paul to go out with one of her work colleagues.

"Look at them," whispered Sophia to her friend. "Who is that girl she is walking with?" she continued.

"Can't you see it's her work colleague, look," said the friend. "They work over there." They glanced over the shoulder of the newspaper seller that had his table next to the white van. The bus stop was five metres away from the van. Sophia's friend slowly eased her head up and spotted the accountancy display sign next to Jessica's office window.

"Jessica doesn't like me, I'm sure she is grooming her friend for Paul," thought Sophia. Out of view, Sophia and her friend moved towards the parked white van and took cover, as she didn't want to be seen by Jessica. Sophia then moved to the left next to the bus stop, extended her arm, and flagged down an approaching bus, watching to see if Jessica was looking their direction. In anxiety to leave, they slipped on the bus from the side door alerting the driver who asked to see their tickets. It was a narrow escape, as Jessica eyes, for some reason fixed on the same bus, but didn't know Sophia was on board.

Sophia grew bitter and suspicious towards Paul ever since that sighting of Jessica and Jade. The chip on her shoulder was never going to go away. Some of the arguments would be accusations of Paul having an affair. Sophia wouldn't name anyone particularly, but in her mind she thought it was Jessica's intention to split then up. As she believed Paul was foolish and easily influenced by his sister, she blamed his weakness for the break up as well. This built up enough resentment for Paul and the family.

A few hours later in Kent, Paul was relaxing with his girlfriend Jade. She was on holiday for a couple of days, and while he was actively looking for work he wanted to make the most of her time off. They had to increase the volume on the TV as the sound of police sirens passing by through the area was deafening. Paul increased the volume and connected the surround sound to it. As he stood up from the speaker he had just connected, he glanced out the window and saw the police cars. He wasn't bothered by them nor interested in what was going on outside. Shortly afterwards Jade heard the doorbell. She alerted him to it but he ignored it. It rang again. He went downstairs to open it. He saw police lights flashing from the car parked up in front of the gate, as he glanced from the side window as he approached the door. He opened the door.

"My name is PC Smith. Are you Mr. Paul Reynolds?"

"Yes," replied Paul.

PC Smith pushed himself in uninvited.

Paul violently fell to the ground, and shouted, "What is this about?"

As Jade heard what was going on she frantically rushed downstairs to his aid.

"You are under arrest on suspicion of rape," said PC Smith, "you do not have to say anything. However, it may harm your defence if you do not mention when questioned something, which you later rely on in court. Anything you do say may be given in evidence."

While PC Smith led him away to the van handcuffed, he saw tears flowing down Jade's face. The look on his face demonstrated how upset and embarrassed he was, especially when he saw his neighbour's son looking from the window. Although, the boy next door was just a teenager, Paul had a reputation to protect and believed the kid looked up to him as a role model. The girl from across the road whom he did not get on with also saw the police cars, but didn't see him get into the car. That brought him some comfort as the cars sped off with him to the station.

An hour later, he was processed and detained at a southeast London police station. He used his call to inform his brother Martin. A duty solicitor proceeded with him to the interviewing room, which was when reality hit him. He was by himself in the room while the interviewing officer spoke to the solicitor outside. It was slightly dark in the room and he felt intimidated. Behind him, he saw a big mirror on the wall. He went straight to it, as he wanted to see how stressed he looked, and how he would be seen during the interview. He tried to stay calm, as he wanted to give the impression he had nothing to fear as he knew he was innocent. However that was not that easy as the reality was he was still tense. The thought that officers, like in the movies, may have been watching him from behind the mirror was not a concern, as he believed his impression would be what would make the difference. He heard the officers coming as he made his way back to his chair. He sat on the right of the desk and his solicitor on the left.

The two officers sat in front of them and one explained that the interview was an opportunity to put forward his side of the story. Paul's eyes widened when he saw the volume of paperwork the officer slammed on the table, then heard the clicking of the tape recorder. He pulled himself up and sat straight, positioning himself ready for the interview. He observed his surrounding to check if there were CCTV cameras. He sat still and felt confident that his behaviour would not give him away. His fingers were twitching as he desperately tried to control his nerves. Fortunately his shaking legs were hidden from view. The interrogation seemed more problematic than he anticipated. Under the table was the damaged leg of the table that was cracked in the middle. He had noticed it earlier. His misguided belief that his trembling legs would snap it in two was a sign that he was not in control, although he knew what he had to do.

The officer read out the charge against Paul again and asked him, "Do you know who the victim is?"

"Not really," he replied.

The officer looked at Sophia's statement. "The alleged victim is, Ms Sophia Wait."

"It's not true," he said and vigorously defended himself, as his fingers twitched harder in anger.

The interview went on for an hour, and then he was sent back to his cell. The police sent both statements to the Crown Prosecution Service (CPS) for consideration who considered it and instructed the police to release him on bail.

As he emerged from the station, he met Martin sobbing outside. The first question Martin asked was whether he had done it.

"Of course not," he replied ferociously, as they got into the car and drove off, heading towards his house. Outside his house were the rest of the family, ready and waiting to greet them when they arrived, and anxious to know more. Everyone was there including Chris, who was fuming with rage. Chris led the way into the house while everyone followed behind. The family discussed their next move, which was the accumulation of funds to pay for his defence. Although everyone agreed to chump up to hire a good solicitor, Chris was the first to dig deep and put his money on the table. He looked everyone in the eye to see who was going to match him.

They realised that Chris was serious. Jessica looked at Martin. Martin looked at Robert. Robert looked at Chris, but realised he was the one that started the chain. Robert doubted Paul's account and had spent the whole morning contemplating that he may have done it. He nevertheless promised to contribute three hundred pounds, slamming down his Bankcard on the table. It was now Martin and Jessica's move. Jessica also promised the same. They all looked at Martin as if they were saying that he was the weakest link. He moved towards his front pocket, and slid out sweets. No one was impressed, as the frustration was building up. He knew that he was messing around so he reached into his other pocket. They now thought he was taking the piss and Chris' forehead started to wrinkle. But before anyone could utter a word Martin pulled out five hundred pounds, and placed them on the table, as if he had anticipated the need for money. Paul felt supported and was glad he was exempt from contributing. He knew he wasn't able to anyway, as he was not working.

A few days later, Paul was summoned to the police station where he was formally charged with one count of rape. His first appearance in court was fixed four weeks from his release date. He realised that he had to get the family together at least a week before that day. The family assembled again, this time at Jessica's house, not too far from the high street where solicitors were easy to access. There were a vast amount of specialist solicitors there to choose from. Some had come recommended by a national newspaper that described the high street as the legal capital of Kent. Mark, their nephew, was sitting on the armchair armed with his notepad, ready to take notes. He was the first to start questioning Paul. He established that the officer had forced himself into the house without an invitation when the door was opened. As there was no need to secure any evidence, or anyone in any imminent danger, he questioned whether the police had followed proper procedure under the Police and Criminal Evidence Act (PACE) of 1984 correctly. Mark also noted that the alleged incident took place nearly five years ago and without forensic evidence it was hard to see how they would have a case against him. While he was doing this, Chris and Martin sat in total silence, and did not contribute to the conversation, unlike the others. The family then came to a decision to appoint a solicitor.

With his experience in the legal field, Mark wanted to be part of the family gathering when they set off to appoint the solicitor. He was disappointed when Paul assured everyone that a friend had already taken care of this and all he needed was the money to pay for the solicitor. The family felt left out and asked who the friend was. Chris was particularly keen to find out. Paul explained that his friend Marcus was popular and had lawyer friends that could do it cheap. But he wasn't aware that this friend was also very close to Sophia. The family had their reservations but trusted his judgment and decided not to probe further. Mark then walked out the room in disappointment. He too felt that he would not interfere and go against anyone and their will.

When Paul met up with his solicitor John, he explained the full story to him. John initially assured Paul that there was no evidence to convict him and he would be acquitted of the charge. For a case of this magnitude, he thought the meeting was too short, and he requested another one for a later date. Paul left the building in a daze without any comprehension of what was in store for him. He didn't understand why he had been accused and this occupied his thoughts so much he ended up in the middle of the road. A speeding car was coming towards him with a police car in pursuit. The sound of the siren alerted everyone to give way, as they gathered on the sidewalk. But Paul didn't even register the sound or commotion around him. Fortunately a stranger spotted the danger and pulled him off the road just as the car swept past close to the kerb. When he came to his senses, he realised he'd had a narrow escape. It was a reality check and he needed to stay focused.

A few days later, he met up with the solicitor again, this time after John had met with Sophia for dinner without Paul's knowledge. John was not comfortable this time round; he was slightly shaking, agitated and sweating quite a lot. Paul was aware of this behaviour but put it down to stress. This time, John astonishingly changed his story, and suggested he plead guilty as the evidence against him suggested that he would get a lesser time in prison; if he was found guilty it would be longer.

"How much are we talking about?" he asked.

"Three years," replied John.

"And if I'm found guilty?" he asked.

"Seven years," John replied.

"Listen, I have been practising for over ten years, so I know a bad case when I see one," said John, skipping through the sentencing guidelines he had in front of him on his desk. "Here, see for yourself. This is what you will get if you pleaded not guilty, and then found guilty by the court." John rolled his chair across the room away from his desk towards his library and found a High Court case, stored on his bookshelf. John quickly looked at his own notes on the top of the case file, and noted the sentence of three years for a similar case. "In this similar case, the guy pleads guilty and got three years." Using his legs as he glided his chair back towards his desk, this made the ride easy on his newly placed laminated floor. John handed the case file to Paul and repeated. "Look at this case; it is also in black and white, as your facts are similar."

Paul looked at both documents; skimming though with keen eyes, as he began to believe what he was told by John. John looked him in the eyes, and though he'd got him.

"I—I can't believe the justice system could be so tough in this country," said Paul. "I didn't do it," he continued. "But—but I can't," instantly John stopped him in his track.

"You can't what, plead guilty?" "Then face the consequences," warned John, as he made visible again those documents. "You have a choice."

"Do I?" "I don't feel like I do," said Paul looking frustrated. "You initially said they didn't have a case against me, what made you change your mind?"

"I have looked deeper into the case, and though your chances are slimmer than I originally thought," said John.

Paul was silent for a while and put his head down on the table, resting it on a handwritten agreement drafted by Sophia from their previous meeting. While his head was on the table, he spotted the familiar handwriting, but thought nothing of it. As he lifted his head, John slipped it under some other files. He told John he would think about it and departed.

On his way home, Paul decided to go to the park near Jessica where he was staying, because he wanted a quiet space to think. But the noise from children playing and the sight of pigeons—one flew so close past his face it almost touched him on his nose as he sat on the park bench—made him realise it was not the right place. An old man sat about four metres from him with a can of beer, partially drunk and singing, which also didn't help. He knew that having too many distractions around him wasn't going to work so he walked off to try somewhere else. He spotted Mark and friends coming towards him on the opposite side of the park walkway. Mark told his friends that he would catch up with them later when he spotted his uncle coming. They carried on walking to find a quiet place to sit.

"I just met with the solicitor."

"Yes, and?" Mark anxiously waited to hear what they had advised him.

"Well, he believes that I stand a better chance if I plead guilty."

"What?" Mark replied. "Why? What reason did he give you?"

"Well, he said that the evidence is overwhelming against me." "He also showed me the sentencing guideline, and a case law that gripped my attention."

"But, I thought you said he told you that you had a good chance," reminded Mark.

"Well, he did, but—"

"But what?" interrupted Mark as he sought to understand how the solicitor could have reached such a conclusion. "Listen DO NOT PLEAD GUILTY," shouted Mark in anger.

A passer-by caught Paul's eves. He was wearing a wig and a black robe, with books and papers under his arm. It would have looked to the man like they were arguing.

"That must be a judge," whispered Paul.

They parted company and Paul went home.

On his way home he looked disturbed. Playing on him mind was what John; his solicitor said to him. His head was down, as he walked across the park grass. He swung his left leg kicking what appeared to be an old football. It flew across the pond in the middle of the park, missing a young child. Paul was unaware how closely it went towards the child. He eased his head up and look to the sky. He got to the house. He slowly walked up the driveway as he turned his head towards his neighbour. His neighbour waved, and he waved back. He got in the house and settled himself down on the sofa.

CHAPTER 8

It was the morning of Paul's first appearance in the magistrate court. Paul was up early as he hadn't slept properly and was bursting with anxiety and fear. He went downstairs to have his breakfast. As he passed the front room, he heard the news report on the statistics of accused rapists. He almost tripped over his jumper while he was staring at the TV. He'd left it there last night before he went to bed. Jessica had taken the day off to accompany him to the court and Jade would meet them there as planned. Chris decided not to show up as he feared the worst and Martin told them he would show up later as he had something to do first. Jessica decided to call a cab which came almost instantly to ensure that they got there on time. On the way, and oblivious to Jessica as she was reading over work papers, Paul watched everyday reality passing him by. He saw a man abusing his girlfriend on the street. A few metres from the traffic lights, he saw a car almost knock over a man as he rushed across the road. Paul realised how different and difficult life could be and that today could hold one of those moments that would affect him for the rest of his life, and he may not be as lucky as the man at the traffic lights was when the car missed him.

When they got to the court his solicitor John asked for a quiet word with Paul. John noted Paul had listened to his instructions and was formally dressed in a grey suit, a sky blue shirt with a contrasting white collar and cuffs, blue striped tie, black shoes and a matching leather bag Jade had given him. Jade who joined him ten minutes later, was on time for the hearing. To his left was Jessica. Behind him slowly walking towards him was Mark, looking at his notes. Next to Mark was Robert, and on his far right was PC Smith waiting for the case to be called. Susan couldn't make it as she'd had to go to work. As they gathered, the sound of a woman's shoes on the concrete drew everyone's attention. Everyone turned and looked round; it was Sophia, and her mother approaching the reception. Both Paul and her eyes met, and she looked away in guilt but with the smirk of a smile on her face. Paul was bursting with hatred. Martin arrived just minutes before they were told by the usher to make their way to Court Five where Judge June Clarke would be presiding.

They went inside, Martin leading the way with Paul following with his head hanging low. As this was his first appearance, Mark told the family that both the prosecutor and defendant would argue for the case to be passed to the Crown Court as the charge was committal and an indictable offence. He told them the Crown Prosecution Services (CPS) believed they had a prima facie case, as they thought there was enough evidence for the realistic prospect of a conviction.

The usher led Paul to the witness box where he waited five minutes for Justice Clarke to appear. He was asked by the usher to confirm his name.

"Paul Martin Reynolds," Paul said and confirmed his home address and date of birth before he was invited to sit down.

Stephen Smith, prosecuting barrister, did not go into too much detail, but reminded the court that he faced one charge of rape. He continued: "These matters can only be dealt with by the Crown Court."

The judge agreed. "This case will next be heard at the Lewisham Crown Court," outlined the judge, as she noted down the details. "This will be presided over by Stuart Driscoll QC," she continued.

Brian Everest, the representing barrister said, "Nothing to add at this stage."

There was no indication of a plea from Paul at this stage.

His bail conditions were set and he was warned of those conditions by District Judge June Clarke. "I must warn you if you breach any of the bail conditions you will be re-arrested."

"I understand," he replied.

The family gathered their things and walked out of the court. First, to leave was Sophia, followed by her mum, her barrister, and one of her friends. While she was walking out going pass the dock, she kept her head straight without a glance backwards. Paul looked at her walking along as she exited the courtroom. He knew what he had to do, and in his mind was to plead not guilty. Martin briskly walked up to greet him as he was leaving the dock. Jade came over too, and greeted him. They decided to go back to Jessica's house for the rest of the day.

The mood was sombre at Jessica's that same evening. Everyone had gathered to reflect on the proceedings and what was to come. Paul didn't want to be a part of it, so he decided to head upstairs in his room for a rest. He'd left his Bible next to him on the bed and opened it to Proverbs. To his right was his electronic tablet computer. He was researching rape statics on persons wrongly accused. He totally forgot his drink and his glass soon overflowed when the ice cubes melted that he'd added earlier to keep it cool. He picked up the remote to switch the TV on but mistakenly switched on his stereo instead. Bobby McFerrin's *Don't worry, be happy* started playing, and he hummed along to the tune. He increased the volume so Jessica, Jade, Robert and Martin were able to hear it downstairs. Jade was the first to move towards the stairs to see if he was OK. As she lifted her right leg to take the first step, Jessica called out to her and shook her head indicating he should be given time to be by himself. Both Robert and Martin nodded in agreement. She stepped back in the sitting room, where everyone was.

"Do you think he will get through this?" asked Jade.

"Of course," replied Martin.

"I'm not sure he will be able to cope at the Crown Court as he was shaken at the Magistrate's earlier," said a concerned Robert.

71

"My brother is a strong boy," Jessica assured everyone. "Biscuits anyone?" She headed towards the kitchen with her half glass of red wine in her left hand and a pen in her right.

Martin knew she had not had a drink in a long time as he'd been in her wine cellar and seen the same bottles still there from a few years back except for the bottle now open on the table.

Upstairs, Paul selected pause on the remote, and started reading his Bible again. He sat up with his back towards the wall where his headboard was resting. The drink from his glass halved after his first gulp down. His tablet was still lying face down on the bed. He turned to Proverbs 12:22 and read aloud: *Lying lips are an abomination to the Lord, but those who act faithfully are his delight.* He then flipped to Psalm 52:2 and read: *your tongue plots destruction, like a sharp razor, you worker of deceit.* The picture in Paul's mind was nothing but hatred, and sorrow, similar to how he'd looked in the courtroom.

The sound of a message coming through on his smart phone drew his attention. He looked at it. It was a message from Chris quoting the same scriptures he had just read. He smiled and kept reading.

Chris wrote, "You will get justice, I will see to that."

He smiled again, and replied, "I know, I know."

He took up the TV remote this time as he remembered he wanted to see the football match, or the highlights from the games he'd discussed with Jade earlier before his court appearance. He flipped through the channels, but could not find the Sky channel. He decided to investigate. He looked at the Skybox, and saw that the data cable had been unplugged. As he connected the cable, he spotted a Christmas CD titled "Silent Night." He wanted to play it, but decided not to, as he thought this would get him into a sombre mood.

He muttered to himself, "I'm going to have a silent day in court."

"What was that?" asked Jade as she silently walked in the room.

"Nothing, just thinking aloud," he replied.

"Do you want some company, or something to eat?" she asked.

"Not really. Where are the others?"

"Downstairs in the sitting room. You look stressed. Do you want me to massage you, to release the tension?"

"No, you have done enough, thank you. "The tension I would like you to release is not possible," smiled Paul, as he reached towards her and kissed her. Shall we go downstairs?"

"Sure."

They both headed downstairs, but before they got to the turn of the staircase, Jade kissed him and assured him that everything would be fine. At the foot of the stairs, Jessica greeted them.

"We felt that you needed time to yourself, so we decided not to disturb you," explained Jessica.

"I understand," he replied. "What's for dinner?" he asked, while heading towards the kitchen pretending to be OK, although deep down he knew it was just a front. He saw the pan on the cooker. He went straight over to it and opened it. It was empty. He looked at Jessica. "Are you cooking?"

"Jade is making dinner today," answered Jessica.

He then walked to the sitting room checking the

73

ceiling for a crack he wanted to fix. As he got to the sitting room, he spotted Robert drinking beer. "Beer. Are you celebrating, or stressing?" he asked.

"Both," replied Robert. "Celebrating that you will be free in a few weeks, and stressing that you may not do the right thing and keep—by keeping your nerves in-check, and ermm, plead guilty." He reached over to Robert and sat next to him. He rested his right arm on Robert's shoulder, and looked him in the eye.

"I always do the right thing, so you don't have to worry," Paul assured him.

"He will draw strength from the divine power," Martin intervened.

"Let's hope so, let's hope so," replied the sceptical Robert.

CHAPTER 9

The uncomfortable feeling for Paul, as he sluggishly moved towards the bathroom, staring in the ceiling looking to god for help. He bent down slowly on his knees next to the shower, with his hands clasped ready to pray. It was the morning of the Crown Court hearing and he was seriously in a dilemma as to how he should plead. Paul contemplated again what his solicitor had told him and decided to plead not guilty. On the prosecution presentation asking for seven years, just as he had been told by his solicitor, he felt that his solicitor knew what he was talking about, and trusted him. He remembered being told that the sentence starting point was five years for a single offence if the victim was over sixteen, and it ranged from four to eight years in custody. All of this played out in his mind. He viewed the support he was getting from his family from the witness box, and had one last look at Sophia. He'd never envisaged being in this situation. The image in his head from the witness box as he looked back in daze, was the life he once dreamt it would be; happiness with Sophia. He looked back on his youth and how friendly they had once been. He didn't think such a friendship would have ended up like this. He thought he had faith in her. He shuffled in his seat looking at the judge, contemplating his next move. He was geared up and ready for the fight before a little voice visited him. Confident as everyone seemed, only Robert seemed to have seen the different look come onto his face in the dock at that moment. Mark winked at him as if he was saying he knew what he had to do. His name was called out by the judge, and he looked poised ready to put up a fight. Mark attempted to explain the procedure to his father.

"I have seen judges indicate that mitigating circumstances will always be taken into account, and will make a difference in every case or at the sentencing, if one pleads guilty," whispered Mark to his father. He was not convinced that Paul was going to do the right thing. "But this will not happen in this case," assured Mark.

It was a crisis monument for Paul as he contemplated and contemplated which way he should plead. The same voice in his head came back to visit him to plead guilty. He looked confused as he stared at the family and the judge. When his case was presented and the judge asked him how he would plead, he surprisingly pleaded guilty.

Martin and Jessica shouted, "No!!!" Jade wept and the family sat there in total shock. The prosecution ask for sentencing that same day and the defence agreed. Mark hung his head in disbelief. Paul didn't seem to realise what he had just done. He looked at Sophia who also looked shocked as she looked back. He saw the guards positioning themselves to handcuff him. This was when reality hit him as to what he had done. He knew how he had pled but hadn't thought of the consequences of doing so. The judge sentenced him to seven years in prison. He started to cry, and thought, "What did I just do?" He was then taken away by the guards to begin his sentence. As he was being led away, Jade shouted, "I believe in you and I love you. Stay strong. I will come and visit you." He smiled and threw a kiss at her as the family watched sobbing.

That same evening, everyone gathered at Jessica's. Chris was fuming with rage. Martin started the discussion by letting everyone know that this was meant to be and they should leave it in the hands of God. There was revenge on Chris' face and Robert was so upset he started to cry as this is what he'd feared. His initial thoughts played on his mind that his negative belief in Paul had manifested in his plea. Susan commented that it was a stupid move Paul had made.

Mark said, "Everyone knows he is innocent, why did he plead guilty? I told him not to."

"I feel like killing her; it's her fault," Jessica said.

"No," Martin counteracted. "Take that thought out of your mind."

"I know what I'm going to do," said Robert."

You won't do anything," replied Martin. While everyone was in rage, Martin appeared to be the calmest. This was surprising because despite his Christian beliefs, he would normally react negatively under such condition. Jessica walked across the room and frowned.

"She is devious, how can we prove that she is?" asked Jessica, looking at Mark.

"Well, you can't appeal a guilty plea, unless you have some really strong evidence to prove diminished responsibility, or some insane loss of mental control; only that way may he appeal it," said Mark. He wasn't sure what he said was correct, but he said it to offer some comfort to the family.

"But is there some strong evidence that she made this all up?" asked Chris. "I'm sorry, but that was a stupid move by Paul, silly if you ask me, let him stay in there." There was anger visible on his face. He walked towards the door looking frustrated. He then turned and sat next to Martin.

"I said, I have a plan," reiterated Robert, "she will confess." Immediately Chris got up again and moved over to Robert. He looked attentively to hear the plan. Disappointedly, Robert told him that he needed to ironed out some issues first.

The conversation continued, while Jade was still upstairs crying.

The next day, Robert called everyone together to discuss his plans. This time they met up at his house. He had come up with a solution and held a book with drawings that looked like a map. He told them he had two plans: plan A and plan B. He explained that plan B would not be revealed until they had exhausted plan A. The wind blew the pages of the book over to plan B but he quickly hid them from view. He knew this was his contingency plan, and he wanted to keep it that way. While he was discussing his plans, he couldn't keep still as he paced around the room with his tea. Jessica and Susan took a sip of their orange juice, while Martin finished his, and asked for more. Mark poured some in his glass and offered everyone biscuits. Scratches were heard from the kitchen door as Robert's dog tried to enter the room. He was locked in as Robert had remembered his meeting with Jessica when he's spilled the drink on his precious carpet. Mark's attention was drawn to the dog and he went into the kitchen to quieten him down. As he headed towards kitchen he thought he knew what his father was going to say, but he was wrong.

"If I can discredit her, then this would be evidence to appeal as she's deceitful," said Robert.

"There are no such grounds for an appeal," replied Mark, "but it's a start to prove innocence."

"How would you do that?" asked Martin.

Listening attentively, as she finished her second glass of orange juice was a wide eyed Susan. The dog insisted on coming in making a rattling sound on the kitchen door. This affected Robert's concentration, so Mark took the dog outside into the garden. Chris said little as he drank his red stripe beer. Piecing together the puzzle was the clever Mark as if he were writing a criminal essay. He asked for everyone's attention as he theorised what he believed had happened.

"Sophia could not accept the rejection, so she made this all up," he suggested. "I knew she talked about Paul playing rough during romance, but he would never force himself on her without her presumed consent. After she had treated him so badly, to the point he could not take it anymore, one way of getting back at him was to—"

"What?" anxiously asked Martin.

"Was to contemplate a deadly-a plan and orchestrate the support of her friends who provided the solicitor who pretended to be impartial on Paul's side, and then—"

"And then what?" asked Chris for the first time breaking his silence.

"And then persuading the solicitor to convince Paul to plead guilty so it would look as if she was telling the truth," Mark concluded. "One thing I must say," added Mark, as he read the Solicitors' Code of Conduct, 2007, highlighted where there had been a breach of rule two of "Client Relations," on page nine. "If the Solicitor breached rule two, there could be serious consequences."

"So, this was purely and simply, a deadly contemplation by all involved to come together to encourage deception," summarised Martin, fuming for the first time. No one had ever seen him so angry, including his wife, as he got up from the sofa, moved towards the kitchen and took out his Bible, which he would use as a means to calm himself down.

Mark assured the family he believed that there may well be a case to answer if he complained to the law society of the solicitor's conduct. No-one knew if Mark's book was up-to-date but felt that he had made a good case against John.

"You are a genius," screamed Robert and Jessica at the same time.

"Anyway, as I was saying," continued Robert, "my plan A is to hire a detective to spy on her for a confession on tape."

"Good idea," replied Chris.

"I would say, a private detective lover," interjected

Susan.

"What do you mean?" asked Mark.

"I mean we should use a detective, but acting as a boyfriend; that way, she will eventually trust him, and reveal the truth," replied Susan.

They continued the conversation contentiously, and decided to act straight away, while Susan drank her fifth glasses of orange juice for the evening. Jessica believed that she had beaten her record of four glasses. Chris nodded to Susan's suggestion and took a sip of his beer. Martin reluctantly agreed clutching his bible in his hand.

"When do we start?" asked Martin, placing his bible in his bag.

"I will let you guys know," replied Robert.

CHAPTER 10

Paul arrived at midday at a south London prison in a van. The guards came to the back of the prison van with keys and opened it. Paul emerged handcuffed and was led straight to the assessment room. Two prison officers walked in: a man and a woman in uniform. They were a sight to behold being tall and well-built and everything about them suggested government authority. The smell of prison and its atmosphere was something he had never imagined until the time of his plea. Now seeing it up close he felt slightly freaked out.

The woman was 172 centimetres tall and her epaulettes and stripes were displayed on both shoulders of her jacket. The pockets on the jacket, cut in a police like curve, were buttoned at the tip. She was dangling her keys in an authoritative manor, as if to say, "I'm in control." Her matching black hat and shoes completed her semblance of authority, reminding Paul of his first day as a cadet dressed in uniform. He became the lead cadet after four weeks for his strength and discipline. He dreamed away into his youth years as he remembered how he'd wanted to be a soldier like his brother Chris. He was woken up from his daze by the introduction of the other officer. He saw how huge and tough these guys looked. He guessed the height of this officer to be 174 centimetres. He was dressed in a white shirt, black tie and black trousers. He was not wearing any jacket but had dangling keys like his colleague.

The whole scene was frightening and intimidating but he looked around to familiarise himself with his surroundings. Both officers drew their chairs and the sound of wood on the concrete floor enhanced Paul's fear. Slammed on the desk were booklets about prison rules, procedures, rights, courses and health care rights. Paul was given a prison number and was told his property would be recorded and put somewhere safe until the day of his release. His category was given as low risk, as he posed no risk to himself, others or to escape. Paul was then told about prison privileges.

"Your 'Incentives and Earned Privileges Scheme' may earn you more visits with family and friends and to spend more money each week," pointed out the female officer. She told Paul about punishments for breaking prison rules and confirmed stories he had heard about the possibility of being kept in your cell for up to twenty-one days if you broke one of the rules. Paul's mood changed after hearing his rights in prison. He bowed his head and paused for thoughts.

"We will not stop you from being in contact with your solicitor," the officer told him. "You will be given up to an hour outside in the open air, as one of your rights."

Paul looked around the room feeling uncomfortable. It was different to what he had been told and seen on TV and he tried to relax his shoulders and lean back in his chair. The glow from the light above his head dazzled his eyes a little bit, as he remembered his sensitivity to certain lights. He was also told that he would be staying in B wing which meant nothing to him but he listened on attentively. As he pondered prayers, and remembered Martin encouraging him to pray, he was told he would be visited by a chaplain within twenty-four hours. When the two officers offered to take him to his cell he asked for a quiet moment by himself. The male officer refused initially, but changed his mind by the agreed look from his female colleague.

The walk to his cell was a defining moment for Paul. Behind him doors slammed and metal bars banged. Paul was introduced to his cellmate Jimmy. They both exchanged pleasantries and there was silence afterwards. The sound of the cell gate slamming and keys rattling frightened him as he spun around so fast he almost fell to the ground.

He quickly rushed to the gate and shouted, "I'm innocent, I'm innocent. I shouldn't be in here."

The guards looked at him and walked away without uttering a word.

"Shouting won't help, my friend," assured Jimmy, as he comfortably relaxed on his bunk.

"How can anyone be relaxed in this place?" thought Paul. He spun around and looked at Jimmy in rage. "What do you know? I bet you are guilty."

"Don't pass judgment my friend," replied Jimmy.

"I'm innocent!" replied Paul. "They have put an innocent man in here."

"Then, if you are innocent, why are you here, my friend?" asked Jimmy.

"Stop calling me your friend!!" shouted Paul. "I don't know you."

"OK, as your wish," replied Jimmy, as he turned the other was facing the wall.

Paul soon found reality start to sink in and he went to the right hand corner of the room and sat with his head in his hands. Above him was graffiti on the grey painted walls. Some of the prisoners' names, titles, and what they were in for were clearly legible. The amount he saw scared him, as he searched to see if he recognised anyone. Anger, grief and coping strategies were all written there, as if you were at a college learning the ropes of the game.

A few minutes later, Jimmy heard Paul sobbing. He was still facing the wall on his bed.

"What have I done, what have I done?" cried Paul. "Why did I plead guilty?"

"You pleaded guilty?" thought Jimmy, as he instantly turned and sat up on his bed. "Stupid man," he said aloud. Paul didn't want to hear that but he felt he deserved it.

"I'm sorry I shouted at you earlier," conceded Paul. "I guess I only have you as my friend."

"What are you here for?" asked Jimmy.

"I'm ashamed to tell you," replied Paul.

"Ashamed?" asked Jimmy, "try me."

"Well, it started with my relationship..." And he began

telling his side of the story.

The look on Jimmy's face was pure sympathy, as he nodded attentively. Twenty minutes later, Paul was still explaining what had happened to him.

"Really, but why?" interrupted Jimmy when Paul told him that he had pleaded guilty to something he had not done. "Why would she do such a thing?" he asked.

It was almost time for outside break and the sound of opening gates and rattling keys could be heard. Jimmy hopped of his bed ready to face the outside.

"We will continue talking outside, where I will show you the ropes of this place to help you survive," Jimmy said.

The guard asked if they wanted to go outside. Paul looked at the cell, and thought outside would be the first taste of temporary freedom and the question was a no-brainer. The guard and Jimmy saw him looking at the ceiling, and thought he was thinking of an answer, but he was actually reading messages left by past inmates about how to survive on the outside. Paul shook his head and the guard thought that was his answer. Paul realised that the guard was about to walk away so he nodded his affirmation that he needed to go outside. The guard opened the door, while they both walked out.

CHAPTER 11

The idea of hiring a private detective was something Robert believed in. However it was not part of the plan for the private detective to fall in love with Sophia. He wined and dined her to total trustworthiness so that she would tell him almost anything as the family requested. The detective was being paid well so he was never going to let his feelings prevent him from getting a pay cheque. So despite his feelings he acted professionally and got some confession out of her but not enough to be used as evidence. She confessed she loved Paul but wanted to hurt him and the family were not surprised. The recording the detective played them explained how she used to sit in silence and contemplate killing Paul but how she could not bring herself to do it. Instead, she had decided she would prefer to watch him suffer in jail.

Robert felt his pressure rising when he heard her accuse Paul of ruining her life. While Chris grew angry when she blamed Paul for the break-up of both her recent relationships and said on the recording how she was bitter and wanted revenge. She told the detective how some of her ideas came from many nights alone in the bath burning her candles. The ruffling of pillows picked up by the recording suggested that the detective had done a good job at winning her confidence and the clarity of the conversation impressed Martin. Sophia also confirmed that friends had pushed her to carry out her plans. The completion of the recording disappointed Mark as he was desperate to get that magic confession they needed and when it didn't come he slumped in his seat in despair. He sighed and looked at the detective as if he wanted to strangle him as he believed he'd had plenty of opportunity to get the confession.

The detective promised he would get it but he was actually battling with his conscience. Still he went to see her again later that same week and positioned his recorder to question her again. She was just in the process of finally confirming Mark's theory but he stopped her intentionally. He knew how important this was and told himself it was just another job but his heart was pounding with love and guilt and he realised he could not continue with the job. He decided it was wrong to incriminate her and almost confessed to her about his own role.

"I have something to tell you," he uttered as he hung his head in shame.

"Stop! All I want to hear is that you love me," said Sophia. "You are the only person I feel I can trust now."

Those kind words not only burnt into his heart but potentially his pocket as well. He knew his job was his life blood and he shouldn't have fallen for her. But when he looked her in the eyes, and saw tears, his heart melted even more. He rolled over onto his back breathing a sigh of frustration. She sat up and took a sip of her tea and saw her shake her head in sorrow. He got up and went into the bathroom to check his conscience to see if he could continue with the job. He couldn't and decided to quit his assignment. When he returned to the room the recording device was no longer under her pillow and neither was Sophia. Moments later she appeared with a knife in her hand.

"Who are you?" she shouted, coming towards him with the knife. His frightened face went red, with mouth wide open.

"I can explain!!" he shouted back in fear. "If you put the knife down, I will explain."

Sophia was in love with him and could not bring herself to hurt him so she put the knife down. She saw the guilt in his eyes and waited for him to confess. He sat quietly on the bed and told her he was a private detective and wanted to get information out of her. He didn't specifically tell her what information but she was convinced he was working as journalist for a newspaper. He sighed in relief at this as it not only gave him a way out without explaining who he really was, but it also bought him some time to prove he loved her. He found out later that his calculation was wrong. When he tried to get close to her, she told him to leave and started to cry. When he didn't leave straight away she looked at the knife in the corner and he decided it was wiser to go.

When he left Sophia was frustrated and angry so she decided to get some cigarettes. She was so upset she didn't realise it was already 10:30 P.M. On her way back she realised someone was following her. She could hear footsteps and the sound of leaves scattering in the wind like in a scary movie. She remembered the horror film she had watched with Paul so many years ago, but this time she didn't have his protection. She decided to walk faster but frantically looked back and forth and saw someone move behind a wall. When she was about two metres from her house her neighbour's cat cried out, frightening her even further. Her heart pounded and she walked even faster, telling herself she needed speed. She fiddled with her keys but finally managed to get them out and open the door. When she was inside with all the locks engaged she finally felt some relief.

The next day Sophia told her mum what had happened and Tina advised her to report it to the police. Sophia thought it was a silly suggestion. She went to the park for a walk later that day as she was not feeling that well. She thought the fresh air would help. When she saw Chris in the park, she stopped and hid behind a tree to watch his movements. He didn't realise she had spotted him but he frequented that area a lot as he had once lived there before her time and was well known to the locals. Sophia was unsettled to see him. She wondered if he would have said hello given she had sent his brother to prison, but she didn't want to confront him so when he was out of sight she walked briskly back home. She didn't think any more about it and carried on with her normal household chores.

She was just about to go and visit a friend when she remembered it was Paul's birthday. She went into her shed and pulled out an old photo album with pictures of them together. The sound of a hammer banging next door reminded her that Saturday was his usual DIY day around the house. She looked around the shed and saw cobwebs and dust gathering on his tool box. It seemed a waste to have it lying around as someone could have used it. For more than three years his things had remained in the shed. Friends had told her to get rid of it but it had never been an option. She knew she wanted to keep as much of him as possible in the hope of a future someday. A very strange hope and future after sending him to prison, she thought.

"Why did I seek revenge?" she wondered feeling guilty while also justifying her actions. She contemplated visiting him in prison but couldn't bring herself to do so. She doubted he would want to see her anyway. When the doorbell rang she rushed to see if Chris had come to see her or the mystery boiler man that had come to her door recently. Instead it was the postman with a recorded delivery mail addressed to her from an anonymous sender. She looked over the postman's head and saw the same man who came to look at her boiler recently. She saw him follow Chris through the alleyway next to the park. Chris seemed unaware someone was following him. She wondered if they knew each other or if it were an attempted robbery. She knew Chris was more than capable of defending himself from what she'd heard from Paul, so she wasn't worried if it was a robbery. They disappeared into the adjoining road next to the bus stop the same place she had been followed. She wondered if they had anything to do with it.

CHAPTER 12

The gloomy atmosphere and loneliness three months after Paul had been imprisoned was taking its toll on Jessica. She missed his company and their regular conversation; he had not only brightened her spirits, but entertained her. They usually spoke at length after she came home from work, with her clients' files under her arm, especially a week before he admitted to the crime in court. She'd agreed for Jade to stay with her for a while so at least there would be Jade to talk to or paperwork to soothe her at night. Jade often volunteered to make dinner too and often cooked her favourite dishes which were very tasty, and satisfying. Since Jade had been staying there her perceptions of her had changed. There was however, still some doubts about her and her boss.

Jessica slammed her papers down on her desk when she returned that night. She'd had a horrible day at work. She felt hot, tired and hungry and violently kicked off her boots to relax—one flew towards her television missing it by a few centimetres.

"Wow, that was close," sighed Jessica as she sat down on her black leather sofa. "It's too hot," she said taking off her top and leaving only her bra on. She didn't realise that Jade was upstairs. She'd left work before Jade but had stopped to do some window shopping and buy the evening newspapers in the town centre. However Jade had taken a cab home as she wasn't feeling well and beaten her back to the house. When Jade heard the TV come on she made her way downstairs to get a drink. Jessica didn't hear her until she came into the room.

"You're here!" exclaimed Jessica crossing her arms to hide her breasts from Jade.

"What are you hiding for? You're a woman like me."

"I left you at work," said Jessica, as she relaxed her arms by her side.

"Yes, you did, but I took a cab home."

"Are you OK?"

"I'm not feeling too well."

"What's the matter?"

"I felt nauseous this morning—like I was going to throw up."

"Well you cannot be pregnant, as it has been over three months since Paul has been in prison. So, it would be impossible to think you are."

"Well, I haven't had my period for three months, but I didn't want to say anything." Jade didn't want to cause any alarm to the family, so she'd kept it to herself. She thought that the family had a lot to deal with. Jessica was now concern and thought she should go and check it out.

"Go and see your GP," encouraged Jessica. "I take it that you didn't cook then? Sorry, that was insensitive. I will make a quick dinner, as I have got some work to do."

"You're going to work now?" asked Jade.

"Yes, you know how it goes, my work never stops. I'm going to make a pasta dish, but I need five minutes to relax first, I'm too tired. I really miss Paul."

"I am going crazy without him. He refused to have visitors, which I can understand, but does he know—" whispered Jade. Paul was ashamed of his decision to plead guilty, and felt it was not time to accept any visitors, not even his girlfriend Jade.

"Know what?" asked Jessica, as she checked the mail on the table next to her, dreading the bills.

"Never mind," replied Jade, thinking it would be a good idea to make the appointment to see her GP.

The following evening Jade and Jessica were in the kitchen having a snack. Pots and pans rattled as Jessica prepared dinner while Jade made herself a sandwich to take to her seven o'clock appointment with the GP.

"Where is the pasta?" Jessica asked, as she slammed the cupboard in frustration.

"OH, pasta again," Jade thought and felt her tummy.

"I think I'm pregnant," said Jade.

"In the bread pan?" asked Jessica, "why would the pasta be in the bread pan?"

"I DID NOT SAY BREAD PAN, I SAID PREGNANT," shouted Jade.

The kitchen was silent. Jessica stopped what she was doing and turned and faced Jade.

"Pregnant, by who?" Jessica enquired, crossing her

arms. Jade looked surprised as if she thought Jessica should know. If Jade knew what Jessica thought of her, she would have looked so surprised.

"Who else?" replied Jade.

"I'm sorry. I haven't functioned well since Paul's been inside. You've known that a while now, haven't you?" Jade moved to the kitchen door and pulled the curtains open; looking out in the garden.

"Yes, I was afraid to mention it. There are a lot of things I don't talk about and I've kept it secret for a while now, but I felt I wanted to share it with you," said Jade.

"Sure, you can share it with me then," replied Jessica, as she leaned against the stove and focused on Jade. "Don't tell me, it's our boss." Jessica finally got it out, but Jade wasn't having any of it.

"What about him?" asked Jade.

"You were—"

"What? What do you take me for, or what are you getting at, Jessica? I'm not going out with the boss if that's what you mean; never have, never will and I'm not pregnant by him."

"I'm sorry—please forgive me," pleaded Jessica, as moved towards Jade and cuddled her.

A car beeped outside.

"That's the cab. I have to go now," Jade said gathering her things.

"Where are you going?"

"To the GP," Jade said as she dashed out of the kitchen.

"OK, bye. See you later," said Jessica, as she walked her towards the front door.

"Bye," said Jade.

Jessica felt embarrassed by the exchange between them. It was their first confrontation. She remembered that just a few weeks ago how she had thought Jade was calm and easy going. She sat down on the floor next to the kitchen door. Facing her were her red plastic spice shelves. On the top shelf she spotted the pasta. She remembered she'd left it there last night. She laughed and reached for it. She opened the packet and emptied its content in the pan. The cooker was on so she reached for the matches in the cupboard and lit it.

It was Jade's turn to see the GP. Her name was displayed on the electronic display board above her indicating she should go to room three. She made her way to the entrance door, not knowing which way to go, as she had not been to see him in a while, and had forgotten the way. She turned right and narrowly missed another pregnant patient coming out of room three. She knocked on the door before she was asked to come in. The door slammed behind her as she made her way to the chair and was invited to sit down.

"Hi My name is Dr. Watson, how can I help you today?"

"I think I'm pregnant," said Jade.

"When was your last period?"

"Three months ago," she replied.

"Why did you wait this long to come and see us?" asked Dr. Watson as he got out his blood pressure machine.

"I don't know," she replied.

The doctor pressed the button alerting the nurse to come in. She appeared seconds later. This surprised him as the nurse had not responded so promptly to his earlier requests and he'd complained to her that patients had to wait so long. He asked her to take Jade to a private area to undertake a pregnancy test. Jade produced a urine sample and was not surprised to find it came back positive. The news brought mixed emotions. She was sad on one hand and happy on the other.

"Your baby is no longer an embryo, it is now a foetus," said Dr. Watson as the nurse left. He explained that after ten weeks the outline of the baby became recognisable and became a foetus.

The look on Jade's face after his explanation demonstrated her continued mixture of joy and sadness. "What does this mean now?" she asked.

"The hospital will contact you and they will take it from there," replied Dr. Watson.

Back home that night Jade broke the news to Jessica who also displayed mixed emotions. She had been eating a biscuit but stopped with it half way to her mouth. She put it back down on the table next to her tea, desperate to learn more.

"While I'm at it," said Jade, "I may as well tell you what I wanted to tell you earlier; I was raped a few years ago. Paul is not aware of it, and I don't want him to know, please." Jade felt she'd become closer to Jessica and could trust her with this information. She'd learned from the police that the celebrity that raped her had spiked her drink and been heavily drugged. She'd been in and out of consciousness and couldn't remember anything but the accused had a phone recording of her consenting. Jade shifted back from the memory to Jessica, waiting for her to agree to keep this from Paul.

"OK," replied Jessica. "Come here," she said and reached out to give her a hug. "Do you want something to drink?"

"No, I just want to lie down for a bit," replied Jade.

"Do you know who raped you?" asked Jessica.

"Yes, but I don't want to say, or get into that now. All I can say is that he is a celebrity."

They continued the conversation, but on a different subject, as Jessica continued to console Jade. Jessica now felt that she was also playing the mother figure for Jade. She knew that this responsibility could become unbearable but she was willing to take on the challenges. Besides, Jessica also felt that it was her duty to Paul to do so.

CHAPTER 13

A few days later Chris and Jade went to visit Paul in prison. This was their first visit in nearly four months since he had been incarcerated, as he felt his decision to plead guilty was a foolish one, and he was embarrassed about his decision. In prison his friend Jimmy was the one that kept him sane.

As Paul was led to the table with his hands cuffed, Chris shouted at the guard, "Is this necessary?"

The guard nodded. They were lead to the open space visiting area, at table 16.

Chris told Paul to keep up his faith as they were working on a plan to get him out. Paul wasn't ready to see Jade and he hid his face in shame, paranoid she had moved on with her life. It was obvious she was not welcome and she walked out of the meeting room crying. She was wearing a large blue coat and a baggy white jumper to hide her pregnancy so he did not notice anything. Chris tried to reassure him that she loved him but he didn't want to know. He suggested to Chris that she had put on weight. Deep down he knew she loved him, but felt useless, and thought she would be better off with someone else.

They chatted for the permitted time and then it was time to go. Jade came back into the room to say her goodbyes but kept her distance with her hands in her coat pockets to continue disguising her bump. This time he was more accepting because he had been reassured by Chris. Jade felt a bit comfortable but kept smiling. When Paul stood up the chair toppled over with a loud bang. Everyone turned to look while Chris bent to pick up the chair. At this point Jade moved closer and leaned over and kissed Paul on the cheek. As they took him away there was a horrible sound of closing prison gates that played on Chris' mind for the rest of the day.

Later in his cell Paul replayed the visit. He was disturbed particularly when he saw Jade leaving with his brother Chris and not him. The graffiti on the interior walls of his cell had taught Paul how to survive on the inside, but there was no message about how to survive thinking about the outside. Beyond that, he couldn't see how he could, with Jade living on the outside.

There were reminders of his outside life however. The wall colours in his cell resembled those of the Magnolia painted surfaces he had in his flat. Blue however was a common feature. The mattress was wrapped in a blue cover and matched his trousers. But he had few possessions really; just the TV and two drawers of things. Paul started feeling sorry for himself again.

"I am such a fool," said Paul to Jimmy. When he'd seen Jade and his brother walk away free, while he was still locked up, made him realise he had thrown everything away. "How could anyone admit to something they did not do? It pains me to see my girlfriend looking like that."

"My friend this is not the first time an innocent person has pleaded guilty in country like the United States," Jimmy reassured him as he tried to fix the blue cover on his side of the bunk. "The evidence sometimes appears so strong that you believe you have no choice but to accept a plea deal. The American legal system is a sham as it does not thrive on justice but numbers and merits. The more you convict, the more respect you get for solving a crime, not understanding that a lot of innocent people are tricked into admitting to something they did not do." Paul started to think this guy is a genius. But the thought of him being in a cell was more on his mind than Jimmy's judicial analogy.

"Look at this room," said Paul, "I shouldn't be here."

"I know, son, I know," sympathised Jimmy.

Crying was heard from next door, while guards patrolled the area slamming doors. It was getting dark as the conversation progressed. A mixed raced guard walked past their cell looking fierce and strong. He looked them up and down, while swinging his baton, and rattling his keys, displaying an authoritative attitude, as if to say he was in charge. He stopped in front of their cell, posed in a position to display his authority, and said in a controlling voice, "Lights out gentleman."

The following day in the breakfast hall, while most of the

prisoners were having their breakfast and looking up at the big screen TV, Paul heard the news reporter saying that the government was considering relaxing prison time by reducing the time foreign nationals spent inside in order to control immigration. A British national listening to the news shouted, "Noooo, not for us guys." The news continued to report that this would not be for serious crimes like murder.

Jimmy whispered, "What is your nationality?"

Paul smiled. Jimmy had been in for five years and would be released in two years time. His crimes were a combination of convictions from robbery to drug dealing. He would have gotten away with it if an old grandmother hadn't seen him selling drugs to a man disguised as a teenager and alerted police. Jimmy referred to the man as his baby faced customer.

As Paul took a bite of a chocolate he'd saved in his pocket, Jimmy told him how lucky he was to have such a close knit family unit. Jimmy, however, hadn't got much support from his family and had received only two visitors since he had been inside.

"From what you told me, your family would do anything to get you out," he said.

"Yes, I'm lucky," said Paul. "Chris is the rebel, and Martin is the saint," laughed Paul. "If anyone was to hurt Sophia, it's Jessica, as she never liked her from the time we started dating." Paul knew their support could go beyond legal avenues but he prayed it didn't ever go further than that.

Sophia had contemplated sleeping at her mum's place since she had been followed as she wasn't sure how safe she was anymore. She was however as stubborn as her father and told her mum that she had decided to stay at home.

"Mum, I have something to tell you," she said. "I'm a bad person, and Paul should—"

Her mum cut her off by assuring her that she should not blame herself for what he had done to her.

Sophia kept a knife under her pillow and decided she should be safe enough. After talking to her mum she watched TV, drank brandy and coca cola and nibbled on some crisps before she decided to sleep. She'd finished half a bottle and when she'd taken her last sip she switched the TV off and flicked off her lamp. The room was pitch black as she pulled the quilt over her. She yawned one more time and then fell asleep.

CHAPTER 14

The neighbours heard the sweet sound of the gospel coming from Martin's house. They also heard Martin playing his saxophone. Singing and dancing in the kitchen to the music was Susan as she prepared dinner. Her favourite spices and herbs sat next to the bottle of olive oil she'd bought from the supermarket. The neighbour to their right was an atheist who didn't like the gospel and often said Christian were hypocrites. Susan spotted him looking out his kitchen window and asked Martin to reduce the volume. Martin reluctantly agreed because he didn't want any trouble. Two weeks ago his neighbour had called the police to complain about the loud music. However when the police came around the neighbours to their left told them it wasn't that bad.

When he decreased the volume Martin could hear something sizzling in the kitchen. The smell of something frying wet his appetite and we went downstairs to examine the cooking. Susan poured red wine into the frying pot to increase the flavour and it produced an even sweeter scent. She added chicken stock, covered it to simmer, and moved over to the dishwasher to check if it had been completed.

"I'm starving, is dinner ready yet?" he asked.

"Not yet, but soon," replied Susan.

"How long?"

"Five minutes," she replied, unloading the dishes from the machine.

He went into the fridge and took out a can of ginger beer. "I heard that Chris went to see Paul. I will go and see him soon."

"Are you getting on with Chris now?" asked Susan.

"A bit," said Martin. "Chris and I are totally opposite. He is a dangerous man—I heard a lot of things about him and I don't know if they're true. We do speak to each other, but I'm a Christian, and he has a bad past. I invited him to church and he refused to even think about it."

Susan served the dinner and laid it out on the table. Martin sat at the head of the table while Susan sat on his right. They both held hands and prayed. Susan got up and got the orange juice and two glasses. Martin took the first bite when the doorbell rang.

"Who could that be?" asked Susan.

"Are you expecting anyone?" asked Martin.

"No," replied Susan, "Maybe it's the neighbour. But we have turned down the volume."

"Well, go and see who it is then."

Susan got up and opened the door.

"Hey, Susan," said Chris.

"Hi Chris," replied Susan. "Come in," she invited as

he greeted her with a hug and kiss.

"Sorry to come unannounced, but it's important that I see Martin."

"Who is it?" shouted Martin.

"It's Chris," replied Susan while Chris made his way towards the dining room.

"Good timing," said Chris.

"It is good timing," said Martin.

"Yes—it's dinner time," said Chris.

"Susan, would you?" asked Martin.

While Susan went to serve Chris dinner, he took a bite from Martin's plate.

"You haven't changed, have you?" asked Martin, watching Chris eating his favourite pieces of chicken. "You have been doing that since we were kids."

"We are brothers, aren't we?" asked Chris. Chris' phone rang just as Susan walked in with his dinner. He ignored the call as it was anonymous.

"Your dinner is on the table," said Susan.

"Yes, thanks," replied Chris. He pulled out a chair to Martin's left but it caught on the rug and as he lifted it clear his phone rang again.

"Maybe it's important," suggested Martin.

"OK, you may be right, one sec," replied Chris. He walked towards the living room.

"Hello, who is this?" he asked.

"You should know this voice," replied the stranger.

"Waitie," replied Chris.

"That's me alright," replied Waitie.

"How did you get my number?" asked Chris.

"We have been in the business too long now not to be able to track down and find people."

"It's been a long time," said Chris.

"It has," said Waitie. "Can we meet in an hour in the café across the road from you?"

"From me? How do you know where I am?"

"You are talking to me."

"When, now?".

"That would be good," said Waitie.

"I can't believe you know where I am, I must be slipping up."

"That's what happens when you get complacent, and leave the business."

"OK, give me ten minutes," replied Chris. He walked back into the dining room. Both Martin and Susan had finished their dinner.

"Your dinner is cold," said Susan.

Chris took the dinner back to the kitchen, and heated it up and then brought it back to the dining room, where Martin was sitting by himself.

"Did you want to tell me something?" asked Martin.

"I just came to tell you I had visited Paul yesterday," said Chris.

"So I heard."

"I have to go now, I'll come back later or tomorrow," said Chris.

By the time Susan returned he had gone.

"Where is Chris?" she asked.

"He left," replied Martin."

"Already? He only just got here," said Susan.

"It was that phone call," said Martin. "I know he is up to something."

Chris walked across the busy road to get to the café. He

didn't know what to expect and was a bit hesitant. A Jeep honked at him as it passed and the driver shouted, "Look where you are going!" Chris realised he had not been concentrating on what he was doing because he was nervous and tried to calm down.

Five minutes from the café, he saw a suspicious looking black sport vehicle parked about ten metres from the café. All the windows were tinted and he couldn't see inside. When he went inside the café there was no sign of Waitie. He pulled from some of his training; both from the army, and that being a hitman and walked around the side of the café with his bag. Three minutes later, a man dressed in a cowboy suit and hat emerged. Passersby stared at him in amazement thinking he was going to a costume party and a few kids on the opposite side of the road laughed. At this point a medium built man who was about six foot tall emerged from the Jeep and walked towards Chris. Chris dipped his hand into his pocket. The man's black leather trench coat was swinging from side to side as he came closer and Chris spotted a gun on the inside. He stopped right in front of Chris and they looked each other up and down. Then they burst out in smiles and hugged each other.

"Let's go in," said Waitie.

"You have got company, haven't you?" asked Chris.

"Yep, in the Jeep," he replied, as he signalled an OK sign to them.

"Five of them," said Chris.

"Yep, you are correct," he replied. Chris had already mapped out the area before showing up for their meeting. Waitie knew what he was capable of, so neither were surprised by the revelations; that there were five men in the Jeep.

"After you," said Chris, as he opened the door.

"Thank you. I can see that you are still a gentleman," said Waitie as they approached their table.

It was noisy inside and Chris wondered if it was the right place for them to talk.

"I like this place; no-one can hear what we are discussing," smiled Waitie as if reading Chris' mind.

The bustle of waitresses and their secluded seating position meant no one would see them unless they went inside the café. This was perfect for both of them. Chris was still uneasy about the meeting, and anxious to know more. Waitie had that look of his usual surprise offer. Chris though he knew what he was going to say.

"The boss wants you back," said Waitie. "You could make some real money like me. I've even got a mansion in the Caribbean now," bragged Waitie as he showed off pictures of his new home. Chris was impressed, and knew what Waitie was going to say. He believed that his family comes first, and wondered if he could ever go back to what he was doing, or even take up such offer.

CHAPTER 15

W aitie knew his boss had a job for Chris, although his boss didn't specifically say so. The conversation he had with him was only about persuading Chris to come back. The celebrity involved in a rape case knew he was guilty of the crime, so he thought there was a possibility of fresh evidence becoming known to the police, or coming to light. This was the primary reason he decided to contact Waitie's boss. The boss was also a close friend of the celebrity.

Chris didn't acknowledge Waitie's suggestion of the boss' request and said nothing. He'd wanted to get out which was one of the reasons he went to the States.

"Did you see the car I'm driving now?" asked Waitie taking another sip of his wine, trying to paint a rosy picture of the kind of life Chris was missing out on. "I have a team that would die for me."

Chris understood what he was saying to him but

111

didn't even bother to consider it.

"What do you say about that?" asked Waitie.

"I want to change my life," replied Chris.

"What life? You mean the life in which you run away to America broke?"

"That's OK by me," said Chris.

"Would you like some more wine sir?" interrupted one of the waiters.

"Yes, bring me another bottle. Can I have the Screaming Eagle Cabernet 1992, please?" asked Waite, demonstrating that he could buy expensive wine.

"That is an expensive wine; you won't get that here," said Chris.

"I will, it has been pre-ordered, and I can afford it."

The conversation continued for forty minutes before they decided to part.

"Here is my card, have a think about it," said Waitie. "We need the finest back in the business, like the wine we've just had, and we can only find that in you."

This went straight to Chris' head a bit, but he kept his emotions in check.

"We have a big job coming up and it would be two million for you—don't answer now, think about it first," whispered Waitie moving closer to Chris' ear. He got up from the table and left two thousand pounds to pay for the meal.

Chris sat there in shock and confusion.

Chris left the café and made his way back to his brother's place, forgetting to change back into his normal clothes.

Susan answered the door.

"Why are you dressed like that?" she asked.

"Like what?" replied Chris, looking at himself in disbelief."Oh, sheesh. I was just at a costume party."

Martin burst out laughing when he saw him. "Still playing cowboys and Indians, like we used to when we were kids," joked Martin with his Bible in his hand, and his glasses resting on his nose.

"This time it's for real," replied Chris.

Martin looked serious and stopped laughing. He'd always had his suspicions about Chris. Anything Chris said in relation to danger he took seriously. Chris told him that he had killed someone as a joke, a month ago, and he'd been very upset and walked out the room. He was convinced Robert, Mark and Jessica were in on the plan to mislead him; by hiding information from him about Chris.

"What do you mean?" asked Martin, thinking that there was some truth to the rumours he had been hearing about Chris.

"Got you," joked Chris aloud but thought, "I can't let my brother know what I used to do in the past."

"Are you going to finish your dinner?" asked Susan.

"No, I'm OK now, I had something to eat outside," replied Chris. "Can I rest in the spare room?"

"Sure, you can," said both Martin and Susan.

Chris took his bag and made his way upstairs to the spare room. He closed the door behind him with the bolt. He remembered he'd left his hat downstairs so he quickly rushed back down to collect it. He took all his clothes off as if he was going mad. He knelt down on his knees in a prayer like position. He then threw himself on the bed. The spring in the bed bounced him up and down before he settled on his back looking up at the ceiling.

"Why me?" he thought. "If I say no, they could kill me." His heart was pounding and sweat beaded on his brow. For a moment the sound of traffic in the streets outside distracted him and he relaxed and fell asleep.

Chris was standing on the roof of a derelict building looking down at the vehicles below. A man had just fallen onto the ground and passersby were screaming as blood gushed from his head. "Call an ambulance," shouted a man. "It's too late," shouted another. Sirens sounded and a few minutes later the police arrived.

"Chris, Chris," shouted Susan.

Chris snapped out of his dream looking stressed and frightened. His breathing could be heard from outside the room door and had alarmed Susan.

"Are you OK?" she asked, "Do you need a drink?"

"No, I'm fine, thanks," replied Chris.

"Can I come in?" asked Susan.

"Yes, in a minute," replied Chris, as he quickly got dressed, and hid his bag. His gun was in the bag, so he was careful not to let them see it. He then opened the door.

"I heard you shouting in your sleep," said Susan.

"What did you hear?" asked Chris.

"I heard, 'he is dead, he is dead,'" replied Susan, as she looked around the room thinking he may have smuggled someone in the house behind their backs. "Do you know that Paul's girlfriend Jade is pregnant?" asked Susan.

"No, I didn't know," replied Chris.

"Have you met her?" asked Susan.

"Yes, I have, we visited Paul yesterday," replied Chris.

"Both of you?" asked Susan.

"Yes both of us," replied Chris. "Jessica arranged it for us, which was when I met her. Where is Martin?"

"He was tired so he went to bed."

"Can I use your shower?" asked Chris.

"Of course you can," replied Susan. "We have extra towels, toothbrush, everything you need. Help yourself."

The next day, Chris got up at about 5 A.M.. He sneaked outside the house, silently closed the door without anyone knowing, and went to the park for a run. He ran for an hour, before another early runner joined him; a blond dressed in a tight running suit. She caught his eye as she passed him on the opposite side. He couldn't resist, and turned around jogging backwards, as he watched her go. He then went to the gym nearby to do his weight training; something he hadn't done in a while. When he got back to the house, Martin and Susan had already left for work. Martin hadn't taken his car so Chris went into his room and took his car keys. He took out a map from his bag and then hid the bag under the bed. He rushed off in the car raking up dust over Martin atheist's neighbour as he cleaned his own car. He looked up and saw Chris driving Martin's car and wondered if the car had been stolen. But he recognised the family resemblance and thought, "That one doesn't look like a Christian," and watched as the car disappeared from view.

On the motorway Chris was doing 80 MPH. He kept an eye out for police patrol cars in his rear view mirror.

He knew he was going faster than the recommended speed limit. He spotted a police car coming towards him in the middle lane and eased down to 70. The police sped past him but one of them looked at him as they passed.

An hour later, Chris arrived at his destination. He got out of the car, slammed the door and took a spade from the boot. He checked his pocket for the map. He went down a slope and slipped on some loose stones, but grabbed onto a couple of branches to prevent himself from falling. It was very windy and his clothes flapped wildly in the wind. He kept on going until he got to a tree, walked five steps backwards and started to dig. A metre down he spotted something wrapped in a plain plastic bag. He heard a sound, and spun around to see who it was. He thought it might be Waitie but he saw no-one. The sound continued so he decided to investigate. He slowly took a knife from his waist and walked in the direction of the sound.

He crept up behind a tree and tried to peek around it but wasn't able to see properly. So he leapt around the tree and spotted a wild dog scratching himself on the ground amongst the dry leaves. The movement frightened the dog and it sped off. He went back to his location and took out the plastic bag. In it was an AS50 semi-automatic sniper rifle equipped with a spying glass on the top. Chris brushed off the dirt and took it back to the car. He wanted to get back before Martin or Susan came back so he sped back quickly. This time he was prepared for any encounters. He knew he had a dangerous weapon and if he was caught it would be trouble so he took a different route to avoid the cops.

Back at the house Chris disassembled the gun, including the optical sight, so it would fit in his bag. He then left a note telling Martin that he had to go out and he would see him later. Chris needed money. He had some stashed away for his kids and he doesn't want to take from it. He considered that he needed money especially to support Jade.

CHAPTER 16

Chris decided to take up Waitie's offer.

"Chris," said Waitie after answering the phone.

"Yes, can we meet at the park?" said Chris.

"What park?" asked Waitie.

"Our usual park in ten minutes."

"OK—see you there," replied Waitie.

Chris sat on the bench in ragged trousers and old ripped Clark shoes. These had once been brown suede but they were now dirty beyond recognition. He also had on a dirty blue jumper with the hood on his head. On his right were two empty cans of beer. Two passersby stared at him wondering if he was homeless or mad. Chris checked his watch knowing Waitie had already been at the park when he called as Waitie sometimes tailed him to monitor some of his movements. The ten minutes had elapsed and still there was no sign of Waitie. He decided to give it another five minutes. Finally a man walked by and sat behind him on the bench.

"Waitie," he said without looking round. "Thanks for coming."

"I take it that you have changed your mind," suggested Waitie.

"I want two million for this job," said Chris. He'd decided this amount would help get Paul released from jail and set himself up for life and out of the business for good. Either way he didn't care if his request was unrealistic, as this would get Waitie off his back, leaving him to continue with his life. Chris knew how to play his card.

"That's too much," replied Waitie. "I'll give you 1.5 million."

Chris had backed him into a corner. Waitie thought it was too expensive but knew if he refused it would cut Chris out of the pie so he had to pay an even cleverer hand. "Take it or leave it," he said.

Chris wasn't good at poker, but he knew a good hand when he saw one. "Deal," replied Chris, as they shook hands and smiled.

Waitie patted him on the back in friendship, as they walked along.

"I need the money to help out my brother in prison and his unborn baby," grumbled Chris, under his breath. "What's the story?"

"The client is a high profile celebrity. He was featured in the news lately for rape and was upfront with us—he admitted he did it."

Chris listened attentively, taking notes.

Chris pretended to take a sip from the empty beer

can, slurring on his speech, as two patrolling police officer approached the bench. The officers stopped to look at them and then continued past. Little did they know that Chris was heavily strapped with a gun around his waist.

"New forensic evidence has emerged which would certainly put him away for a long time," explained Waitie.

Chris knew exactly what Waitie was going to say, so they both said: "This is where I/you come in," at the same time. The story was convincing and Chris knew that Waitie wouldn't have asked him if he didn't think he was the right man for the job. Speaking in code, Waitie continued the briefing, giving Chris the intelligence he needed so he knew what to look for.

"Telephone Interception by Waitie and his men suggest that she will be visiting the countryside next week," said Waitie. "More information and a deposit will be left at our regular spot, but no pictures. You will have enough information to make an accurate hit. I want you to kill her and make sure she is dead. You know the risks. We've known each other for years; we don't want to get on the wrong side of each other, so I'm counting on you." "To protect our client we need to take out the victim."

Waitie knew there was little difference in the training and hits between them. He knew if they fell out it would be a disaster. So he didn't want to upset Chris but he felt he had to show some authority. They stayed out of each other's' way for a reason.

"I'm a professional, leave it to me," assured Chris.

Jade was on the phone with a friend planning a trip to Birmingham and the sights they would see. They had agreed to go the next week but Jade warned that this might not be possible. After ending the conversation she decided to write a letter to Paul to inform him about his baby. She looked on Jessica's desk for a pen and writing pad. She wasn't able to find one, so she decided to search deeper. She lifted up some of her papers, and among them was a handwritten letter. She respected Jessica's privacy, so she moved it aside and continued to search for the pen. On top of the shelf above the computer, she spotted the pen holder with four pens inside. She took one and found some A4 paper under the desk next to the printer. She took this back to her room and began writing:

"My dear prince,

Please don't give up on us, continue to fight, I believe in you. Sorry to break the news to you like this, but I cannot keep it in any longer—I'm pregnant. The baby and I are doing well, and I'm three months pregnant. I may be going to see my friend in Birmingham this weekend. "PS and you are the father." Bye now."

Chris called Jade from the park to find out how she was doing as he felt he was in a position to help her and his obligation to Paul automatically expanded to her.

"How are you Jade?" asked Chris.

"I'm fine," replied Jade.

"I don't want you to worry about anything. I have got some work, so while Paul is away, I will make sure you and the baby are looked after."

"What kind of job?" she asked while she reached for an envelope to seal the letter.

"I don't want to talk about it over the phone," whispered Chris, still dressed like a mad man. He had spotted an old enemy so he ducked his face from view.

"OK, I understand," replied Jade, as she sealed the envelope, while her voice break.

"I will have enough money to help fight for Paul's release as well," Chris assured her. "Is Jessica home yet?"

"No," replied Jade.

"I may be away for a couple of days," said Chris. "But feel free to call me at anytime, if you need any help."

"Where are you going?" asked Jade.

"I don't know yet, I think it might be Manchester," replied Chris.

Jade didn't tell Chris she might also be away.

When they had finished talking Chris left the park, at ease after talking to Jade. He felt that a burden had been lifted off his shoulders. Walking towards the exit, he didn't care whether he was spotted by his worst enemies; he was happy and thought that perhaps now he was sorted for life.

CHAPTER 17

A week later, Jade left on the Monday for Birmingham and Chris left on the Tuesday. When Jade arrived at the train station she saw her friend waiting in the car park. She walked carefully down the stairs to the exit and inserted her ticket to open the barriers.

"Argggggggggggghaaaaaa," they both screamed, as they had not seen each other for years. They hugged for two minutes, not letting go. The excitement attracted the attention of other passengers from the same train and they looked on smiling. Two ladies whispered to each other how nice it was to reunited with someone you hadn't seen in a while. They were in fact long lost sisters and hadn't seen each other since they were six. Their father was waiting by his car and also spotted Jade's reunion. He reminded them they had been in the same situation a few weeks ago too as he took their luggage.

While they were still hugging, Margaret felt her bump.

"Wow, look at you. I can't believe, you are pregnant," she said with one hand on her shoulder, and the other pointing to her tummy.

"I am, I am," replied Jade, smiling and happy to see her.

"Let's go," said Margaret.

"How far away do you live?" laughed Jade.

"Not far," replied Margaret. Margaret took her luggage, and placed it in the boot of her car. She opened the door and let her in the front. "How is Paul?" she asked as they drove off leaving the station.

The sisters and their father were still there smiling, watching them drive off.

"The last time we spoke, you told me that you were going out with this Paul," said Margaret.

Jade didn't want to get too much into the conversation about Paul, so she dogged the question. She knew she had to come clean, as they had been friends for years, and she had never lied to her, but wanted to put it off as long as possible. For that moment, she kept her silence.

"What have you done to your hair?" asked Jade, changing to subject. "The last time I saw it was red. You are blond now. Why did you colour it?"

"To keep the guys off," joked Margaret.

Chris rented a car, kitted up, and left early in the morning to avoid the traffic. He had to stop near where he had hidden his gun as this was the secret spot Waitie had left the money and the instructions. When he got there, he saw clues as to where else to look. Codes they had developed over the years doing this type of work had made it easier for him to navigate properly. Clouded with anxiety to get on with the job, he picked up the photograph, although Waitie had suggested he wasn't going to leave one. He didn't have time to look at it, and thought he may look later, so he continued around some trees, scratching away branches looking for the money. He found it and the directions in the same spot. He checked his watch and lifted his head up to the sky when he heard the thunder. It looked like it might rain. This was not the first time Chris carried out hits without looking at the picture. He trusted Waitie, and didn't think it was necessary.

Chris thought he was going to Manchester but discovered the map was for Birmingham but he got in the car without hesitating and drove off. He moved over to the fast lane on the M1. His favourite jazz music was playing as he checked the speed reading on the dashboard. He was going at 80 MPH. When he spotted a man driving a Porsche he felt tempted to race him, but he smiled and ignored him. The man was persistent and drove closer to Chris, pushing to see if he could persuade him to race. Chris heeded to temptation, looked at the man, selected fifth gear, and floored the accelerator pedal. Chris immediately jumped ten metres in front and the man responded. Chris knew his car was no match but he continued to compete and sped up to about 85 MPH. The man caught up with him and teased him again; this time Chris moved up to 90 MPH. But the thought of a police patrol ahead prompted Chris to reduce his speed. He knew he had kit on him that would land him in prison, so he changed lanes and settled in the slower lane. The man was persistent and tempted him again, revving his engine. Chris didn't acknowledge him and maintained his current speed. The man looked disappointed but finally sped off. Twenty minutes later, Chris spotted him at the side of the road being searched by the police. As he passed, he waved at the man, and smiled.

Margaret helped Jade to take the luggage to her room. When they went back downstairs Margaret wanted to hear more about Paul, so she brought up the subject again. Jade continued to avoid the question and this rang alarm bells in Margaret's head. She knew something was not right. She decided to leave it for a while, and changed the subject. Jade knew that she knew she was hiding something. She saw it in her face. They looked at each other, and smiled.

"Let's go and have something to eat," suggested Margaret.

"Good idea," replied Jade.

They sat around the table. Margaret decided to make a sandwich for both of them because she knew that Jade liked chicken sandwiches.

"How far gone are you now?" asked Margaret.

"Four months," replied Jade, as she took her first bite.

Margaret laughed at her speaking with her mouth full. She thought she sounded funny. Margaret poured apple juice into Jade's glass because it used to be her favourite. But Jade found her tastes had changed now she was pregnant and told Margaret she would rather have orange juice. Margaret obliged and poured her another glass.

"What happen to your job?" asked Margaret.

"I'm on holiday now, but I may give it up soon. I'm feeling tired these days."

"Well you just have to ride it out until your maternity leave starts," suggested Margaret. "You will need the money," she continued drinking Jade's apple juice herself.

"I know," replied Jade. "Chris promised to help too."

This opened up an opportunity for Margaret to enquire about him and Paul. Jade realised what she had done but it was too late for her to retract her statement.

"Who is Chris?" asked Margaret.

"He is Paul's brother."

"Paul's brother? Why would Paul's brother want to take on his responsibility?" asked Margaret.

"I'll tell you all about it tomorrow on our walk," promised Jade, picking up crumbs of chicken left on her plate.

"OK," replied Margaret.

Jade's glass was empty. She was still thirsty and wanted to ask for more drink. Margaret read her mind and offered more. Before Margaret could comment on her sudden greed, she assured her that it wasn't her but the baby. They both laughed. They continued lunch until Jade felt tired and went to have a lie down.

Chris got to his hotel in time for breakfast. He'd already picked up food on the way there. He paid in cash for the room and checked in to number eight. It was on the fifth floor so he went up in the lift as taking the stairs was unrealistic with such heavy bags. When he arrived he headed straight to the bathroom and began sweeping the place for bugs. Although he had no reason to doubt Waitie, one of the rules in his profession was not to trust anyone. When he had finished he fell back on the bed as he felt tired from the journey. His towel was wrapped around his waist but was becoming loose. He heard the doorbell. He sprung up, reaching for his pistol under his pillow. He tightened his towel, and walked towards the door. He looked through the hole and saw it was the hospitality girl. He placed his gun back under the pillow, and opened the door.

"Hi, can I help you?" he asked, resting his elbow on the door frame looking her up and down.

"I'm sorry, but I believe I forgot to clean this room, and the bed," she replied.

"I think everything is fine," he assured her.

She looked him up and down as well in his towel. She had long blond hair and her uniform was rather sexy. Normally she would have caught his eye. She spotted her ID that she'd dropped on the floor in the room when she was in there earlier and asked if she could get it. When she bent to pick it up her short skirted uniform revealed more that he needed to see. He wondered if this was a distraction, or a setup, so he reluctantly ignored her. She walked out the room, smiling at him as she said goodbye. After she had left, Chris switched on the TV. His favourite film "Hit man" was on. Waitie called to see if everything was going according to plan and Chris assured him it was.

The next day, Jade and Margaret went for a walk in the Cannot Hill Park. Chris had also been sent here to find his target. He'd been there since 6 A.M. planning his position and familiarising himself with the area. He lined up half a mile from the main park in a derelict building. He assembled his rifle from the corner of the building and waited for his target. He was dressed in his old army uniform, and tied a purple head band around his head. His black army boots were laced up properly to prevent him tripping over. Both sleeves were rolled up past his elbows for comfort. He was very nervous as he had not done this for years.

He looked through the optical sights attached to the top of his rifle. He'd been given a description of his target and who that target would be travelling with. At this point he hadn't looked at the photo he'd picked up at the secret spot. The information and location given to Chris was enough to accurately pinpoint the intended target. Chris remembered in hit training between him and Waitie to work blind. This was based on trust between the two. He waited, and waited, but there was no sign of his target. Meanwhile, coming into focus was Jade and Margaret. As they walked and talked, Jade stopped to fix her shoes. Chris took another look, and spotted Margaret; the target's accomplice. Chris didn't spot the target, but waited as he positioned his finger on the trigger. Jade then stood up, but Chris wasn't able to match the description with the target as she was hidden behind a tree, so he waited for a better view. Jade's back was in direct focus for Chris. He was convinced this was the right target, and he didn't need to see more. He took aim as Jade's head came into position and prepared to squeeze the trigger. A child playing in the park kicked a ball that hit her on the left leg and she turned. Her face came into direct focus for Chris just as he was about to squeeze the trigger.

"For fuck's sake," Chris said when he spotted it was Jade. He took out the photo and looked at it. It was Jade. Chris realised his trust training was flawed, and wondered what Waitie knew. He blamed himself for not looking at the picture earlier.

He immediately engaged the safety pin on the rifle. He was so shocked he knew he could have mistakenly triggered it. He let go of the rifle, spun back against the wall and sliding down until his knees were bent close to his chest.

"I almost killed her," he kept on whispering to himself. "If Waitie knew she was part of my family and still sent me on this mission, I will kill him."

By this time, Jade and Margaret had already left the location. Chris took up his phone and called Waitie.

"Hello, is the job done?" asked Waitie.

"What do you know about the target?" asked Chris, "Do you know her family?"

"Why all this questions, is the job done or not?" he continued to ask.

"WHAT THE FUCK DO YOU KNOW ABOUT HER?" asked Chris in anger.

"Calm down, I don't know her family," replied Waitie, "why?"

"She's in is my family," replied Chris.

Waitie went quiet for while, after whispering, "For fuck's sake."

"Is she dead?" asked Waitie.

"No she is not," said a relieved Chris.

"How is she related to you?" asked Waitie.

"She is my sister-in-law," replied Chris.

"There is a lot of money at stake here and you know the rules: if she is not your mother, daughter, or sister, why is she not dead?" asked Waitie.

"Fuck off. You hurt a bone in her body and you answer to me," replied Chris, and hung up the phone. Chris went back to the hotel, collected his things, and checked out. He rushed back to London.

CHAPTER 18

Jade and Margaret sat on the park bench having ice cream. Spring had just ended and the sun was out, although it was not that warm. Jade looked up in the tree above her and spotted a pigeon. She moved from beneath him just in case, while Margaret laughed as they both knew what could happen. Jade noticed parents and their kids picnicking out on the grass. This was something she had dreamt about doing since she was a child. She was pleased that she would now be able to do it, although she would have to wait for a little while as Paul was inside, to have a proper family picnic.

Suddenly Margaret jumped up and screamed as she fanned something away. She attracted the attention of others in the park as she spun and ran off. Jade was laughing. It turned out that it was a bee. Neither of them were a fan of bees so they decided to move somewhere else. They found a better place to sit without pigeons or bees and Jade thought the time was right to discuss Paul. So she finished her ice cream, wiped her hands, and positioned herself as if she was about to tell a story.

"Paul was accused of rape," she said, while she wiped off the last speck of ice cream from her top.

"Really?" said a surprised Margaret.

"It's not what you think. He said he didn't do it and I believe him," said Jade, looking Margaret in the eyes, expecting her to understand. "His ex girlfriend, *Sophia Wait*, accused him of rape. There was no evidence, but he was coerced into pleading guilty."

"If he wasn't guilty, why plead guilty?"

Jade looked at her in disbelief, and said, "I believed he didn't do it, and he was persuaded to incriminate himself," replied Jade, which surprised Margaret because her words made her think Jade was no longer an accountant's secretary but a lawyer.

"How long will he be in for?"

"Seven years."

"Seven years? I'm sorry Jade, I thought it would be more like two or three years. Let's go home, you look tired." She felt sorry for Jade, and didn't want to upset her anymore.

As they got up from the chair, a pigeon landed where they had been sitting. Margaret and Jade looked at each other and laughed, as they continued to walk.

Chris was frustrated so he stopped at his local pub to order a gin and tonic. He sat on the outside garden bench at the back of the pub thinking. He had to do something to help Paul even if he had to kill someone. The mission Waitie sent him on was still bugging him. Although he wanted the money he also wanted out of the business. He wiped the frost off his glass that had built up over time because it was so cold. A girl came over to chat him up but he ignored her as he had other things on him mind.

"My innocent brother is in prison, and I can't do anything to help," mumbled Chris.

The girl got the drift and walked away. As she did so she stumbled between two chairs, drunk as a bat. Many of the patrons were pissed and behaving badly.

A man stumbled and knocked over Chris' drink. Chris got up in a rage, grabbed him and took him outside, hitting his head on the pavement. He was knocked unconscious and Chris sat back down to complete the remainder of his drink, as if nothing had happened. Four of the man's friends surrounded Chris shouting, "We are going to kill you." Two had baseball bats. Chris didn't acknowledge them and this sent one into a rage. He felt the response was not satisfactory so he decided to shove Chris. Chris grabbed him by the arm, pulled out his gun and pointed it at his head as if he was about to squeeze the trigger. The others ran away. Chris felt a hand on his arm.

"Leave it, Chris."

It was Waitie.

"How did you know I was here?" asked Chris.

"That's not important anymore," said Waitie. "You almost killed the man."

"Why are you here?" Chris asked in an angry voice.

"I may have another job for you," replied Waitie.

"Did I tell you I needed another job?" asked Chris, as

he fixed up his clothes and shoved past him.

Waitie was still trying to manipulate Chris to get him to do his dirty work. Waitie took out some cash and paid the pub owner for the damage and turned to Chris. "Look at you, you need money, and you are who you are; a professional killer."

"I don't feel like talking now, so leave me alone," warned Chris.

"I will respect your wishes but we will keep in touch," replied Waitie. He knew he was playing with danger and what Chris was capable of.

Chris decided to meet up with some of his friends in East London shortly after he left the pub. He wanted to have a rest. Although he was drinking, he wasn't drunk. Before he saw his friends, he spent five minutes in the park gathering his thoughts.

Jade got back from her trip and was looking happy Jessica was not home yet, and appeared to be running late. Jade was counting the days until her first scan. She knew she had left it late because she'd hidden her pregnancy. Looking at her calendar she realised it was scheduled for Thursday. She heard the key rattle in the door. Jessica was home.

"Hi," said Jessica, as she hugged Jade, expressing how much she'd missed her.

"Hi," replied Jade.

"How was your trip?" Jessica asked, resting her bag on her desk in the corner. Not looking at what she was doing while taking off her shoes, she almost knocked over Jade's drink that was on her desk.

"It was nice, I haven't see Margaret for ages. We went to one of Birmingham's famous parks," said Jade holding her tummy, and scrunching her face, as if she felt a pain.

"Are you OK?" asked Jessica.

"Yes, I'm fine, the baby just kicked," smiled Jade. "I have my scan on Thursday."

"This Thursday?" asked Jessica, as Jade nodded.

"I haven't heard from Robert in a long time, is he OK?" asked Jade.

Yes, he is," replied Jessica. "I spoke to him today, he said he was in East London, or Stratford somewhere."

"East London, why?" asked Jade.

"I don't know," replied Jessica.

"Has he revealed his plan B yet?" asked Jade.

"Not yet. Martin also said he had saxophone practice in East London," remembered Jessica. "Actually, I think its Stratford."

"That's where Sophia live," Jade asked in a rhetorical way.

No-one asked about Chris, but Chris was already in Stratford East London.

"I just remembered that I have to drop something off in Stratford, do you want to come?" asked Jessica.

"Maybe," replied Jade as she continued to rub her tummy. The baby turned again. This had been going on for ten minutes. "It seems like everyone will be in East London tonight," said Jade. She sat down on the sofa, straightening her legs, as she thought this would help the kicking baby.

"Yes, it seems so."

"I'm off now Susan," said Martin.

She wondered why he was going so early.

"What time do you think you will be back?" she asked, while tidying up the kitchen. She thought he may be up to something because he had worn his new Deserts and taken other shoes with him. He told her that he needed them for practice. This wasn't a bother to Susan, as he did this all the time. He was dressed up nicely.

"Are you really going to practice?" asked Susan.

"I am indeed," replied Martin, wondering if his wife thought he was up to something. Susan always made her jealousy obvious. "Don't wait up for me, I may be a bit later than normal tonight."

Susan knew that this would not be the first time he had gone to practice and stayed out late. She knew that when he met up with his friends, they normally chatted for long lengths of time so she was not worried about the time.

"I'm off now love," he slammed the door before Susan could even say bye.

Susan took up her Bible and started to read it. She had a funny feeling about Martin going out that night. She did get paranoid and superstitious from time to time. She thought something might be wrong so the Bible was her comfort. An hour later, she was still reading her Bible, blinking and dozing off to sleep. Her mind was still on Martin. She rang Jessica for reassurance but she did not answer the phone. She tried Robert but he also did not answer his phone. She thought of calling Jade but decided not to. It was now eleven and she'd had no word from anyone. She decided that she couldn't hold out any longer, so she went to the bathroom and freshened up. On her way back, she saw that the light had been left on in the kitchen, so she switched it off. She climbed into bed, and within five minutes, she was asleep.

CHAPTER 19

It was twelve o'clock when a shadow moved across Sophia's front door. Deep in sleep, she didn't hear the glass she was drinking out of smash after it fall when she turned hitting the table attached to her bed. The shadow stood outside the house as if it was a member of that household opening the front door. She didn't have her security lock on that night. Her door was opened, with what appeared to be a key by the intruder who went straight to the kitchen, took out a knife, put it back down then picked it back up again. Sophia slept on. The intruder searched the drawers, obviously looking for something and mimicking the moves of a robber. The intruder was wearing gloves, and dressed all in black. Even in the dark, it was clear that the person was wearing branded shoes. They left footprints on the carpets. The intruder went into the living room, and searched more drawers. Papers and valuables were scattered all over the floor. The intruder slowly walked up the stairs holding on to the railings, as one of the steps creaked. The intruder stopped, and waited, then proceeded with caution. It was difficult to tell if the person was a man or a woman, as it was very dark. On reaching the top of the stairs, the intruder checked the rooms. One of the rooms was open and the other was closed.

The intruder pushed open Sophia's room, and stood over her in the same way as in the movie she and Paul saw. As she lay still on her back, he took hold of one of her pillows next to her and placed it over her face. She instantly woke up suffocating as the intruder overpowered her. She grabbed on to the sheet, stretching for her knife with one hand. She took the other hand and grabbed on to the clothing of the intruder, but its strength was too much for her. She kicked as she struggled and gasped for air. By this time her heart started to slow and her chest constricted as she gasped for air. She was dying. She made one final attempt to fight, but her weakening oxygen depleted body had nothing left. The bed shook with her dying movements until she tried to take breath and stopped moving. The intruder held the pillow still watching for anymore movements. She was dead. The killer gently removed the pillow and checked her pulse to confirm she was really dead. The intruder then slowly went down stairs, opened the front door checking to see if anyone had seen anything and closed it.

Tina was worried the next day as she hadn't heard from Sophia. This was unlike her. She decided to visit her. It was twelve midday. Tina pushed her key in and opened the front door. She shouted, "Sophia, Sophia, are you there?" There was no answer. She spotted footprints leading upstairs. She thought they were of Sophia's boyfriend. She was still worried, so went upstairs. She saw Sophia's body on the bed, but thought she was sleeping. She called out again, but still got no reply. Tina wanted to be sure, so she shook her trying to wake her up. She felt her pulse, and there was none. A frantic scream alerted the neighbours who came to see what was going on.

"Call an ambulance, and the police," shouted Tina. She tried to talk again but the words couldn't come out.

They called the police, who came five minutes later. The ambulance came shortly after. It took three officers to console and restrain Tina as she kicked, and cried, and threw herself to the floor. She finally went to a corner in one of the other rooms and cried her eyes out. The police asked her to leave, and cordoned off the area as this was now a crime scene. The forensic team arrived just as the police were setting up an appointment to meet with her to ask her questions as part of the investigation.

Two days into the investigation, the police went to Tina's house.

"Good morning, my name is Detective Stuart," introduced the officer. "Is this a good time to talk," he asked and Tina nodded. "When was the last time you saw your daughter?"

"Two days ago," replied Tina, as she continued sobbing. Detective Stuart moved closer to her and handed her some tissue.

"Would you know who would want your daughter dead?" he asked.

Stricken with grief she replied, "No." Her voice cracked. She sniffled and looked at him. She looked drained and tired.

Detective Stuart decided that was probably enough questions for the day and left the house. He gave her his card to call him if she had any new information. As he was leaving Paul's solicitor John, who Tina knew, and another friend arrived. They passed the detective on his way out. Tina invited them in and closed the door after the officer had gone. The friend hugged her, and so did the solicitor who looked disturbed and guilty as he believed he may have been partially to blame. She offered them a drink with swollen eyes as she continued to cry. The tissue Detective Stuart gave her was soaking wet. She moved to the left corner of the room and threw it tin the bin. John reached for some more on the table and handed it to her. The friend said he had his suspicions who the murderer was and wanted to know the date of the funeral.

"The police said they will not release the body until they have completed their forensic investigation," said Tina. "This means the funeral will have to be put on hold until then."

Paul's solicitor John tea fell and splattered on the floor. He was shaking with nerves.

"Clumsy," thought Tina, as she cleaned up his mess. There was no more tissue as he handed her the rest to clean up the floor.

The meeting ended and they left her house feeling sad. When they had gone Tina remembered that she had an emergency number for Sophia's dad, whom she hadn't seen for a while. Their last encounter a few years ago was not a pleasant one. Due to the nature of the breakup and her pride, she had never used it. She reached into her ten-year-old diary and nervously dialled the number. She was reluctant to do it as she thought there is no way he could still have the same number, but she tried anyway. It rang twice before it was answered.

"Can you co-co-come over please?" sobbed Tina.

"What is it? Calm down," replied Sophia's father.

"Please come now, Waitie, I can't speak over the phone," she said.

"This sounds serious," he replied. He feared the worst, as he thought about his daughter. "OK, I'm on my way." He hopped into his Jeep, and rushed over to her house.

The drive should have taken twenty minutes, but he got there in ten. He vigorously knocked twice on the door. She went and opened it. She hugged him without hesitation, as he slowly placed his arms around her, trying to work out what the call was about.

"She is dead, Waitie, she is dead," said Tina.

"Who is dead?" he frantically asked, while he pulled her from his chest with his hands resting them on her shoulders.

Your daughter," she replied.

"MY DAUGHTER? How did she die?" he asked, fuming with grief and anger. "I told you to call me if something ever happened. When did she go into hospital?" he hysterically asked, with his hand on his head, pacing up and down.

"No, she wasn't ill, she was murdered," said Tina.

143

When Waitie heard that, he sat down in the middle of the sofa, in shock, wiping away tears. He walked to the kitchen with his hands in his pocket. He didn't say another word. Tina sobbed in the corner of the room. Waitie went into the garden. Within minutes he came back into the house with his hands on his head. Tina saw tears fall from his eyes, as he tried to keep his composure.

"Have you got a drink?" he asked, as he sat this time on the arm of the chair.

"I have got some brandy," replied Tina as she attempted to head for the kitchen waiting for a response from him.

"Let me have a glass please. Have the police been notified?"

"Yes, they have," replied Tina.

Waitie sat quietly for a few minutes. He took a gulp and drank all his brandy down, making a sound as if his throat was scorched by the strength of the brandy. He went back to the garden and made a phone call. Tina looked from the kitchen, but she was not able to make out what he was saying. One thing she didn't want to do was to disturb him, so she decided not to join him outside. One thing was certain, he was so angry that the glass shattered in his hand when he had his second drink.

"Because of my work, and the fact that you asked me to leave you both alone, I stayed away from protecting you both," said Waitie. "It seemed this was a mistake. Someone will pay."

"This is no time to blame anyone," said Tina.

"I missed her so much, I went to see her recently pretending to be a boiler engineer," said Waitie, as his face dropped and eyes twitched.

"So it was you! She told me about it," said Tina.

Waitie knew that he would not do anything until after the funeral and he would need help to catch the killer. He did not want to interfere with the police investigation but he wanted justice.

"Please no more killing Waitie," suggested Tina. "I know what you are like."

Waitie did not respond to her. "I need to make another call," he said, as he proceeded to the garden again. He waited for the phone to be answered and then said, "Chris, my daughter has been murdered."

"What? Your daughter, I didn't know you had a daughter," replied Chris. "I'm sorry to hear this, my condolences to you and your family. When was this?"

"Last night," he replied, while contemplating war, ignoring what Tina said about more killing. He thought no-one could kill his daughter and get away with it.

"What is your daughter's name?" probed Chris.

"Her name was Sophia," replied Waitie.

Chris was silent.

"Are you there Chris? Chris?" called out Waitie. "I think he hung up on me," he said to himself. Waitie checked the phone and saw the call was still in session so he wondered if there was a network issue. He moved it back to his ear for one more try.

"I'm still here," replied Chris. He knew a war was about to start as he knew what Waitie was capable of.

"As you didn't do that other job, can I have the money back?" asked Waitie, thinking that he was going to need all the resources he could get. In the back of his mind he wondered if Chris was the right person to hunt the killer down.

"Sure, but you promised another job," replied Chris.

"Now is not the time," said Waitie.

Chris wondered what Waitie knew about his daughter's involvement with his brother's imprisonment. He also knew the tricks of the profession of a hit man. He figured out that Waitie had been following him around and wondered why. But if Waitie wanted to kill him he would have already.

"Waitie, I need to give you time to sort out things. Let me know when is the funeral," suggested Chris.

The phone call ended. Chris made his way to Martin's. He was thinking about meeting with the others in a couple of week's time. He also knew that Jade was not safe as Waitie was driven by money, and despite knowing what Chris was capable of, he didn't regard in-laws as close knit family. Chris now had a dilemma on his hands. He was not a coward, but he didn't want to start a war that might endanger his family's lives so he knew he had to be vigilant.

CHAPTER 20

Detective Stuart was meeting with his boss, the Detective Chief Inspector (DCI), to discuss Sophia's murder. Stuart was heading the murder investigation team and needed to follow all leads to establish the cause of death and who was responsible. As he reported his findings in the case, with a notebook and pen in front of him, he highlighted what was needed to complete the investigation. The blinds in the office were open and the DCI sat on the desk staring out the window with one leg touching the floor. The informal meeting was not usual, besides the DCI knew Stuart was the best man for the job.

"What have you got for me?" asked the DCI.

"A young woman was murdered, although we are still waiting for the complete report from the coroner's office," said Stuart, as he adjusted his glasses on his nose, looking over it at his boss' face. "I understand, looking at the report; that a community and partnership team frequents the area, educating the community on the consequences of murder. I have my Family Liaison Advisory Team (FLA), and Homicide Task Force (HTF), providing all the necessary assistance needed for this case, so I'm fully equipped to deal with the matter."

"OK," replied, the DCI, while he contemplated any extra support he could offer. "So, what leads have you got so far?"

"We know that she had enemies—someone was sent to prison for raping her. We learnt that she recently reported people following her, also from the initial forensic reports we know that the killer wore branded shoes,"

"Right," said the DCI, before walking towards the window and flicking one of the blades on the blinds to see what his other officers were doing.

"Her father is allegedly a hit man, although we have no real evidence to substantiate this," continued Stuart.

"You seems to have everything in place, so I will leave you to it, but report back to me in two weeks on any further developments," said the DCI as he made his way to the door. "By the way," he turned around, with one hand on the door lock, "have you interviewed the family of the convicted person who admitted raping her?"

"Not yet," replied Stuart.

Later that day, the doorbell rang.

"Susan, go and get the door," asked Martin from the shower.

Susan emerged from the kitchen, with her apron on, and onions in her left hand. When she opened the door Detective Stuart identified himself by showing his ID, and told her he was the investigating officer for the murder of Sophia.

"Can I come in?" asked Detective Stuart.

"Sure," replied Susan, as she showed him to the sitting room.

"I need to speak to Martin, is he here?" asked Stuart, as he made his way to the sitting room. Detective Stuart tried to be friendly and suggested they had a nice place. Susan offered him a drink, which he refused. He told her that he couldn't drink on the job.

By this time Martin had finished his shower, and walked straight in the sitting room, with his towel on.

"I'll go and put some clothes on first officer," Martin said and left the room. He came back as quickly as he could but he wasn't too steady and looked a bit nervous. "How can I help you, officer?" Martin asked trying to compose himself.

"Sophia Wait was murdered two weeks ago. I understand she went out with your brother some years ago and then accused him of rape and he is now serving a sentence in prison for that. Is that correct?" asked the detective, as he prepared to write down his answer.

"Yes," replied Martin.

Susan was not too worried so she left the room as she believed this was routine questioning.

"Where were you on the night of the murder?" asked the detective.

"I was at saxophone practice in East London with friends. Do you think I had something to do with it?"

asked Martin.

"I'm not saying that. "Were you anywhere near Stratford on that night?"

"The centre is in Stratford, so yes," he replied. Detective Stuart noted down his answers, and reached in his pocket.

"Here is my card, if you have any information, please do not hesitate to call me," he suggested, as he made his way towards the front door.

"Sure, will do," replied Martin and then went to his bedroom without saying a word to Susan.

Susan joined him. By this time she was becoming concern. "What was that all about?" she asked.

"The police are just doing their job," he replied. He didn't say much after the police had left, and Susan started to wonder why. Martin knew that his family would be suspected but not to this scale. He had done some work on Sophia's house, including changing the lock to her door which he believed may be a factor in her case. Chris also had a ways of getting things done and picking locks was part of his trade, Robert used to visit Sophia a lot, and Jessica hated her. All of this would make his family prime suspects.

"Why would anyone want to hurt her?" asked Susan. "Despite her deceptive behaviour, I would not want to see her dead—I always thought leave her to God," continued Susan, while cleaning the room. She spotted a key on the floor, which she had never seen before, but Martin assured her that it was for the church storeroom and she remembered using a key like it.

"Would any of you be capable of doing such a thing?" asked Susan.

"I would," joked Martin, as he ironed his shirt for work the next day.

Susan switched on the radio to listen to her favourite story. There was a breaking news report: "The police believe they have a very good lead in the murder of Sophia Wait. They are working on a number of theories that could lead them to the suspect."

"That's good," said Martin.

"This would be welcomed by the family as this would take the heat off us," agreed Susan.

"I believe Jessica knew her father; they were at school together," said Martin.

"Do you know him as well?" asked Susan.

"All I know was that Chris hung out with him sometime ago, but I have never met the man," said Martin, on the verge of completing his trousers. He placed them on the hanger and began to clean his shoes.

"What is that on your shoes?" asked Susan.

"It's black tar. I stepped in road works coming from work yesterday," replied Martin.

"Which shoes did you wear to the practise a few weeks ago?" asked Susan.

"One of my new brands, why?" asked Martin, as he yawned, changing into his night clothes. He told Susan he was tired and wanted to sleep.

Susan indicated that she would be up for a while.

CHAPTER 21

The following day, Jessica went to Robert's house. She came to see him as she was short of cash and wanted money to book a holiday. She'd seen a deal which fell three weeks into her pay cycle. She assured him he will get the money back as soon as she was paid. The notion that Jessica wanted cash was unusual as she was considered the well off one in the family. Robert made her dinner, and told her that he would do an internet transfer.

Meanwhile, Mark was in his room playing his Play station three (PS3). He was unaware of what was going on downstairs, but it didn't matter to him anyway.

"Yes," he shouted aloud as he scored in his *FIFA 10* football game. England and France were playing and he was always keen for England to win. "Goal!" he said as he busied himself with the controls, twisting from side to side as if he was on the pitch. When the doorbell rang he remembered he was supposed to ring his girlfriend, but if he was to much into his game he often could be bothered. "If it's my girlfriend, I hope they tell her I'm not here," Mark said to himself. "I don't want to see anyone now, I'm too busy."

He searched for his drink next to his bed with one hand, unaware he had knocked it over while playing Grand Theft Auto IV.

A sudden power outage surprised Mark. The connection to the box was still active and the lights were flickering so he wasn't sure what had caused the blackout. He looked down to his feet and realised he had kicked out the extension that powered the TV. With the sudden silence he became aware of voices downstairs, one which said, "I'm Detective Stuart." Mark didn't bother to reconnect the TV and rushed downstairs to see what was going on. Half way down the stairs, he realised he had no shirt on. He rushed back upstairs and put one on.

"I'm investigating the murder of Sophia Wait and I'm looking to speak to Robert," said Detective Stuart.

"That's me," said Robert.

"I just need to ask you some questions, I'll be brief."

"Can I offer you a drink, officer?" asked Jessica.

"No, thanks," he replied shuffling the pages in his notebook. "What is your name?"

"Jessica, Robert's brother," she replied.

The detective put his glasses on and checked his records. "I also need to ask you some question as well."

"Were you invited in?" interrupted Mark appearing at the door, wondering if he had followed procedure.

"No," replied the detective.

"I suggest you go back outside, and wait until you are

invited," said Mark.

"May I ask who are you?" asked Detective Stuart, as he made his way back outside.

"I'm Mark, Robert's son—a trainee criminal solicitor and you could be breaching Police and Criminal Evidence Act PACE by inviting yourself in," he replied.

The detective realised he had not conducted his investigation by the book. From that moment on Mark scrutinised him like a hawk and listened to every question. For Robert it was one of his proudest moments as a father as his son safeguarded them from police abuse.

"Sophia was murdered at about midnight. Where were you then?" asked Detective Stuart, looking at Robert and waiting for an answer.

"I was in East London," replied Robert defensively, glancing at Mark. "But I don't believe I was still there at that time."

Mark saw Detective Stuart note Robert had been in East London that night, but fail to note he may not have been there at the time of the murder. Mark wondered if he should flag the detective's conduct, or wait until the officer tripped up so they could later sue or complain. He thought he should do the right thing, so he said, "You must write down my dad's second response, otherwise, you may be breaching section 23 of the Criminal Procedure and Investigation Act of 1996."

Surprised by his intervention, the detective felt a bit uncomfortable. He posed the same question to Jessica, and this time took down everything she said.

"I drove to East London with Jade that night," Jessica explained. "I also believe I left there before the time of the murder. Any further questions officer?"

"No, that's all for now." As he walked away, he turned and looked at Robert. "When you were in East London, were you in Stratford?"

"I was in Stratford, but still not sure that time." He opened the door, while Jessica closed it behind him.

When Detective Stuart left Mark texted Chris to warn him they were questioning the family. He asked Chris to tell him if Stuart turned up because he wanted to be there for any questioning.

"I was so nervous," said Robert.

"Me too," said Jessica.

"Thank God I was there," said Mark, as his proud father hugged and thanked him.

"I can see my hard earned cash has not been wasted on your studies," bragged Robert. "Where were we before the detective turned up?"

"In the dining room," said Jessica leading the way. "It's dinner time."

Mark sat proudly at his usual spot, while Jessica sat facing Robert. Robert got up to serve the dinner. He took out a roast chicken from the oven and started to slice it up. The steam and the aroma coming from it made Mark's tummy rumble. Jessica also couldn't wait for her portion and took a small piece to taste.

"Wait, your turn," smiled Robert.

"Can I get a drink, Dad?" asked Mark.

"Sure," replied Robert.

A wide variety of food was placed on the table for self service. Jessica took food first, then Mark followed after. She served her salad and vegetables on the same plate.

"I kind of feel sorry for Sophia, because I don't think

anyone deserves to be murdered," said Mark.

Robert carried on eating without a response. Jessica nodded.

"I have some history with the family, so I will miss her," said Jessica. Jessica did not want to get into her secrets, but realised that her private affairs may come out one day. Too many members of the family had spotted that personal letter on her desk.

"How can you be so cold?" muffled Robert, with his mouth full, as he expected her to show more sympathy than she'd showed. Robert also thought she was being sarcastic.

"I'm not—I'm a realist," replied Jessica. "On a different note, I didn't think Chris was so close to Paul."

"He is, but Chris can be secretive," said Robert.

"I think Martin knows more about Chris, than we do, but he may be protecting our feelings, which is understandable," said Jessica. "I'm close to Martin, but he has never said a word about Chris in that way to me or what he does for a living."

"We are a loving family anyway, so no matter what we do, we will stick together," said Robert.

They continued chatting until it was time for Jessica to leave. Mark wanted to continue his game, but looked at his watch, and thought it was too late. Robert wouldn't allow it anyway. He knew Robert could be strict sometimes.

CHAPTER 22

Meanwhile, it was Chris' turn to be visited by the police. The police liked to come unannounced to secure evidence in their investigation. Chris went outside to empty his rubbish into his wheelie bin. He lived in a rough neighbourhood where his neighbours were always fighting. They were also nosy and at any commotion you would see them looking through their windows. When Chris was on his way back to his flat, he heard a car pull up behind him. Chris turned his head behind him and looked over his shoulder. This time it was Detective Stuart and a colleague. The DCI had advised they take a colleague when visiting that area.

"Hi Chris, I'm D—"

Before he could finish Chris interrupted and said, "I know who you are."

"Can we come in?" asked the detective, stopping at the door, after Chris had gone in. He remembered Mark was on his case for not following police protocol, so he waited for an invitation from Chris.

"Yes, and my nephew Mark will be here shortly, if you don't mind," suggested Chris.

The name Mark rang a very uncomfortable bell in the detective's mind, as he had thought to speed up the process before he got there.

"Sure, that's fine," replied the detective.

Chris' front room was small and only had one sofa, so he could not accommodate too many guests. The other officer stood at the door as there was nowhere for him to sit.

"Would you like to sit?" invited Chris, while fixing the cushion on the sofa.

"No, thanks, I don't think I will be long," replied Detective Stuart. "Where were you on the night of the murder, about say 12 midnight?" he asked. As usual he used his pen and book to take notes.

"I was in East London, and I was there until late, but I was with friends," replied Chris.

"I need all your shoes, except the ones you are wearing now, for forensic analysis. Could you hand them over now please?" asked the detective. The shoes prints from the crime scene eliminated the shoes Chris was wearing. "I will process them here and now, and hand them back to you. My colleague is part of the forensic team, and came with his equipment."

Chris handed over seven pairs of Clarks including some of his trainers to Detective Stuart, who then handed them to his colleague who took them to the police van for forensic examination. Moments later, the police officer believed they had all the necessary information, and left Chris' flat in a hurry as if he had another suspect to catch. But the truth was that Detective Stuart rushed the job to avoid confrontation with Mark. It was also convenient for Chris because he had all his kit inside the house and was worried that they could have presented a search warrant and searched the flat. This could have sent him away for life.

After they had left there was a knock at the door. Chris though it was the police again, so he rushed outside the back to hide his kit in the shed before opening the door without enquiring who it was.

"Have you forgotten something sir?"

"Yes," smiled Kerry, as Chris raised his head up to the sound of a woman's voice.

It was Chris' girlfriend, the mother of his kids.

"Kerry!" smiled Chris, "come in."

"Who were you expecting?" asked Kerry.

"No-one," replied Chris. He did not want her to know too much about the situation.

He offered her something to drink, and asked her about the kids. Like Waitie, he kept her in the shadows, as Waitie had done with Sophia for her protection. Chris believed this would guarantee their safety. None of his family even knew about his children.

"I thought you had left London for good as we had agreed, but I didn't know you had come back until recently," mentioned Kerry. "I know it's safer this way for me and the kids, but when are you going to stop doing what you are doing, and spend more quality time with them? They need you."

Chris sighed and the anguish and frustration showed on his face. He didn't want to hear that type of comment as it did nothing but bring stress and sadness to his heart. "I'm working on a plan," he reassured her. "What happen to your blonde hair? Why did you dye it brown?" asked Chris, as he desperately tried to change the subject. It didn't work.

"A plan, how long will it take? How long must they wait? That's not good enough."

"Listen, I have got enough on my plate as it is at the moment, just leave me alone," said Chris in frustration. The last thing he need was a lecture. He was working on a plan to get out of the line of work, but he could not tell anyone in detail. This was part of the reason he left for the States nearly six years ago.

"Have you heard about the murder in East London recently?" asked Kerry, finally changing the topic.

"Yes, she was going out with my brother Paul," answered Chris.

"She was a sincere and decent girl, I have been told," said Kerry.

"Yeah right—not to my brother," thought Chris. "How is Jason doing now, he is twelve now isn't he?"

"He is doing fine," replied Kerry.

"And Eboni, how old is she now?" he asked.

Ten," replied Kerry.

"I regretted some of the decisions I made in my younger days," recollected Chris, "but the best time was with you."

"Really, yet you left me, why?" asked Kerry.

"You know why," he replied. "You haven't touched your drink."

"I know, I'm just happy to see you," smiled Kerry.

"Have you got a boyfriend now?" asked Chris.

"I promised that I would wait for you, and I have," replied Kerry, as she took the first drink of her orange juice.

"Look it is still dangerous at the moment, can you wait a little bit longer for me?" he asked.

"I only want you so you better be quick, or my patience may run out," smiled Kerry.

"And that I don't want. I would love to have you spend the night with me, but it is still too dangerous." He looked out the window. "When you were coming to see me did you apply code one?"

"Sure, I always do, you have taught me well," she replied.

"I know I have," said Chris.

"Here is the latest photo of your children," said Kerry handing him a picture. "They look more like you as they grow. I think it's time for me to go now." As she was about to open the door, she remembered something. "I almost forgot, one of your friends came round about a week ago, he said his name was Waitie. He said he came around once with you, but I cannot remember him. He was playing with the kids, saying that they have grown up nicely."

"Whoa!" said Chris. "I have never brought him around to the house, that's a lie." He could see the concerned look on Kerry's face. Chris did not want to cause any unnecessary alarm, so he kept his cool. "If he comes back again, do not answer the door, and stay put," he warned. "Always check your window first and if you see him anywhere near the house ring me without hesitation, or leave the house if you can safely, and stay at your mum's for a while. I will tell him not to visit again, so this is only if you see him."

He walked her to the door, and kissed her goodbye. The sad look on Chris' face was noticed by Kerry. Kerry turned around and waved at Chris. He waved back and watched her go.

CHAPTER 23

Paul had started to write a book about his life and was working on it while his cell mate Jimmy was outside the prison yard. But when he heard the news about Sophia's death he was disturbed and couldn't concentrate. Her voice kept on coming to his ears, especially when she told him that she loved him. When Jimmy returned he saw at once that Paul had something on his mind. Paul lay on his back staring at the ceiling and twisted and turned restlessly as he tried to come to terms with her death.

"Why did you not come out today?" asked Jimmy, as he hopped on the bottom bunk. The bed smelled fresh; they had changed the blue mattress cover and replaced it with a purple one.

"Did you hear the news?" asked Paul.

"What news?"

"Sophia is dead!"

"Really? That must be good news for you."

"No actually."

"What do you mean by no? The bitch put you away for seven years. How could you not be happy?"

"What Jimmy doesn't realised is that I'm not a violent man," Paul said to himself. The emotions in the cell between the two were quite different. Paul was more forgiving, while Jimmy was the opposite.

"She put you away," said Jimmy looking serious at Paul.

"No, I put me away, I just hope none of my family are involved."

"Why would you think something like that?"

"I have a very dangerous brother called Chris," said Paul. "I know a lot of his secrets, which I have kept with me until now."

Chris sounded familiar to Jimmy. He wondered if it was the Chris he knew. Paul saw his face and wondered if he was hiding something.

"He is a hit man, isn't he?" asked Jimmy.

"Do you know him?"

"No, but I have been in the world of criminality to know when someone talks about one by reading their facial expressions," said Jimmy, although in his mind he still thought it may be the same Chris. "I also know a lot of people." They continued the conversation until Paul decided to continue writing his book.

Jade's scan was rescheduled so she showed up at the hospital and when her name was called she went into room seven. As she entered the room, she was told to hop onto the bed.

"Is this your first baby?" asked the technician.

"Yes," replied Jade. "How long will the scan take?" she asked, as she positioned herself on the bed as gel was poured on her tummy.

"Usually fifteen minutes," replied the technician.

"What do you look for?" asked Jade.

"We look for serious structural abnormalities, check the baby's size and how advanced your pregnancy is," replied the technician.

The scan was done successfully and Jade discovered that it was a boy. Jade couldn't wait to pass on the news so she telephoned Jessica to let her know. Paul came across her mind as did Sophia. She was sorry to learn of her death as she didn't believe anyone had the right to take a life. Jessica was ecstatic and so was Chris when she told him the news.

Detective Stuart had made a significant breakthrough in the case. He questioned the neighbours, one of whom said that he saw the killer. The neighbour was up late that night, and spotted a man in the house. His statement was not clear, but enough to assist in the investigation. More forensic analysis came back from the lab with damming evidence and he re-visited the brothers and took more forensic evidence; some of which were still in his possession. He then decided to release the body for burial. Tina made the funeral arrangements and invited the family. On the day of the funeral, there were only a few people at the church. Chris went to the burial ground as Martin couldn't make it. All were dressed in black and both Chris and Waitie wore dark glasses. They stood next to each other and Chris saw the tears flowing down his face.

Before anyone else could see them, Waitie turned away and wiped them away with his handkerchief. Waitie was kept in the loop by Tina as to developments in the case. Neither of them were aware the police had re-interviewed the brothers. Chris was told by Mark before his interview, but that was just about it. The detective kept it from them, as he feared that the information might get in the wrong hands and tip off the suspect before they could secure more evidence. The wind blew and the well-wishers cried. Waitie saw how hurt Tina was so he moved towards the grave and hugged her. He whispered to her, "It's my fault." As the minister prayed over the body while it was lowered into the ground, Waitie could not bear it any longer, and went to his car. Chris followed in an attempt to support him as best as he could.

"You have got beautiful children, take care of them," said Waitie.

Chris didn't like the sound of that, and although he told Waitie not to visit his family again, he was still worried as to what Waitie knew.

"I need your help to find the killer," said Waitie. Waitie thought appealing to Chris' conscience would be a good way of getting the best in the business on his side. He desperately wanted Chris to second him, but he knew that Chris answered to no one. "I want to personally torture whoever did this to my angel. I will give you all my savings, which I saved up for my only child. Now there is no point keeping all this money, so when you are ready, name your price. If you can't do it I will have to do it myself, and then leave this game and turn my life around, however I can't do that before the son of a bitch who killed my daughter has paid with his life."

It was surprising for Chris to hear Waitie say he wanted to leave the game. At one point Chris thought he was enjoying the benefits from the contracts so to hear him say that was confusing. Chris thought that this may have been a result of his daughter's death.

"Even if it's one of your family members, if I pay to carry out a job and it's my daughter, yours, or anyone else's it must be done," said Waitie as Chris listened attentively.

Chris knew this was a serious statement for him. At one point, Chris thought he was referring to Jade's situation. Chris understood he was grieving so he did not take his comments literally. "What does he know?" Chris wondered. Chris moved his hear round and started to look for Waitie's men. Waitie was unaware what Chris was doing. He turned and looked at Chris.

"If you don't, I will kill you myself, that's how serious this is to me."

Chris' automatic reaction kicked in. He knew that the time was up for him and Waitie and he had to now keep his distance. Chris was prepared to die for his family, especially his children. The situation was tense and he knew he had to make arrangements for a hide out for them to stay. Chris had hidden his gun nearby just in case there was trouble. There was no sign of Waitie's men around which seemed surprising, but it didn't mean they weren't there. Chris looked again this time across the road from the cemetery. He spotted a white jeep. It turned out to be a passerby.

Waitie offered Chris a lift, but he refused it. He wanted to be on the safe side, given what he had just heard. On his way back from the grave Chris spotted one of Waitie's men parked nearby so he turned around and took the other exit. He knew one of them had to be there. Chris now knew that he had to call up his long time friends for help. He contemplated going to the U.S. again, but this would mean running away again from his kids. He was not prepared to do that this time. Chris wanted to end this once and for all, but with Waitie on his hands, he knew it would not be easy. If his brother had not been imprisoned by his daughter, which made the family a prime suspect, he wouldn't be in this predicament. Chris realised that in order to keep his secrets from his family, he had to get a new identity. He knew this would not be easy, but he was determined to turn over a new leaf, and repent of his sins, and he was prepared not to let Waitie spoils his plans. If Waitie was in his way, he would take him out.

Chris got home safely. He took his funeral clothes off and took a shower. Although he disregarded Waitie's threat as circumstantial, he was on the alert. Before he went to the bathroom, he activated all the secret CCTV cameras surrounding his flat. He also activated an infrared motion sensor and his alarm system. He knew what he was up against, so he had to be prepared. Moments later, he came out the shower, and went to his wardrobe. Some of his equipment was lying on the ground, and in a specially designed box. He opened his drawer to get the key for the box. Inside were his passports—one for the UK and another for America. Chris' expired Chinese passport was also there. He took it up and checked the picture in it. He was thinking he could use it again if needed. But this was not an option for Chris, as it meant leaving his kids. Chris weighed up the two; fight, or flight. This time he is going to fight.

Chris shoved them aside, and took out his key for the box. In the box were night vision goggles, a video camera and photos of himself and friends in the army. Also contained in the box was his old bug sweeper. The last time he checked, it was not working. He thought it might have been the batteries. Next to the motion sensor was a picture of him and Waitie in their late teens. They had known each other since they were kids, but had always kept their personal lives a secret from each other. The sight of the photo caused him pause for a while, as he could not believe his good friend may have now become his worst enemy. There was no other way out given the circumstances, so he had to face up to reality, and accept that this was the real thing, and the friendship may be no more. He knew it was either him, or Waitie, and he wasn't prepared for it to be him. This time he was not prepared to strike first as, he did in school when he first met him. Chris paused and looked back on when he was at school.

The playground was bustling with laughter, noise and gimmicks from kids playing at lunchtime. The boy who was not allowed to take is gun to school ignored the rules. He moved slowly behind the bike shed. He spotted his target. He aimed, and squeezed the trigger. The water hit the boy who was releasing his bike for a ride.

"Who did that?" he asked, as he spun with rage.

"I did it, and what are you going to do about it?" said the other boy with his water gun.

"Well I will show you what I can do," said the boy with the wet shirt. He rushed quickly in an attacking posture, charging towards the other boy knocking the gun out of his hand as it flew up in the air. The other boy watched it going over the bike shed. He looked in rage, as he followed it with his eyes falling to the ground. The water gun smashed in pieces, as it hit the ground with such force. He got even angrier. They started to fight. An older boy, who was approaching the scene, rushed towards them and broke up the fight.

"What is your name?" he asked the boy who had the gun, as he held him in the waist of his trousers.

"My—my name is Chris," he answered with rage breathing heavily.

"And you?" he asked the other boy, grabbing on to his wet collar.

"My name is Waitie," he replied.

"I'm considering taking you both to the head, but I will let you off this time. Now go to your classes, and don't let me ever see you guys fighting again." He let them go, as they rushed towards their classes. The bell went three minutes ago, so they had to rush back to their lessons. He watched them to make sure they were going into their classes, instead of fighting again. They entered and he walked away.

CHAPTER 24

A large organisation was about to transfer their contract to the accountancy firm Jessica worked. Jessica's thoughts had been on the funeral, but she had been able to compose herself professionally in her presentation the day before she provisionally secured the deal. She'd been brilliant and the directors of G&M Computers thought that they would move their business to her company.

The organisation was responding to the government's call for the weeding out of tax evasion which was the primary reason the company wished to switch companies as the directors believed that their previous company wasn't doing a good job. They had been very impressed by Jessica's business plan to be transparent and fair. Jessica's boss was happy for her initiative which would potentially bring big business to the company, so he called a meeting.

He used the large meeting room because he needed to

have all the major players present. Extra chairs were brought in to accommodate everyone. Jessica knew there was going to be a surprise, but didn't know what it would be. The acting PA, during Jade's absence, brought in bottles of wine and champagne for the celebration. Jessica knew that the deal with G&M Computers was in its final stages and wondered whether it had been completed and signed off. The invitation email sent to everyone had just come through in her inbox. The time was set for 10 A.M but she popped into the room at 9:30 A.M. to check out the settings. Cakes, biscuits, crisps, and fruit juice were all laid out on the table. Flowers were placed in the middle of the table as they often were when the company landed a big contract. It was Jessica's favourite choice: a combination of lilies, gerberas, roses and carnations.

At 10 A.M. everyone made their way to the meeting room except Jessica and a colleague who were finalising work and checking emails. "Come on," shouted the colleague when they had finished and she and Jessica made their way to the meeting room. When they got there, everyone was already seated and waiting. Jessica was the last one to sit. The boss raised a bottle of champagne and hit it twice with a fork to get everyone's attention.

"Thanks for coming at such short notice, but I have an important announcement to make. Jessica hasn't been herself recently since the death of her ex in-law, but she was able to keep her focus, and secure a lucrative deal," announced her boss, as he prepared to pop the cork from the champagne. "Sometimes she looked so terrible, as if she herself was guilty," joked her boss, "but despite all of this, she managed to present the deal professionally, and pulled it off. Thank you very much Jessica and congratulations with your success."

Jessica smiled with pride and blushed.

"I would like everyone to raise their glasses and propose a toast to the company's success through Jessica's hard work," said her boss.

Everyone rose and toasted Jessica.

Jessica stood up and said, "I would like to thank everyone for their support during this difficult time; I couldn't have done it without you guys and family support. I can also inform you that Jade is pregnant, and is coming back next week," said Jessica.

After the announcements of Jade's pregnancy, the usual office whispers started. Someone shouted, "Tell Jade congratulations."

"I will," responded Jessica, as she took her first taste of the champagne.

In the meantime, Chris decided to pay some of his friends a visit. He had no choice but to dip into his savings and buy a Jeep. His first stop was an ex-army friend, AKA Tiger, a specialist sniper awarded for bravery, and the best shooter he knew.

"What are you doing here? I thought you were in America," said Tiger after embracing Chris on his doorstep. "Come on in. We haven't seen you in ages, what brings you to this part of the world?"

Chris sat down on a chair that Tiger brought out for him.

"Drink?" offered Tiger.

"Beer, please," he replied.

"Room temperature or chilled?" asked Tiger.

"Cold for me please."

"Don't tell me, you need my help."

"Bingo," smiled Chris. "I will tell you about it another time, but be on the alert for a call. I know you would never let me down. I need my life back, and most importantly, I need to protect my children and my family."

When Chris got up to leave, Tiger stood and shook his hands and said, "You can count on me, my friend, you can count on me."

The next stop was an ex-gang leader, AKA Bulla. He was a gangster equipped at street fighting and breaking locks. When Chris buzzed his door a little boy answered, with a woman standing behind him.

"Didn't I tell you not to open the door unless you know who it is, or call me to do it," shouted his mother.

"Your mother is right little man," said Chris.

"I'm sorry, I'm Chris, is Bulla here?" he asked.

"Yes, go and get your dad," said the mother, as the little boy rushed upstairs.

On his way down the stairs, Bulla spotted Chris. "Hey, hey—what brings you to this part of the world?" asked Bulla.

"We can't talk here, let's go into my Jeep," said Chris and they walked outside. "I can't say much now, but I may need your help."

"You know I have got a family now, and I don't like that role anymore," replied Bulla.

"I know, but I need your help, there will be something for you at the end of it. I can't stay as I'm in a rush but I will be in touch," said Chris.

"OK," replied Bulla, as he watched Chris drive away down the road, before he went back in his house.

Next on the list was a computer wiz, AKA Genius. As the name suggested he specialised in computers and was the best hacker and code breaker around. He was also a fighter and he knew how to shoot.

Chris found him at a noisy exhibition centre, packed with exhibitors displaying their new inventions and technological enthusiasts. It was so noisy it was hard to hear yourself think. Chris moved through the crowds until he spotted the man he wanted to see. He grabbed him from behind with one arm, and held a plastic knife to his neck.

"Please don't hurt me," Genius shouted, as onlookers watched to see what was going on, believing that a murder was about to be committed.

"Shut up, you coward," smiled Chris.

Recognising the voice, Genius felt the knife and discovered it was plastic. "Chris, how do you know where to find me?"

"It wasn't difficult. You are easily profiled. Besides I had to find you as I need your help," said Chris, as he dragged him to a less noisy spot.

"Anytime," replied Genius.

"I will be in touch," said Chris, as he walked away waving goodbye.

Chris' next visit was the main man he needed. He was a

mechanic, doctor and engineer, AKA the supplier. The supplier fixed everything and supplied everything.

Chris drove past his garage but missed it at first as a new building had been erected making it difficult to identify. But the supplier himself had not changed that much. When Chris honked his horn the supplier stepped outside and recognised Chris in his Jeep.

"Oh my God, Chris is that you?" asked the supplier.

"It is me alright."

"Are you here for good now?"

"With your help, I will be."

"You are not into trouble again?" asked the supplier, as he stroked his beard.

"I hope not after your help; can I count on you?"

"Of course you can."

"I'll be in touch, bye."

"Bye," he said as he watched Chris drive off until he had disappeared from view.

Not far away a man was walking along the roadside. He actually knew the supplier, in fact he knew everyone and was known as the insider. He specialised in police connections and was the first to know what was going on, on the inside, and everywhere.

Chris pulled up beside him and asked, "Do you need a lift?"

The man without looking said, "No, I'm not going far."

"Yes, but you need a lift," insisted Chris.

The voice sounded familiar to the man but he ignored Chris. "You owe me money."

"I know my friend, but I will pay you with interest,"

assured Chris.

The man smiled and got into the Jeep.

"You have good links, and I need your help again, only this time it will be the last time I need to call on you. Will you help me?" asked Chris.

"Yes, but only after you have paid me," smiled the insider.

"Here is £2000. Keep the change. Now will you?" asked Chris, as he looked in his face for an answer and drifted off the road.

The insider pointed out that he was drifting, before he straightened the wheel. "Yes," smiled the insider.

Chris dropped him off at his destination, and saw him going into the bookies. Chris smiled; he knew he had been unwilling to help because he needed money to gamble.

The philosopher, AKA Jimmy, was a thinker, strategist and a motivator. He was last on Chris' list. He knew Jimmy was in prison, but unaware that he and Paul were sharing the same cell. Jimmy was due to leave prison soon, and so Chris decided he might not need his help any time soon. Chris had completed his mission, and was ready to take on Waitie if it got to that stage.

CHAPTER 25

The police investigation was like something out of a Cinderella movie with confiscated shoes in boxes all around the room. As part of their investigation they had to check the prints found at the crime scene against pairs of shoes. The team of officers working on the case found that the private detective hired to get information from Sophia had been seen in the area around the time of her murder. The police met up with him and found his alibi was shaky but substantial. However footprints found at the murder scene were from branded shoes and eliminated him as the prime suspect.

The police had confiscated other items from Paul's brothers as well including keys, gloves, and a hat that had not yet been fully forensically examined. The police needed to speak to a few more people, before passing the items to the team that would thoroughly piece together the puzzle. When they discovered the knife in the kitchen had been picked up and then put back down on the surface next to the stove, they theorised the killer may not have intended to kill Sophia. However, the police agreed amongst themselves that this might be contested in court if the evidence led to the correct person.

The police also found notes, letters, and a plot to accuse Paul of rape. The investigating team didn't think this was relevant, as they knew she was dead, and it was not her they were investigating. However they found names of people that may have colluded with her to convict him. The police brought this to the attention of the CPS lawyers and they advised them to hand over the evidence to the family after they had completed this case.

The police became aware that Paul's plea had been made under the duress of his solicitor and evidence to support this was found in Sophia's diary. The police were also following another line of enquiry that matched Robert's plan B. They found evidence of this plan but no other relevant details. Armed with all this information, Detective Stuart believed he had enough evidence to arrest the suspect. But before he could arrest anyone, he had to seek a warrant and knew it would be best to get one under section eight of PACE from the magistrate.

The police then received a tip off that all the brothers were meeting at Jessica's but weren't sure it was reliable. Detective Stuart wanted to make sure their timing was right so he planned his next move for the evening and arranged a meeting with his boss to let him know. In his hands was all the paperwork to present to the DCI. On his way to his office, he took the CPS' files on Paul but decided not to bring them up at this stage. He knocked on the door twice before he was invited in by the DCI.

"What have you got for me on the case?" asked the DCI. "I heard that you have made a big break through, I hope you are right, otherwise your job could be on the line. What I don't want, is another alleged wrongful conviction,"

"I'm confident that we have our man, or woman," replied Detective Stuart, not giving much away at this stage.

The DCI realised Detective Stuart wasn't too sure if his suspect was a man or a woman, but decided not to questioned him about that.

"The only question is, whether the killer had the *Mens Rea* for murder," said Detective Stuart seriously with his glasses in hand. "That's for the lawyers to decide but they have got a clever nephew that challenged me recently; I believe he is studying to become a solicitor."

"A promotion is in sight if you get a successful conviction. Have you been in touch with the CPS?" the DCI asked pointing to some paperwork when another colleague entered the room about a matter they had discussed.

"I will need a holiday first," smiled Detective Stuart.

"What happened to that rape case you were working on?" asked the DCI, as he knew it was a high profile case, and wanted follow up on the matter.

"I put it on hold until this one is over. This takes priority as you know sir," said Detective Stuart. He was on a mission as his case files were very large. He was one of their best officers but didn't always get it right. "My next task is to go after Waitie."

Stuart wasn't aware that his boss had met Waitie on a few occasions, nor would he even contemplate any wrongdoings from his boss. The insider also knew the DCI, as they had worked on projects that secured many convictions in the past.

"The best person to get information on Waitie is the insider. I have got his number," said the DCI.

"Is he a police informant?" asked Detective Stuart his eyes widening.

"He is not, but we go back a long way," said the DCI before he was interrupted by another officer. He told the officer to wait while he wrapped up the conversation with Detective Stuart. "You definitely will need a break after this case. By the way, how is your family?"

"They are fine thank you," replied Detective Stuart. He wanted to talk in private and looked at the other officer meaningfully.

The DCI picked up on this and told the officer to come back in a couple of minutes.

"Is your son at university now?" asked Detective Stuart.

"Yes, this is his second year, he is studying criminology," said the DCI.

"Really!" said Detective Stuart, "that's really good. I like how you are drawing him into the profession."

"Why not? Keep it in the family. Anyway, I'm busy, so I will leave you to it. Keep me updated."

Detective Stuart walked out the office and went to get his lunch out of the fridge. While he was doing so the DCI rang on his mobile instructing him to delay the arrest until further notice. He wasn't too happy with the delay but there was nothing he could do about it but follow orders. He placed his lunch in the microwave and heated it up. He then quickly walked back to his office.

He sat around his desk, and eased open the lid of his home cooked lunch. He placed Sophia's case file aside, as he was instructed to pause for a while, and picked up the rape case. He settled himself down, having his lunch while going over the case. His mobile phone vibrated. Not wanted to be disturbed, he ignored it.

CHAPTER 26

Kerry was preparing to move in with her mother for a while, as instructed by Chris. This was to keep them safe.

"Come on kids, we are going to spend some time with Nanny," she said.

"Why Mum?" Jason asked.

She knelt down and held on to both his hands, and looked him in the eyes. "You remember how I said we would spend time at Nan's, well now is that time," she softly said. "Now, be a good boy, and pack your stuff." She knew this move would not be good for the kids, especially if it was long term, because they were so used to their own space, friends, and usual visits to the local library, but she had no choice if she needed to keep them safe.

Kerry stood on her stepladder and reached for her suitcases on top of her wardrobe. "Oops," she said as she almost fell. Kerry regained her balance, and pulled down the first one. She struggled with it even though it was empty because she had to lift it down from such a height. She finally got both suitcases onto the bed.

"Your hair was twisted in a plait recently, why did you loosen it Jason?" asked Kerry, as he walked into her room. "Go and get your bag and start packing, it's behind the door next to the computer in the front room," directed Kerry.

Kerry went into her wardrobe, and took out most of her clothes. She felt the need to choose what she wanted to take with her. She also thought it might be a good idea to pack her cosmetics stuff, as she didn't know how long she would be gone for. Eboni had already packed her bag the day before. As she continued to pack, Kerry peeked through the window, and she saw a suspicious looking man watching the house. She was scared, but wondered whether it was someone visiting her neighbour.

The suspicious man was tall, black and wearing a hooded top. She wondered why he was dressed like that as it was boiling hot. That gave the game away. She initially thought it was one of Waitie's men. She continued her packing. Five minutes later, she looked again, and this time the man wasn't there. She moved the curtains, and looked properly and her eyes met his. She quickly closed the curtains, took up her phone and called Chris.

"Chris, Chris," said an anxious Kerry, her hand on her chest. Her heart was pounding. "A man is watching the house," she continued. "I'm scared, what should I do?"

"Describe him to me," said Chris, in a calm voice.

The description she gave him, matched his friend, Bulla.

"It's my friend, I asked him to keep you safe," said Chris.

"You could have told me," replied Kerry.

"I didn't want to cause any alarm," assured Chris.

"Well, you sure didn't," she responded sarcastically.

"Are you packed, are you all ready?" asked Chris.

"Not yet," replied Kerry.

"Well let me know when you are as he will be dropping you off at you mum's," assured Chris.

"OK, will do," replied Kerry.

When it was time to leave Kerry did some last minute checks. She was tempted to tell her best friend where she was going, but remembered what Chris had told her about doing that. Despite giving her assurance to Chris she could not resist the temptation so she rang her friend to say goodbye and ended up telling her what was happening.

"This is our secret," said Kerry.

"You can count on me," replied her friend.

Kerry wasn't aware that her friend knew Waitie, but her friend did not know about the situation between Chris and Waitie, and despite being friends for years, had never mentioned him to her.

"Why can't you tell me exactly where you will be staying?" asked her friend.

"I just can't, OK," said Kerry.

"Why not?" insisted her friend. "It's not that I'm going to tell anyone; don't you trust me?"

"Yes, I do, but I wasn't even going to mention it to you until I got there. I thought I would call you from there but I thought I should do it now instead," replied Kerry. "Please respect my privacy."

185

"OK," said the friend.

By this time, Bulla was waiting outside. He spotted a suspicious car, so he moved to his car, and positioned his gun on the car seat. Three men were in the car and they slowed down as they got near the house. One of them pointed. Bulla knew he would not be a match for all three men, but he had no fear, and was always ready for the challenge. He realised it was risky, so he honked his horn again. Kerry was just finishing her conversation with her friend. The friend wanted to talk more, but the constant sounding of the horn prompted her end the conversation and complete her checks. She indicated to him from the window that it was time to get the bags. Bulla came and collected them. As they were leaving, the kids looked back in tears. Kerry was also crying.

CHAPTER 27

John was at his office expecting an important client, but the earlier appointment still had not left. John did not want the man to wait, so he contemplated how he could finish the conversation. Fortunately the client picked up that he was watching the clock and began to wrap it up. John nodded in agreement as if he understood everything his client was saying even though his thoughts were elsewhere. He looked at his phone, and rang the secretary to inform her he wouldn't be much longer. Five minutes later he rushed the client out and asked the secretary to send his waiting client in.

"Sorry to keep you waiting, I was wrapping up matters with my previous client."

"My name is Waitie, it was my daughter that was murdered recently, but I'm not here for that. I'm here to ask a question about a case," said Waitie, while he slowly sat down on the seat closest to the door, rather than the one closest to the window.

"I heard about you, and I was told that you are respected in the community, but I didn't know you were Sophia's dad," said John.

"Then you must of heard about the high profile rape case recently reported on TV, seeing that you are prominent around here," said Waitie, as John looked shocked, remembering the case with Paul.

"You mean the case with Paul?" said John.

"Paul, who is Paul?" asked Waitie.

"Not to worry, wrong man," replied John.

Waitie looked confused, but he was too focused on the reason for his visit, so he didn't pay much attention to what John had just said. "I'm talking about Jade, have you heard of her?" he asked.

"No," replied John, while he reached over to collect some court papers next to Waitie. The name on the paperwork brought back memories of the on-going high profile cases that had re-opened recently.

"The police say they have new evidence; what are our options?" asked Waitie as he handed John paperwork on the celebrity case.

John matched the case Waitie was talking about with one of the cases in the folder. "We just have to wait and see. If the girl decides not to testify or cooperate any further then there's hardly much they can do," suggested John, as he rocked back into his chair.

"Umm, if we kill her then she wouldn't take part," thought Waitie, as he stared up in the ceiling in deep thought. "So, are you saying we cannot do anything at this stage?" he asked, as he re-focused his attention to John.

"That's correct," responded John. Rocking forward and pulled his chair closer to his desk, and picked up a filing folder.

"OK, I'll be in touch when such a time comes," said Waitie, as he got up to leave. John handed him his card. The meeting was over, and it was time for him to go. Waitie reached towards the door to open it, but remembered seeing him at the funeral, and turned around, and asked, "I saw you at the funeral, have you met my daughter?"

"Yes, we were friends," said John.

Waitie left the office. On his way to the exit, he brushed pass the flowers that were situated next to the door, revealing to the receptionist what appeared to be a gun. He took out his phone just outside the office and dialled a number. The voice was a female one. He asked about accounting matters, and offered to meet up with her for dinner. The look on his face at first suggested that she did not agree to his invitation, but after further persuasion she accepted.

At the end of the day John locked his door to leave the office. He checked under the receptionist's desk to set the alarm as she had already left. Before he set the alarm, he looked around the office and noticed the place was untidy. John eased off his bag, took his jacket off, and began to tidy up. The magazines on the table in the waiting area were scattered all over the receptionist's desk and some were on the table as well. John rearranged them in order. He poured sweets in a jar and checked the flowers next to the exit to see if they needed water. Finally John stepped back pleased with what he'd done, so he put back his jacket on, grabbed his bag, and opened the door.

As John was about to set out on his journey, he remembered the alarm was not set. So he went back and bent forward, stretching his long arms out trying desperately to reach it. He made another attempt, this time sliding on his back as the button was under the desk. John managed to set the alarm and slam the door shut behind him. John knew about security issues in the area so without hesitation he rattled the door checking to make sure that it was locked. John went around to the back of the building, and pressed the button on his key fob, releasing the doors of his BMW car. He didn't want to soil his clothes on the polish he'd used that morning to clean the car so he slowly glided into place behind the steering wheel. Before he drove off, he moved his head around to check in his surroundings and see who was around. That's when he spotted Chris from across the road gazing at him. John turned his head and looked again, before speeding off. Chris disappeared behind a parked van when he looked the second time.

On his way home, he decided to pick up a few things at the supermarket. In the car park, he spotted Chris again. By this time, he thought that he was losing his mind, or Chris was following him. This didn't deter him from getting his shopping and coming out with two bags in his hands. As he entered his driveway, he spotted that his wheelie bin was in the middle of the walking path. Someone must have shifted it, as this was not the way he had left it that morning. John wheeled it back where it normally sat. He then looked behind him, and opened his door.

"Ah," he said as he went in, "What a day, I'm so tired." He didn't know seeing Chris and Waitie would bring back such distressing memories. John took a shower and ate a quick dinner and got into bed. "You have to help her, she is our friend," a voice whispered in his head. "We have to meet up with her to discuss the plan. You are a lawyer; all you have to do is to contemplate a plan, a deadly one."

That voice was Sophia's friend Marcus. "I saw you at the funeral, do you know my daughter?" Waitie's voice echoed in his head. John thought he was going mad, so he went downstairs to have a drink. In the dark corner of the kitchen, he thought he spotted Sophia smiling at him. He closed his eyes and opened them again but the image was gone. "This is not happening," he thought. By this time, John's throat was dry, so he went into the fridge, and took out the water. He poured it into a glass. He drank it sweating and shaking. He was haunted by Sophia's voice and thoughts of what took place leading up to Paul's trial. "Maybe I was tired, maybe I was hungry, but it's hard to understand what just happened," John thought.

Tormented by his conscience, he held his head in his hands. "I have to tell Tina about what we did," he thought. "It's our fault she is dead." John took up his phone; it was 9 P.M. He searched for Marcus' number, while his hands shook with nerves.

"Hello," answered Marcus. "What do you want, do you know what time it is?"

"Yes, I know," said John. "I need to see you, can you

191

come down to my office tomorrow?"

"What for?"

"I can't discuss this over the phone but I did an interview with a BBC programme about Paul's case; they tracked me down. Look you have to come and see me."

"OK, I will see you tomorrow."

John fell asleep shortly after the conversation with Marcus.

CHAPTER 28

Meanwhile, that call created the same effect on Marcus.
He went out to get some cigarettes at the shop. "Paul is in prison, and Sophia is dead," thought Marcus. Marcus decided to walk the long road home after buying cigarettes. It was a dark and rainy night. In the rain the streetlight reflected a rainbow like view into the darkness. When Marcus got to the park, about a hundred metres from where he lived, he heard a woman screaming. He decided to investigate the matter.

The park was dark and wet. The voice sounded similar to Sophia's. Marcus didn't believe in ghosts, so he dismissed any idea of hallucination and treated it as a genuine call for help. He moved closer to what looked like a woman. Walking closer to the figure, he stumbled on a piece of wood, and fell with one hand hitting the ground. It was pitch dark. He looked round in fear. No one was there. His focus shifted to the spot the voice was

193

coming from but no one was there. He started to get concerned about the matter.

Marcus was already half way into the park so there seemed no point turning back. As he proceeded the rain started to get heavier. He approached a tree. Marcus considered waiting under the tree until the rain subsided. As he got to the tree, a man came from behind it, looking him in his face. All he could see were two eyes staring wildly at him. He was so frightened he clutched at his chest.

"Oh, sorry," grumbled the man in a deep slurred voice, clutching a can of beer. He was a homeless drunk that frequented the park.

Marcus walked faster looking back every few minutes. When he spotted the exit he blew a huge sigh of relief. It was a welcome sight.

Chris knew about Marcus but didn't know exactly who he was, and Marcus didn't know him either. But Chris was in the area. He spotted a man walking alongside the road and pulled over to ask for directions to the supermarket. Marcus told him that it was five minutes away from where he was if he carried on straight.

"OK, thanks," replied Chris.

By now it was almost 11:30. Marcus finally got to his door, and checked behind him, to see if anyone was following him. He quickly got out his keys, and opened his door. When he got in, he was soaking wet. He headed towards the bathroom, and grabbed his towel. As he came out he almost ran into his flatmate who had just returned home. Marcus' flatmate let out a frightened shriek and laughed.

"Are you OK, man?"

Marcus knew his flatmate was always trying to frighten him, especially when he was in the bathroom. "Yes, I'm fine," he replied. He went straight to the kitchen to get himself a drink; he took a beer, and lit one of his cigarettes. He then moved back to the sitting room, and sat in the sofa. His flatmate realised he'd been unsuccessful and saw Marcus' face was distant so he gave up and went to his room.

"Oh my God, if it wasn't for my own twisted, personal feelings, Sophia would have been alive now," thought Marcus, believing the killer to be one of the brothers. "I had sexual feelings for her, but she didn't. I don't understand why I encouraged that deception. That deception backfired and became deadly, now how will I live with myself? And what about Paul? He trusted me. He is going to kill me if he hears any of this."

It was now 12 A.M. in the morning. By this time, he'd had three beers, and was half-drunk. Marcus went to his room, lay on his back on his bed, and switched on the TV. There was a report on the news that the police had made a significant breakthrough in Sophia's case. It also reported that her father was an alleged dangerous man. The reporter on the news stressed that this was an unconfirmed report and speculation. Marcus came to the realisation that it would be best to tell Tina everything. This would relieve some of his pain and might comfort Tina. However, what he didn't realise was this might have deadly consequences. Marcus was tired from all his thoughts and now coupled with heavy drinking he fell asleep with his door wide open.

Chris was still in the area and the insider pointed out to Chris where Marcus was living.

The following morning, John went into his office early. He knew he wouldn't be able to concentrate on any work for the day until he had met Marcus. Marcus had been scheduled to show up twenty minutes ago. John waited an extra thirty more minutes before he decided to call him. Marcus did not pick up his phone. John thought he might be on the tube or perhaps there was a network issue so he didn't worry at first. He tried again and the phone rang without an answer. It was then John started to worry and when he heard a strange noise from the other room next to his office.

John frantically shouted, "Who is there?"

There was no answer.

"I said who is there?" he shouted for the second time. He called out his secretary's name and still got no answer. "I'm going to call the police," said a scared John. John got up from his seat, and reached for his baseball bat in the right hand corner of his office. He held it high above his head and tiptoed to the other room. No more sound was coming from the room anymore. John vigorously pushed the door open and rushed in. A stray cat ran out and down the stairs. John chased after it, opened the door, and let it out. "I must have left the window open last night," thought John. As he was about to close the door, Marcus arrived.

"Hi," said John in a frightened voice. "I thought you were dead."

"No, were you calling me? I was on the phone, sorry," apologised Marcus. "What are you doing with that bat?"

"I heard sound coming from the room next to my

office, so I went to investigate. It wasn't anything."

"The reason why I called you here is that I had some strange experiences last night and I was hallucinating," said John. "We have to tell the truth, we have to first tell Tina." I want a clear conscience."

"I agree," said Marcus. "I heard voices as well last night. What did you tell *Our View*?"

Our View was a popular TV show that investigated alleged wrong that resulted in a miscarriage of justice.

"They wanted to know about Paul's case," he said, "they believe he was wrongly convicted. They wanted to know if I had anything to do with his guilty plea, and whether he was under solicitor's duress to plead guilty, as no normal person in their right mind would plead guilty under such circumstances, except in America I suppose."

"But this would have serious legal ramifications," said Marcus looking worried and disturbed.

"Leave the legal bit to me."

"OK."

"Shall we call Tina now and arrange a meeting with her?"

"Sure."

They called Tina on the company's speakerphone so they both could hear the conversation. Tina agreed to meet them on Thursday, as Wednesday, the next day, she was due at some appointments. The meeting was set for 11 A.M. John would book the morning off, and Marcus checked his diary, which was free for that day. Marcus left just as John's secretary reported for work. She thought he was a doggy early morning client that John didn't want her to meet. She smiled and waved at them. Marcus waved back while closing the door.

CHAPTER 29

Thursday in south London at 9 A.M. John and Marcus met up at his office as agreed. Marcus waited in the reception area, while John was finalising a case bundle. The barrister was coming to pick it up. The instructions were given to his secretary. His locum solicitor would be on site to cover for him in case there were any emergencies.

"The bundle is ready for the barrister to be picked up," said John to his secretary, while fixing his tie. "The respondent's bundle is also there, and can you make sure that the locum solicitor goes through the case and the settlements with the barrister?" John took up his jacket and walked towards the door while his secretary nodded. He opened the door, and held it open. "I will be back before four."

Marcus closed the door behind him.

The secretary saw them both heading towards the car

from her window. She remembered his face from his visit on Tuesday. This time she didn't think it was a doggy client, but maybe a relative. John loosened his blue tie, as he remembered that there was no need to keep it on as the trip wasn't formal. He opened the buttons on his purple shirt, as it was too hot. Making himself comfortable, he rolled up his sleeves, before getting into the car. They both knew that it was now or never.

"We are doing this for Sophia," said Marcus, as he fastened his seatbelt.

"Sure," replied John, as he did the same. John reversed out onto the road almost hitting the shop keeper next door stocking his shelves at the front of his shop, close to the road. "Sorry," he shouted before they sped off to East London. "I warned him that his stuff was too close to my driveway, and the road," thought John as they got underway.

Thursday 10:30 A.M. East London. It was hot and humid and about 27 degrees Celsius. It felt even hotter in Tina's house. Tina was learning to cope with the death of her daughter, and the heat during the hot summer days. She was preparing for her appointment with John and Marcus and put biscuits and cakes on a tray on the coffee table. Her lovely flowers were relocated to the right hand side of the table to make way for the tray of snacks for her guests. Cubes of ice set to cool drinks for her guests were in the refrigerator. In the corner next to her book shelf she had her remote control fan on. She was still sweating. Tina increased the speed on the fan remotely. She realised

it was swinging to dispense air evenly through the room. Tina was still hot, so she took the remote, and waited for it to swing towards her, then clicked on the swing button so it stopped on her. "That's better," she thought.

Tina looked at the clock on the wall. It was 10:50 A.M. She thought she needed some kind of recording system, because she didn't know what to expect, and she wanted to secure some evidence. She saw a voice recorder app on her phone and a note pad. Tina was not that familiar with her smart phone but tried to navigate to the recording icon. She then pressed the record on her phone and spoke. It recorded. She stopped it, and decided it was not necessary.

It was 10:55 A.M. when she heard a car pull up. She looked through her window, and saw it was John and Marcus. She opened the door waiting to greet them.

"Hi," said Tina.

"Hi Tina," said John, as he kissed her on the cheek twice.

"Hello Tina," said Marcus, as he did the same.

"Come in. Have a seat," she invited

John sat next to her, while Marcus sat on the chair in front of her. Tina got up from her chair, took the tray and offered them biscuits. John took some biscuits, and Marcus took the cake.

"What do you want to drink?" asked Tina.

"What have you got?" asked John.

"Tea, beer, juice, coffee and water."

"I will have juice," said John.

"Water for me," said Marcus.

She went and got them what they wanted. John did not know where to start and tried to pluck up the courage to tell her. Marcus looked the more uneasy of the two. Marcus gulped down his water as he was hot. He was also clearly enjoying his cake. John was the opposite; he sipped his juice, and only had one bite of his biscuit.

"It's hot in here, do you mind swinging the fan?" asked Marcus.

"Sure," replied Tina.

Marcus walked over to the fan to do it manually but it suddenly started swinging before he could do anything. Marcus thought Sophia's ghost was in the house and he stepped back looking at the fan. "How did that happen?" he asked.

"It's remote controlled," smiled Tina, looking at his frightened face. "You thought it was a ghost?" still smiling.

"There is something I need to talk to you about, and if you don't speak to us after we have told you, then we wouldn't blame you. "It's about your daughter," John said.

Tina listened attentively. "What about her?" she asked, with tears in her eyes.

"Would you like to go first?" suggested John to Marcus.

"Yes," said Marcus. "First, once again I must say we are sorry for the loss of your daughter and I take some responsibility for it."

When he said that, Tina wondered if he was partly responsible for her murder too. If so there could be more than one killer contrary to what the police said. Tina for some reason always believed that it could be more than one killer.

Marcus saw the way she was looking at him and

quickly removed any doubts from her mind. "No, I don't mean that I am the killer, what I mean was that I was the orchestrator behind Paul's conviction," he continued.

"How is that? He raped my daughter, how are you to be responsible?" asked Tina.

"Well, when Sophia came crying to me after he had left her I was really mad. I thought of my own selfish feelings for her, and not her, herself," said Marcus. "I encouraged her to do something about it."

Tina and John both went for a biscuit at the same time. Neither were looking at what they were doing as they were intent on staring into Marcus' eyes and John grabbed her hand by mistake. They laughed, and apologised to each other.

"She was upset, and I played on her emotions. I deceptively came up with a plan by encouraging her to go to the police, and report that he had raped her. This was wrong, and I'm truly sorry," said Marcus.

"OK, so you encouraged her to do something that was deadly, serious and wrong, what has that got to do with blaming yourself for her death?" asked Tina.

"Well you see, if I had not done that, Paul wouldn't have gone to prison, and his brother wouldn't have killed her," said Marcus.

"You cannot blame people for her death, we don't know who killed her—leave the matter to the police," said Tina. "He did rape her, didn't he?"

"No, it was all made up," said Marcus.

Tina stood up with her hands on her head, and mouth opened wide. "You're joking aren't you?"

"No," replied Marcus, his head down.

"So, what have you got to do with it?" asked Tina, as

she looked at John.

"I'm afraid I have something to do with it," replied John.

"What part did you play?" asked Tina.

"I encouraged him to plead guilty," replied John.

"So all of you, including my daughter, sent an innocent man to prison," shouted Tina, as she walked out the house and sat on the balcony looking down on the floor. Moments later, she came back and said, "If I knew my daughter well, she wouldn't have done that on her own. I'm really upset with the pair of you, but I don't blame you for her murder. I do blame you John for abusing her trust. I looked up to you as an honourable man, but you have let me down. So what now? Are you going to go to the police with the story?"

"I can't, this would ruin my career," said John.

"Well you have ruined another person's life, so you have to come clean."

"I sort of have, on a BBC programme," assured John, "that's the best I can do."

"Is there anything I can do to soften the blow?" asked Marcus.

"Pray," said Tina, as she contemplated telling Waitie. She believed however dangerous as it may be, he needed to know.

John finished his drink, but Tina was so upset she didn't even bother to offer more. She explained to them that she needed some fresh air. This time she went into the garden. From the kitchen window, they could see her on her mobile and became worried she was calling the police. Marcus told John what she was doing, but John assured him that she wouldn't do that.

Tina was on the phone to Waitie. "I have got some news for you, but you have to come and see me."

Waitie was busy with a mystery woman he'd made an appointment with after seeing John. She called out to him to pass her a towel from the hotel they were booked in. Tina recognised the voice, but kept her cool as she was not with him anymore.

"I have shocking information that may piece together the puzzle in Sophia's killing," said Tina. "When can you make it?"

"Maybe later, maybe tomorrow," said Waitie.

It was obvious to Tina that he'd stopped what he was doing, and she heard him asking the mystery woman about a letter he'd written her. The call ended and Tina went back in the house. John and Marcus were still there.

"Thanks for the information, thanks for being open and honest—and thanks for saving my daughter's life," said Tina, in a sarcastic way. "You have done your damage, now it's time to pay, or repair it." Tina packed up her tray, switched off her fan, and took the empty cups back into the kitchen. Her daughter's face was vivid in her mind as she looked through the kitchen window and saw one of her toys hanging up in the shed. She wiped away her tears and went back into the sitting room. "I'm upset now, and I need some peace and quiet," she told them.

John and Marcus realised they were no longer welcome there anymore.

"I hope you will do the right thing, and I don't want to ever see you guys again, now could you please leave?"

asked Tina as she wiped her face again, while trying to hold back tears.

They left and she went to her bedroom.

CHAPTER 30

The next day, Waitie decided to visit Tina. It was Friday afternoon, and he thought it might be a good idea to get food for her, so he bought her favourite—KFC chicken. He thought natural tropical juice would also go down well with her. At the same time, Tina was at home feeling all sexy and hot. She knew how Waitie didn't love her, which was why she had told him to leave shortly after Sophia was born. Nevertheless, she still had feelings for him, and wanted to make them known. One way of doing so was to try to entice Waitie to reveal his emotions as he'd done in the past. Tina wanted attention and comfort now she had lost her daughter and Waitie seemed the obvious one to give her that. What mattered to Tina was to see him looking her best.

Waitie told her that he would be there at 4:30 P.M. so she was cleaning up and getting things organised before he came. Tina knew the main reason was to inform him of the revelations by Marcus and John. She finished her chores at 2:00 P.M. with enough time to have a shower and choose what she wanted to wear. It wasn't as hot as it had been when John and Marcus were there, so there was no need to have the fan out, nor was there any reason to dress provocatively. She got into the shower, and came out ten minutes later. Tina had her towel wrapped around her. She went to the full length mirror on her big wardrobe.

At mid forty, Tina thought she was still in as good a shape as she was 22 years ago, when she had Sophia; enough to impress Waitie. Trying to look her best, Tina went back to the bathroom and grabbed her makeup kit. She started applying it. Ten minutes later, she was done. Tina looked in her wardrobe and took out a very short skirt. She was size fourteen, so she thought a size twelve skirt would do just fine to make her look sexier. She squeezed into one and it fitted perfectly. Tina had always attracted plenty of attention from younger men thanks to her curvy and sexy figure. Tina's intense workout programme at her local gym had paid off.

Tina then reached for a V-neck top that displayed and revealed her curves and cleavage to the extent that leaning forward could cause an accident. It was also short and stopped just above her navel. Despite how much it revealed when she lean forward, Tina was happy with it. As she was at home, she decided to wear flat heeled shoes. Smiling and feeling good about herself, Tina sprayed on her favourite perfume, in the hope of luring Waitie into her bedroom. Her hair was placed in a style that normally attracted Waitie's attention; he had complimented her on it on numerous occasions.

Tina's loneliness for a man had been building up for years. She felt Sophia's death would draw Waitie closer to her. "I have no-one now. No daughter, no man, no Waitie," thought Tina. "I can't live like this any longer, and the only way to try and get this off my mind, is to find a man, even if it's for some comfort." The desire for a man was taking its toll. Somehow, the death of Sophia made her more vulnerable, almost for any man. Tina decided to cast her net. She felt that Waitie should be the first. The woman Tina believed snatched her man away from her meant that she was still bitter. She was out for revenge, and she would use her vulnerability to her advantage. What she was unaware of, was the unpredictability. She was unaware how Waitie would react. Whether he would fall into her trap, or whether he would even contemplate being with her again. Waitie had to know about Johns and Marcus' revelation, so this is the time to take her chances.

It was almost time for Waitie to show up. Tina rushed downstairs to see if he was there and heard the sound of a Jeep outside. It turned out not to be him, so she went back upstairs to complete the final touches on her face. The doorbell rang. Tina checked her hair, her make up, and pulled up her skirt even shorter, before dashing downstairs to open the door. Waitie looked her up and down, and smiled, before he walked in.

"You look really beautiful, what's the occasion?" he asked, thinking it wasn't hot enough to be dressed like that unless she herself were feeling a bit hot under the collar.

"Thank you," she responded, blushing, and feeling

desirable. "I just saw these clothes and wanted to put them on," explained Tina.

"Really?" smiled Waitie. "You said it was important, what it is?" asked Waitie, ignoring her sexy look, although he looked attentively at her cleavage when she deliberately bent forward to offer him a biscuit. "No thanks, actually I brought you some chicken."

"Really, that's very kind of you, thanks," she said as he took the bucket off him. "Let me get some plates."

Tina got two plates and placed some pieces of chicken on them and set them down on her coffee table. She was getting thirsty. She reached for her favourite natural tropical juice and poured some into both glasses. Both she and Waitie loved it so much they had seconds. Before long they had finished the two litre bottle of juice and half the bucket of chicken. Waitie was the first to pack it away and clear the table. Tina decided to step things up a bit so as he walked back to the living room she brushed passed him, her soft breasts pinning him back on the doorframe, as they looked each other in the eyes. It was strange after yesterday's revelations why she would have the courage to entice Waitie, but in her mind, she believed that it would be the best time to get some comfort, as she hadn't had any since Sophia died, and who best to do it, but the father himself. Tina knew she was also vulnerable.

Tina wanted Waitie to check her bedroom window. She believed there was a draft and it was particularly annoying during the winter. Waitie used to be a builder, so she knew he could fix it. They went upstairs to check on the window. Waitie examined the seal around the window and spotted the problem. He assured Tina that the next time he came round he would bring his tools, including his caulking gun to do the sealing. Tina was happy for the offer and another opportunity to see him again.

Waitie's mobile phone fell down and Tina was quick to bend over to pick it up so he could see what he'd had once. He looked at her seductively, moving closer. She picked up his phone, and turned around smiling, not realising he was now right behind her. They looked each other in the eyes. Tina decided to make the first move, so she held his hands, and sat on the bed.

He went with it in a daze, reminiscing about old times. Waitie started to feel heated as he stared down her bosom. But he realised this was not what he had come here for so he snapped out of it, by saying, "This is not what I came here for, although I find you irresistible."

Tina was flattered, but disappointed. She kept her dignity, and bravely brushed it off. "Yes, I don't know what I was thinking. Let's go downstairs to discuss why you are really here."

They went downstairs. Tina had discovered her mobile phone had recorded the confession by John and Marcus and decided to play it to Waitie, but before she told him about it, she gave him the choice to listen if he wanted to.

"I had a visit from John, and Marcus yesterday. This was the reason I called you," said Tina. "They told me some shocking things. I have it on tape, do you want to hear it for yourself?"

"You mean the solicitor John?" asked Waitie.

"Yes," she replied.

"No, you tell me what they said first, and then I will

decide if I want to hear the recording," he replied, as he feared the worst. Waitie didn't want any new revelations that would anger him.

"Well, they told me that they were behind the deception to incriminate Paul," said Tina.

"Paul? The chap that went to prison for her rape? John told me something about that," said Waitie. He was unaware about the family structure. Waitie still didn't know that Paul was Chris' brother.

"Marcus cooked it up, and John persuaded him to plead guilty," continued Tina.

"So was Sophia raped?" asked Waitie.

"No, she wasn't, it was all a plan, because he left her," explained Tina.

"What are you saying to me?" asked Waitie, as he sat down looking lost. "So my daughter was capable of something like that?" Waitie felt responsible that he'd not been there to teach her right from wrong. He'd kept out of her life because he'd always thought his type of work would put her in danger, but he realised now, ironically, that he'd been wrong. To rectify things he now needed justice and he would do whatever it took to get it. "I want to listen to the recording," he said.

Tina unplugged the phone from the charger, navigated to the recording app and selected play. Waitie listened attentively.

They were half way through the recording when Marcus and John had already confessed when Waitie said, "I don't want to hear anymore." In his mind he had already decided that they would pay with their lives. He was angry but tried hard to disguise his feelings so he wouldn't give the game away. "I have to go now."

"Please don't do anything stupid, nothing will bring her back," suggested Tina.

"Really," said Waitie sarcastically in his mind, as he smiled and walked towards the door. He knew nothing would bring his daughter back, but his justice, would bring comfort to him. He opened the door, turned and say goodbye. Tina watched him go. She moved towards the door as it slammed.

CHAPTER 31

Saturday morning, 10 A.M. Central London.

Waitie called a meeting with his staff in a rented office block in central London. At the appointed time five men arrived dressed in suits and ties and carrying attaché cases and folders as if ready to sort through a crisis. A laptop computer and a projector were brought in for them. All of this was a disguise for what was really going on, for in each of the cases the men carried a knife and a 9-millimetre pistol with extension clip, while Waitie, already waiting for them in the room, he had a 357-magnum handgun.

They sat down while Waitie got out his notes and made a plan. Chris was not involved in this as Waitie and his team were capable of handling the mission and Waitie had some suspicions about him anyway. He wanted to know if everyone was loaded and ready, so he asked for all briefcases to be unlocked and placed on the table. The sound of the flapping briefcases mimicked that of a director's meeting. The cases had been pre-prepared and had maps and directions in them. The guns were underneath the papers. He checked to make sure everything was intact.

"There has been a new development, gentlemen," said Waitie, as he walked around the table looking at everyone in the same way an army general would, with his cane under his arm. In this case the most dangerous of the group was the leader.

The men looked serious and ready.

"This is not a dangerous mission, but mistakes could make danger possible," he said.

One of the men was pouring water from a jug, another was playing with the flowers closest to him. Although these men were killers, there was always a coward in the pack, and it was obvious to Waitie who that was.

"I want you to find two men and bring them to me," said Waitie, as he stopped by a man he regarded as the weakest link because of his failure in previous assignments. His cowardice had almost got them all killed, but because he and Waitie had known each other for a long time he'd given him another chance. However, he was intimidated by Waitie standing over him now.

"On page two is the address of target one, and on three, target two," said Waitie, as he illustrated his mission. "Target one is the main fish. Target two, is not so important but I need him as well. These idiots contributed to my daughter's death and they will pay. Remember, I want them alive. Any questions gentlemen?"

The weakest link nervously put up his hand. "What if we cannot find them?" he asked while everyone looked at him.

"I will find them, and then let you know. Any more questions?"

"No," came the murmur from the group.

"Off you go," said Waitie, as they got up from the table.

It wasn't that difficult to find the targets as Waitie's men were experts. The main fish was first. John wasn't that difficult to find. One of the men staked out his house while the other kept a low profile. At 9 P.M. that evening they moved in. Two approached the house while the others waited in the park.

Marcus' recent encounter in the park with the drunken man had taught him a lesson and he decided not to take that route at night again. Waitie's men waited in the park expecting him, but when he didn't show they realised they'd been wasting their time and approached the flat instead. They knew it was a shared accommodation so they would have to go incognito, but tried their luck and knocked on the door. Marcus opened it.

"Hi, sorry for the late intrusion," one of them told Marcus, "but my car has broken down and I need to take my girlfriend to the hospital. She's about to give birth. I need a push. Would you be so kind as to help?"

Marcus looked out the door beyond him and saw a desperate woman in the Jeep who appeared to be in pain. The idea was to lure him away from the flat and it worked. As he got near the jeep, the woman jumped out at him and pointed her gun to his head.

"Get in the jeep," she said.

Marcus was frightened as hell and turned around to face the nozzle of another gun. He had no choice but to cooperate. They drove for five minutes down the road, next to the bus stop adjacent to the park, where they picked up the others. They took him to John's house. One of the men picked the lock and went into the house to search it thoroughly, but John was no-where to be found.

"It appears he has been given a tip off," one of the men suggested.

They spotted a man walking away from the side of the house, who bore a resemblance to Chris but he wasn't their target so they'd left him. Chris had seen them and knew something was going down.

They took Marcus back to the place where they had the meeting. Waitie thanked them for their work and told them that he now only needed his right-hand man, Jason. Marcus was gagged, blindfolded then handcuffed, and put in the Jeep. Jason didn't know where they were going. Waitie was driving and didn't want to reveal his location.

They had turned the music up in the Jeep to drown out the sound of Marcus begging in the back. Although he was gagged it was clear to them what he was saying. Jason realised that they were heading towards the motorway. He knew Chris and Waitie had a hideaway spot off the motorway, but didn't know exactly where it was. Waitie asked Jason to remove the blindfold off Marcus' face. As Waitie drove past a flyover, Marcus spotted a private road sign titled Death Valley, and he started to shake even more. A hundred metres from

Death Valley, was another road with no name. Waitie took that turn and continued along it. The dusty track made it impossible to see clearly where they were going but Waitie was familiar with the area and their journey was trouble free. Ten minutes later, deep into the woods, he came to a complete stop, next to a cliff.

"GET OUT OF THE CAR," shouted Waitie, as he held the door open.

Marcus was still shaking as he got out of the Jeep.

"Should I remove the gag from his mouth?" asked Jason.

"Yes," replied Waitie.

"Please, please, I didn't mean to do it," said Marcus, as Waitie took out his 357-magnum.

He flicked out the barrel, to check that it was fully loaded.

"You have messed with the wrong man's daughter," said Waitie with fire in his eyes.

Marcus was still handcuffed. Jason stood him next to the cliff. At the bottom was the river. Waitie pointed the gun to his head.

"Please I'm begging you."

Waitie ignored him and fired one shot to his head which took out a chunk from the back of his skull that flew over the edge of the cliff. Blood gushed from Marcus' face and he saw the sky spun as he fell to the ground. Now on his back he could see the light from the moon as he tried desperately to raise his head before his vision started to blur. He knew it was the end for him but he tried to turn to see Waitie's face. His breathing slowed and his heart rate dropped as he faced death. Within moments he was dead.

Jason took off Marcus' bloody clothes and burnt them to destroy any forensic evidence which could implicate them in the crime. Waitie didn't want to hang around so he walked back to the vehicle, waiting for Jason. Jason stayed five minutes longer, while he used his kit to destroy any remaining evidence. He rolled the body down the cliff so it would look as if he had fallen. They got back to the office block at twelve midnight.

"I need John, and I need him fast," said Waitie, as he cleaned his gun.

"We will have him, we will have him," promised Jason. "How did you know about all of this?"

"Tina told me that they confessed to her, but don't tell her a word about our involvement."

"Sure," said Jason.

Waitie knew that the only difference between him and Jason was money and experience. They were both ruthless killers. Waitie threw £10,000 on the table and told Jason he should pay the others, and that he was paying in advance for John. Jason knew that he had to get the job done, given that he was being paid in advance. Waitie would never do such a thing if he didn't think he was up to the job. Jason took up the money, and they both left in the Jeep.

CHAPTER 32

Two weeks later, the insider met up with Chris and told him what happened to Marcus. From their discussion the insider worked out Marcus's connection with Chris and the role he'd played in Paul's imprisonment. Chris had tried to stay as far as possible away from Marcus to avoid temptation because he didn't want to get drawn back into the world of being a hit man, but he wondered if Waitie had something to do with his death. If he did Chris knew now that Waitie was serious about getting revenge for his daughter. He hoped Waitie still wasn't aware of his family's involvement with the case, but that too was probably just a matter of time. When he found out Paul had hurt his daughter there would be trouble. Chris was prepared for anything. He knew Waitie would go after John next and Chris was happy for him to do the dirty work of killing the men.

A woman was walking her dog next to the river, throwing sticks for it to chase. The wind picked up and the river was lashing against the rocks so the woman rested for a moment on a stump. From here she threw a stick and the dog went after it, but didn't come back. The wind was ferocious and the woman grew worried and began to look for the dog. She had only walked three metres when she smelled something rotten. She continued until she heard the dog barking. She called for him but he didn't respond so she followed the barking as the smell got stronger. It was so bad she had to put her hand over her nose. From around the corner of a rock, she spotted her dog's tail wagging. She called to him again but he would not come. So she went a bit closer even though the smell was almost unbearable. As she drew closer she spotted a decomposed body. She screamed and ran back to where she had come from. Her dog chased after her. When she was some distance away she took out her mobile phone and dialled 999 for the police. The area where the body was found was just on the outskirts of East London so the East London police division picked up the case. The commissioner's prerogative to assign cases to the best team in the region and headed by Detective Stuart was exercised in this case, by the advice of the DCI.

Martin had been asked to come down to the East London police station. When he showed up he was told to wait until an officer came for him. He heard the police whispering that a Martin would be arrested in connection with the murder of Sophia Wait. The police came out and called him in. They handed him a file with evidence from Sophia's diary which would help in clearing his brother's name and might even free him. He looked shocked but happy for the information. The Martin he heard the police was talking about was brought in by another officer as he was leaving.

Waitie's team was on the hunt for John. John had heard over the news that the body of the man discovered had been identified as Marcus. The news reporter said, "His dental records helped to identify him. The coroner's reports certified and confirmed the death. The coroner's post-mortem confirmed that he died from a single bullet to the head."

John decided to pack his bags and leave. John looked through his window and saw a suspicious looking man. He didn't know it was that the same man Waitie had sent to kill or capture him. Jason was not at the scene. John quickly packed his bags, took his passport, papers, and a train ticket to Heathrow.

When he went out the back door he realised there was nowhere to go. He realised confessing to Tina had been the wrong thing to do but it was now too late. He was scared and frightened. He opened the shed to hide but it wasn't safe. He was sweating. He heard keys rattling in his front door. John called the police but he was too nervous to talk. He looked up and saw an escape route over his wall. As he climbed up the wall the man picking his lock stepped inside and spotted his movements in the back. The man rushed to the back door and fired two shots. Both missed him as John jumped into his neighbour's garden. He was gasping for air. He knocked on his neighbour's back door. They let him in. Without saying a word, he ran through their house on to the street. They realised that a gunman was chasing him. He ran as fast as he could to the tube station. He got on to a tube and got away. No one saw him again.

When he was on the train he saw the same man he'd seen outside his office and at the supermarkets. It was Chris.

"I have got a gun, and I am going to kill you," Chris said as he sat down next to John. There was no one else in the compartment so Chris showed John the gun. "Waitie and I are close, but how did he find out about your little plan?"

"How can I trust you?" asked John.

"You can't, because I want to kill you as well."

John decided to tell Chris everything. He had little choice anyway. When he had finished Chris looked at him.

"Tina? You told Tina?"

"I have helped your brother by going on *Our View*."

"Too late for that. Alright, go on and get your plane. I will find you when the time is right, and trust me, I will."

Waitie was waiting at the meeting spot for reports on John's capture or death. A white Jeep pulled up and Waitie looked out his window. John wasn't amongst the men so he assumed they had caught and killed him.

"Did you get him?" asked Waitie when they walked in.

"No, we missed him. We shot at him but he got away," said one of the team.

Waitie got up from the chair so fast it hit the wall behind him. He went to Jason, looked him in the eye, and pointed his gun to his forehead. "I WILL FUCKING KILL YOU INSTEAD," he shouted.

Everyone was scared. They knew Waitie could do it without even flinching. Jason wasn't scared but concerned.

"I tried my best boss, and I will get him, but I don't appreciate you pointing your gun at my head," said Jason, in a calm but concerned voice.

If anyone else had said this they would have been killed on the spot, but Jason had no fear. Jason was also Waitie's best man, and even though he thought Jason's lack of fear was a problem, he also needed him.

He took the gun away, and said, "The next time I will kill you."

Jason knew he wasn't joking. He now had three options: kill Waitie, leave the group, or get John. He believed the latter was the better option. The group decided to split and go home until the next search. Four rode in the white Jeep while Jason, as usual, rode with Waitie in his black tinted Jeep.

CHAPTER 33

Waitie got a call to meet up with his mysterious accountant friend, only this time Tina saw them together. They were spotted going into a posh restaurant on Piccadilly in West London. Waitie was dressed in navy blue trousers with a grey blue striped shirt to match. His bow tie was nicely placed and suited for the occasion. His date was wearing a long, lacy fishtail, V-neck, blue dress. This was the fashion at the time, and anyone wearing it was considered rich. As they entered the restaurant, the waiter greeted them and showed them to their reserved table.

The table was beautifully set with a white covering and multi coloured flowers in the centre. It caught the eyes of other jealous customers who wanted to know if it was reserved for a particular occasion or a celebrity. Two glasses and a bottle of red wine had also been placed there to start things off. Tina decided to make her presence and feelings known so she followed them in to the restaurant. Waitie did the courteous thing by holding out the chair for his guest to sit down. He then moved around to the opposite side. Waitie put his serviette in his lap and she did the same. The waiter came over to take their orders after they had examined the menu for a while.

"The lady should go first," said Waitie.

"For starters I will have the Jerusalem Artichoke Soup, with truffle and hazelnut please," said the mystery woman, as she watched the waiter take the orders.

"And for you sir?" asked the waiter.

"I will have the smoked salmon with bergamot, lemon and radish."

As the waiter moved off, he almost bumped into a lady coming towards the table. Waitie saw their exchange but didn't pay much attention but when he looked at her again he realised it was Tina. His shocked face alerted his guest who also looked disturbed to see Tina. Tina was the first to speak.

"Would you mind if I join you?" she asked.

"Hi Tina," said his guest, as they'd known each other for years.

"Hi," she replied.

"Hi Tina," said Waitie, as he drank some of his wine for the first time. "This is not the time and place, I'm having a private dinner with my guest."

"Your guest, oh please, she's always been your lover and you left us for her," said Tina.

Waitie's guest kept quiet. Waitie knew she was talking about her and Sophia.

"I won't spoil your evening, so take care, both of

you," said Tina, as she walked away towards the exit.

"Are you still seeing her?" asked his mystery woman.

"No, but we had a daughter, so we have to communicate," he replied.

When Tina went outside she saw Chris and they stopped to chat. It would be possible to see Waitie and his guest from where they were standing so Tina positioned herself in a way where it would be impossible for Chris to see them.

"Someone will die, if he sees them together, so I better avoid the confrontation," she thought to herself.

Meanwhile, back in the restaurant they had finished their starters and were ready for the main course. They were laughing and winking at each other as if they were in love. The atmosphere was romantic. Waitie leaned over and touched her hand, stroking it, and stared into her eyes. She looked happy. As he was about to say the L word, the waiter interrupted them to take their order for the main course. Again, she ordered first. This time she ordered lamb, turnips, shallots and Lancashire pudding. He went for the most expensive on the menu: native lobster with carrot fondant, ginger and lime. The juice from the lamb slowly seeped out on the plate as she cut through it with her knife. The aroma drew his attention so he took a piece of hers to taste.

"This is really good," he said, as he chewed and swallowed quickly to try another slice.

"Leave it, you have yours," she joked. She had never been a lobster lover, so she wouldn't even try his.

"Why are we meeting in secret like this?" she asked.

"You know why. You don't want your family to know," said Waitie not realising he already knew one of her family members.

"I'm sorry to hear about your daughter," she said, expressing her condolences for the first time. "If you need help, please feel free to let me know."

Waitie's phone rang. He looked at it and saw it was Jason. He didn't want her to know about his regular business, so he ignored it, and set it to silent but it kept buzzing and she started to get suspicious. He had told Jason not to disturb him so he wondered if there was news on John. Waitie politely asked her if he could take the call outside, but by then the phone had stopped ringing. "Phew, that was close," he thought. Waitie had a lot of respect for her, so he would not do anything to jeopardise the relationship.

It was time for desert. He was not too keen on sweet stuff so he opted for a healthier option of yogurt parfait with raspberries and lime. "I will choose for you," he said, as he searched the menu for a dessert to her taste. "Let me get something that is as sweet as you," he suggested while he attempted to charm her. Waitie had to try his best to win her over as he had fallen out with her for many years.

"The special lady will have praline mousse, white chocolate, muscovado sugar and ice cream please." He smiled and looked at her thinking he'd made a good choice.

She loved his choice, which warmed her heart a little closer to him. "You are a very nice man, I don't know how anyone could think of you as evil," she said.

What she said touched him, and concerned him. Waitie thought someone was going around revealing his dirty side. He also thought that he needed to change his bad ways.

"Did you have a good time?" he asked.

"Sure, thanks," she replied.

They got up from their table; she went to the toilet, while he paid the bill. It was time for them to leave. Waitie took her hand, and opened the door for her. They went to his Jeep, where he took her home. She didn't want him to know where she lived, and he respected that, so he dropped her off near her house. Before she went, he kissed her, and said his goodbyes. Waitie knew, apart from his daughter, she was the only woman that could soften him or make him a better person.

CHAPTER 34

Jessica came home with a smile on her face and told Jade she'd met her dinner date on a visit to one of her client's office. She hadn't been out on a date for many years and was humming Mariah Carey's lyrics, *I still believe some day you and me will find ourselves in love again.* She went into the bathroom singing and didn't even notice her dress was stuck in the door.

Jade wondered who this lucky person was, but she knew that Jessica was a secretive person so she didn't bother to probe. She also knew that Jessica would not attract bad men with money. But being girly she naturally wanted to know more, so she decided to ask about the evening instead.

"Where did you go; movie or restaurant?" she asked.

"We went to a posh restaurant," replied Jessica. "Girl, the table was nicely set, the wines were top brand, the food was very expensive, but very nice, and the man..."

"What about the man?" Jade asked.

"He's rich," blushed Jessica.

"You go girl," said Jade as she folder her clothes. "You deserve it, it has been a while. Are you going to see him again? Your face does kind of say it all."

"What do you think? Of course," she replied.

Jade was unaware they had known each other for a long time.

Meanwhile, Tina felt disappointed and rejected. She had lost her daughter and she had no man to get the attention she sorely needed. It was taking its toll on her. She didn't want to stay single for the rest of her life. Tina had a slight crush on one of Waitie's men. She had got his number through some deal that Waitie wanted her to carry out. She knew that he wouldn't want her to go out with any of Waitie's friends, but she didn't care because, as to her, she had needs as well. She also remembered her recent encounter with him and his guest in the restaurant.

Tina took up the phone and dialled the number. The phone rang for a few minutes, without answer. She persisted, and the phone was eventually answered.

"Hi, I need your help, can you come over please?" asked Tina.

"Sure," replied Jason. If his boss' ex needed help he could not refuse.

She dressed similarly to when Waitie visited only this time her skirt was a bit longer.

Five minutes later, he was there. She opened the door, and he was shocked to see her like that, so he averted his eyes, and asked her if she was expecting someone else. However, she persuaded him it was safe to come in.

"You see, I have to be honest, I loved Waitie but he didn't love me. But I've also had a crush on you for a long time," she told him, not knowing that Jason wouldn't even contemplate crossing that line. She knew she was lying, and she still have strong feelings for Waitie.

"Have you been drinking?" he asked.

"I had a shot of brandy and coke, but that's just about it," she replied.

"Why did you call me here, what do you want me to do for you?" asked Jason.

"I just want to talk," she replied.

"OK, we can talk, but I will not take advantage of a vulnerable woman," he continued.

She respected his comments, but wanted more from him.

By this time, he realised he'd be in trouble if Waitie came and saw him there. As Tina walked towards the kitchen to get him something to drink, he couldn't help but notice her ass.

"Wow, she is buff, Waitie is missing something—OK get a grip of yourself," he thought in his head. Jason looked on until she emerged back from the kitchen. Her V-neck top was also revealing, and her large breasts, got him going again. Jason knew how his boss would feel about him being there, but he feared no one. He also knew that Waitie was aware that he was just as ruthless as he was.

"Here you go," she said, bending over showing off her chest as she handed him a beer.

"I do find you attractive, but I have to respect my

231

friend," said Jason, as he took the bottle opener and popped opened his beer.

"We are not together anymore. We haven't been for many years," she replied.

"Well we could be friends."

She liked the sound of that and she smiled and nodded. He was turned on by her looks, appearance and her perfume, but he had to compose himself in order to show respect. Jason was unaware why she was doing this and whether she really meant it and wondered if was trying to get back at his boss. Jason also knew that would be a dangerous game for him as he didn't believe in people leading him on for a joke. Jason knew what Waitie was capable of in circumstances like this, and the boss' ex could pose a challenge to him. He had beaten up women that had done that to him in the past which he was not proud of.

The phone rang and it was Waitie. He didn't ignore it.

"Jason, where are you?" asked Waitie on the phone.

"I am at Tina's," he replied.

Tina was furious about his honest response, but Waitie knew that he didn't tell lies, which was one of the reasons he respected him. Tina thought it was going to cause an issue, so she started to worry, but ironically, he was happy he was there to talk some sense in her head.

"She came and interrupted my dinner with my date earlier, I was embarrassed," said Waitie. "I respect her but she needs to let go now. Talk some sense in her head for me please. By the way, why are you there?"

"She called me to do something for her," replied Jason and Waitie decided not to question him anymore.

"OK, come and see me tomorrow, I may have a job

for you."

"Waitie and I are hunting down the person that caused your daughter's death," said Jason when he got off the phone. "What Waitie doesn't know is that I may know the killer." He was surprised he'd told this to Tina, as he knew Waitie wouldn't be happy, but he must have felt her pain and after he had seen her looking so sexy he had changed his mind. He softened a bit. Jason grappled with the fact that she was his boss' ex, but he was willing to bend the tree a bit for her. "I have my suspicions, but one of this person's family members can be dangerous so I have to approach this with caution. Now, this little secret is out, you're definitely my friend now—maybe one day we'll be more than that."

The comment built up Tina's hopes. "You are a sweet man, your secret is safe with me. I heard on the news that police found Marcus' body; he was identified by his dental records as his body was so badly decomposed. Did you hear the news? Could it be linked to this theory you are suggesting?"

"I haven't heard that news," he replied and ignored the question because if he answered he would have to tell the truth as it was against his principles to lie. He was very clever with his answer. "That one was close," he said in his head. Jason never told lies unless he felt his life depended on it. "I have to go now."

He rose steadily to his feet from the sofa, and she stood up with him. They were very close to each other and looked each other in the eye. Jason moved forward. She thought he was going to kiss her, but he was looking at the tattoo engraved on her neck. He then went to the door.

"When can I see you again?" asked Tina, leaning seductively on the doorframe.

"Let me get back to you on that," he replied.

She closed the door behind him, and rushed to the window, as if she was a girl in love.

CHAPTER 35

The next day back at Waitie's usual meeting place, he met up with Jason.

"Did you convince her to let go?" asked Waitie.

"I don't think it was my job to do that boss," smiled Jason. "Have you got an assignment for me?"

"I have got an unfinished job to do; it's big money. I asked Chris to do it, but it turned out to be one of his brother's girlfriends," explained Waitie. "I don't know how to approach this. But the man is paying big bucks for this job. If I do it, then it will be war between me and Chris, and if I don't, then my boss will get upset. It's hard to reconcile the two." Waitie knew he is no match for his boss with too many connections. He had never refused the boss request. Jason looked at him in surprise.

"Your boss?" asked Jason.

"Yes, you will never meet him. Only me and Chris have met him, and know of his whereabouts, although sometimes it's hard to find him. Before John ran away, he told me that we should wait for the evidence from the police. They say they will present it, but the client still wants us to go ahead with the killing. I want you to find where she lives, and let me know, but be careful, because Chris will kill you without flinching."

"I know he will," replied Jason.

A few hours later, Jade was outside talking to a neighbour. The neighbour's son's birthday was coming up soon. She was telling Jade about it. It was obvious to the neighbour she was about seven months pregnant, so she wasn't sure if Jade would be able to help with the decorations. A car pulled up. The window rolled down. Unaware of any danger, Jade didn't take any notice.

"Excuse me, I need to get to Fisher's Quarters road, how do I get there?" asked the stranger.

"Go to the top of the road, and turn left at the traffic lights," directed Jade.

"Do you know, Paul?" asked the stranger and Jade thought it might be one of his old friends she didn't know.

"Yes, he is my boyfriend, why?" asked Jade.

"Not to worry, I'm Jason, and you are?" he said.

"I'm not telling you my name, I don't know you," said Jade.

"I'm so sorry," said Jason, as he was about to drive away.

"I'll see you later then Jade," said the neighbour, as she walked back to her house, while Jason recorded the name. Jason didn't know if she was living there, so he tried to enquire further, but Jade wasn't having any more of it.

Emerging from around the corner was Chris, but by this time Jason had wound the Jeep window up and was about to drive off. It wasn't the usual Jeep they normally drove or Chris would have recognised it. Chris moved his right arm towards his waist; going for his gun, but Jason had driven off.

"Who was that?" asked Chris.

"I don't know, he said his name was Jason," replied Jade, as she made her way into the house.

"Jason!" said Chris with a loud voice.

Jade was freaked out by his reaction and thought she had done something wrong.

"Not to worry," he said, as he didn't want her to be suspicious. Deep down in his mind, he knew that Waitie had sent him and was on to something. But what puzzled Chris was that Jason could have carried out the job easily. So Chris was thinking that maybe he may have had a change of heart.

"Have you seen Jessica?" asked Chris, as he sat at her desk and switched on her computer.

Jessica didn't normally hide anything and that handwritten letter was there. Chris was not known for reading anyone's private letters, but like anyone, it was hard to avoid if it was right in front of him. The letter stated how sorry the person was and how he would do anything to make it up to her. His initial thought was some poor old guy had done her wrong and wanted to get back together with her. Chris didn't pay much attention to Jessica's affairs as he needed to get on and do what he had gone there to do, but as the letter was in front of him, he glanced at it from time to time. As Chris carried on using the computer, he glanced at the letter again and this time the name Tina caught his attention. Before he could look further, Jessica walked in.

"Hi everyone," shouted Jessica, still in her happy mood after her evening out.

Both Jade and Chris responded. She asked how Chris was doing and moved closer to hug and squeeze him. He was surprised to see her in that mood. Jessica would normally come home tired, and ask what was for dinner and then continue working at her desk. Chris asked how she was.

"I'm fine," she said as he hugged her.

All that was on Chris' mind was securing Paul and his girlfriend. He felt it was his obligation to do so.

Chris decided to contact the insider. He wanted to know more about this celebrity that wanted Jade dead. "I'm going outside for some fresh air," he said to the women as he opened the door to make the call to the insider.

"Insider, I need your help," said Chris. "A certain celebrity wanted to kill my sister-in-law Jade, what can you tell me about him? He raped her and got away with it thanks to his connections," he said looking around to see if Jade and Jessica were eavesdropping. "I need everything on him, and I mean everything."

"OK, I'm on it," said the insider.

Chris contemplated a deadly plan to kill this man. He believed this was the only way with the sort of money at stake. He believed Waitie would eventually get someone to do the job, and deny that he was involved. Chris thought it was time to pay Jason a visit. He ended the conversation, and walked back to the house.

Jessica was in the kitchen, while Jade was sitting on the sofa watching TV.

"What is on telly?" asked Chris.

"EastEnders," she replied.

"OK, I will leave you to your soap, I'm off. And remember, don't talk to strangers, or give out any more information," warned Chris.

"Yes Dad," joked Jade, as Chris closed the door behind him.

Later in New Cross, South London, Martin needed to work out, so he decided to go to the gym. On his way, he spotted a man with Chris, whom he thought he'd seen 15 years ago. It was only guesswork and he wasn't sure if it was one of Chris' old friends.

Waitie and two others gathered outside a pub in South London. Sitting in Waitie's Jeep was one of the guys who had been on the mission to capture Marcus. He was visible from the window who Waitie ask took cover in the back in case there were any unexpected encounters. Also in the back of the vehicle was Jason on his mobile phone and dressed in army green trousers and t-shirt and like a soldier.

Waitie was in the pub drinking. Martin was tempted to go over and say hello, as Martin walked towards Jason. As Martin drew closer Waitie stood up but still didn't recognise him and showed Jason a picture of Jade. Martin was wondering what was going on, so he stood back and paused at the newsagent next door. Martin saw Chris approaching the men so he took cover in the shop. He looked mad and Martin knew something wasn't right. He kept cool and paid for some chocolate and kept watching, prepared for anything.

Chris moved towards Jason from behind without him noticing. By this time, Jason had come out of the vehicle. The man that came with Waitie and Jason in the vehicle didn't see Chris approaching; it was his job was to spot danger. It was clear that Chris had all in his grasp should he decide to launch an attack. Jason was surprised to see Chris.

"Hey killer," greeted Jason, looking friendly and happy to talk. "What brings you here?" he asked, wondering if it was his recent visit to Jade.

"What brought me here is you and your boss. Both of you are messing with the wrong man's family," said Chris.

Waitie saw the look on Chris' face and decided to see what was going on. He positioned himself for anything. There was no need for him to join them as he believed Jason was capable of handling the situation.

"OK," said Jason seeing that Chris was serious. He decided to probe more into why he was so upset. "What is the problem now?"

Martin was still watching and the shopkeeper began to wonder if he was hanging around to steal something. As Martin explained he was hiding from his brother he saw what appeared to be a gun on Jason and started to worry. He knew Chris had no fear, but he didn't think Chris would be stupid enough to approach a man with a gun with such anger. He knew that Chris had seen the gun but kept on arguing with the man. Jason tried desperately to keep his composure, and didn't want the situation to escalate further.

"Why did you visit my family earlier today?" asked Chris.

The other occupant in the Jeep came out and was standing behind Chris in a combat position with his hands in his jacket. Martin saw it was two against one and it was getting dangerous, so he decided to intervene.

"Let me tell you and Waitie something. If either of you hurt any of my family, I will kill both of you," said Chris.

Jason didn't like the threat and thought he'd had enough, and pulled his gun. Waitie spotted what was going on, and rushed outside, followed by the other man in the Jeep who had also pulled out his gun.

"Fucking put that away," said Waitie to both of them. "Just leave it now Chris," he said, knowing what both were capable of. He feared for the trigger happy Jason, rather than Chris.

Jason saw no fear in Chris' eyes. He knew what he was up against and wanted to be the first to draw because his plan wasn't to intimidate Chris but to shoot him. Waitie saw that in his face, which was why he thought it was necessary to cool the situation down. Martin rushed to Chris' aid.

"What are you doing here?" whispered Chris between his teeth, as he tried to protect Martin.

"I was watching what was going on, and feared the worst. I thought they were going to kill you," Martin said.

Chris winked to Martin as he didn't want them to know that they were related. He knew his family would be a weakness in their eyes and they could use Martin to get Chris to submit.

Waitie looked around. He had never thought Chris

would come alone, which was one of the reasons why he'd shouted at Jason to put his gun away, so he assumed Martin was his accomplice. He also knew how dangerous Chris was and that if a fight started Waitie could end up being killed. Waitie had no way of knowing Chris' intentions and how prepared he was, so he was playing it safe.

Martin seemed to gain assurance from Chris telling him everything was under control but Waitie was still not sure if Chris had more accomplices. Waitie looked up at the nearby buildings to check for signs of a sniper. He wasn't scared, but was smart, as he knew what he was up against. Chris persuaded Martin to go. He wanted to get him out of harms way. Martin trusted his brother and reluctantly walked away.

Five minutes after he had disappeared down the road, Chris looked at Jason. "You have no idea what you have done. You pulled a gun on me," said Chris, but he knew that there was nothing to stop Jason from shooting him, not even Waitie.

Jason also knew that Chris could have killed him as well. "Waitie saved you," said Jason putting on a brave face.

"If I see you anywhere near my family again, you know what will happen next," said Chris.

"Gentlemen, calm down, there is no need for this," said Waitie.

Chris walked away, and got into his Jeep across the road.

"YOU ALMOST GOT US KILLED TODAY," shouted Waitie, at Jason. "What were you thinking. You were acting like a wild dog. Do you really know whom you are dealing with? You think you know him? Let me tell you a secret. I'm nowhere smarter, or more dangerous than he is; I saved us today. No-one pulls a gun on Chris and lives to tell the tale."

"You mean I saved us—I went to his family house following your instructions," said Jason. "That's what he was mad about."

Meanwhile, Martin called Chris to see if he was OK. He wanted to know more about the strange encounter. Chris downplayed the situation as a long time friendly feud.

"The one that pulled the gun, was he just showing off?" asked Martin.

"I had everything under control," said Chris.

Martin was reassured and they ended the conversation. Chris took up the phone to call the insider. The phone rang twice, before he picked up.

"Hi mate," said the insider while eating his lunch.

Chris could hear him chewing and gulping down his meal.

"You sound really horrible, mate. What flavour juice are you drinking—Mr. Natural?" asked Chris. Chris knew that he loved his natural juice.

"Natural pineapple and raspberry," answered the insider.

"What have you got for me?"

"The man played for St Catherine United. He is one of their top players," said the insider, as he burped over the phone while talking.

Chris thought that was disgusting, but he knew what he was like, so he ignored it.

"He lives up Essex, and he has a wife and two kids.

He hangs out at a night club at 15 Millett Square, and his name is Milton Fernandez," said the insider.

"Hold on," said Chris, as he searched for another pen, as the one he was using stopped writing. "Carry on."

"He knows PC Smith, the arresting officer that arrested your brother," continued the insider.

"How do you know about my brother?"

"Come on, you know who you are talking to."

"Do you know his address?"

"55 Magnet Road, EX 16 8LP—his telephone number is 06798654271."

"Thanks for the info, I will come back to you if I need more."

Chris picked up a voice disguiser. He installed it on his phone and called straight away. Chris dialled Milton. The phone rang once, and then was answered. Before Chris could say anything, he said, "Waitie I thought you would have had the job done by now."

"It's not Waitie—call him, and your boys off the operation on Jade," said Chris, as he heard the sound of his children talking, and calling, "Daddy, Daddy."

"Who is this, who is this?" asked Milton.

"Never mind who this is, just leave Jade alone. I heard your kids in the background. You live at 55 Magnet Road, EX 16 8LP. If you want to have a peaceful life, and see your kids growing up, call off your dogs," said Chris.

The phone went silent.

"Who—" said Milton, but Chris had already hung up the phone. He looked at his kids in the garden playing and moved closer to them. He looked frightened and concerned. He hushed them into the house, while looking back frantically.

CHAPTER 36

A month later, Paul sent two invitations to Robert and Mark to visit him. The prison emailed them their visiting order number (VO) and the duration of their visit was 60 minutes. They knew that they had two hours to drive, so they got up at 5 A.M. Mark was first up. He rushed to the bathroom because he had thirty minutes to leave the house to beat the traffic. Marked rushed his shower, and was out in ten minutes. Robert went in after him.

Mark took the iron and pressed his brown knitted jumper and ripped jeans. It was late September, and it was starting to feel cold. He also ironed his dad's trousers and shirt. When Robert emerged from the bathroom they had just ten minutes to get ready. Mark was already dressed so he went to the kitchen and poured out hot water into two cups to make tea. The toaster went and the bread popped up and he smothered it with melting butter. As he was doing this, he almost knocked over his dad's tea.

"Hurry up Dad, time is getting away."

Robert came down and they finished their breakfast, grabbed the necessary prison details, got into the car, and drove off. Two hours later, Robert pulled up near the prison parking bay. The automatic gate opened, and he drove in.

"Can I have your VO please and identification," asked the prison officer.

Anxious to see Paul, they'd forgotten to have their VO ready. The prison officer waited for Mark to hand it over.

"You may be searched as a precaution," said the officer.

"No, you are not searching me. I am not carrying any drugs or illegal substances to my uncle. There is nothing in the rule book that says it's mandatory to search. If you insist I will need to speak to a senior prison officer," objected Mark.

"OK, we will not give you a thorough search, but only the basics."

Mark agreed to this.

"All checked and verified. You can go through now," said the officer. The officers took their photographs and fingerprints before entering.

They went into an open room of people visiting family. On entering the room they saw Paul sitting in the far right corner on table 22. He smiled when he saw them. Robert greeted him first. They hugged and smiled at each other. Mark also hugged him. The woman sitting next to them was speaking too loud; Mark had to ask her to lower her voice.

"You are looking OK," said Robert.

"You are looking well yourself," replied Paul. "Come here my soon to be top lawyer nephew," said Paul as he hugged Mark again. "How is everyone?" asked Paul, as he shuffled to show off his book to Mark.

"Did you write this?" asked Mark, as he skimmed through.

"Yes I did," smiled Paul. "Poor Jade. I miss her so much. Are you guys looking after her?"

"Sure, especially Chris," said Robert.

"Rumour has it that it was one of you who killed Sophia," whispered Paul, as he looked to see if the prison officer heard what he said.

The officer was supposed to be within hearing and viewing distance of all prisoners.

"Where did you hear that from?" asked Mark.

"You know prison, we hear everything."

"You know we wouldn't do such a thing," replied Robert.

It was 25 minutes into the visit, and the conversation had become interesting. Paul had told them about his friend Jimmy had inspired him and helped him survive prison. Jimmy was like Paul's psychologist, philosopher and counsellor.

"I got Jade's letter, that she is carrying my baby. I'm so happy, my first child," said Paul. The look of happiness on his face was visible for them to see. He told them he was aware that they were working on a plan for his release. Paul suggested to them that he knew that the police found this plan and evidence, and handed it over to them.

"You seem to know more than us and we're on the

outside," said Robert.

"You have been kept well informed," said Mark.

"Is Chris behaving himself?" asked Paul.

"Well I haven't heard much about him. However, Martin told me that a gun was pulled on him while he was having an argument with what appeared to be old friends," said Robert.

"So how is the solicitor studying going Mark?" asked Paul.

"It's going OK, a few more months to go," replied Mark.

"Good to know. Hurry up and come and represent me," laughed Paul, while he checked his watch, and looked at the officer. "I also heard that Sophia's well connected dad is looking for the murderer. I'm pretty confident that my family was not capable of doing such heinous acts. The only person capable of doing this would be Chris, but I don't think he would go that far. It's not easy in here. I'm glad that you guys haven't given up on me. I'm also confident that the truth will come out, and I will be freed soon, so we can all be a family again."

"We will never give up on you," said Mark.

The time had come for the visit to end. Both Robert and Mark looked sad when they were told time was up. Paul held back his tears. It did not help that the woman next to them was crying aloud. Her husband had been given a life sentence for murder.

"Tell Jade I love her," said Paul as they hugged. As he was taken away he called over his shoulder, "Tell everyone hi for me, and tell Jade she will see me soon."

Mark and his father stood there until he was out of sight before they left.

CHAPTER 37

At East London Police station, Detective Stuart was officially assigned to the murder of Marcus Shepard. Due to his disappearance since the murder, John was the prime suspect within the line of enquiry. Detective Stuart asked his colleagues not to disturb him unless it was very important and walked into his office. On his table were forensics reports on Marcus' body and other evidence in a folder. He closed his door, shut his blinds so no one could see him from the outside, and switched on his instrumental moods CD.

Detective Stuart played this whenever he evaluated and examined forensic evidence. Before he opened the package, he sat in his office chair and adjusted it for comfort. He kicked his feet up on his desk, and then turned his office light down using the remote. He started to reflect and meditate. He relived the conversation at the crime scene:

"What have we got here?" said Detective Stuart.

"It's a homicide but the body is very decomposed," said PC Smith, as a team of the Scenes of Crime Officer (SOCO) field forensic men combed the area for clues. Five men dressed in white suits were on their knees scanning the ground for evidence.

"Any clues so far?" asked Detective Stuart, while he walked around observing the surrounding area.

"Well, the preliminary theory suggests that he fell from that cliff, but that appears inconclusive. Another theory suggests he was murdered," said PC Smith.

"If that is the case, then whoever did it must have been an expert, leaving the body here so it's so decomposed most of the forensic evidence has been lost," said Detective Stuart.

"I have sent a team to examine the top of the cliff, to see what they can gather," said PC Smith. "He could have been pushed or fallen to his death. But what reason would he have to be there by himself?"

"Maybe he killed himself," suggested Detective Stuart.

One of the forensic team made a shocking discovery. He approached Detective Stuart, and PC Smith, and suggested to them that a hole found in Marcus' skull was consistent with that of a gunshot wound.

"This has changed the game if the report we have just heard from your team is correct," said Detective Stuart. He walked towards the river. He scooped up some of the river water and looked at his rippling reflection. He then walked back to the scene, and stood right under the cliff. He spotted bloodstains on the rocks.

Detective Stuart was interrupted from his reflections on

the case by a phone call. He took his feet off his desk, and answered it.

"When you have some time, can you come and see me in my office. I need to know where we are with the investigation on the man found at the bottom of the cliff," said the DCI.

"Yes. I will be with you after I have gone through the forensic report," said Detective Stuart. He took up the report and started to read it. It contained some interesting revelations and he made some notes for the DCI. He stood up, and leaned forward away from his chair as he continued to read. He got up and paced up and down as he rationalised his thoughts. When he had finished he called his boss back and said he was ready to come and see him.

Detective Stuart went into the DCI's office and proposed his theories and suggested lines of enquiry. "I had a quiet recollection on my visit to the scene, before I read the forensic report."

"OK, what have you come up with?" asked the DCI.

"The decomposing body was found by a woman walking her dog near the river at the bottom of the cliff. Giving the nature of the body, forensic report suggests that he was murdered. The pathologist couldn't determine the time of death, as it had been more than 36 hours, and therefore we cannot prove that a suspect was there at the time," said Detective Stuart as he walked to the window looking down from the seventh floor. "This may pose a challenge for us. The window of a five and a half hour theory can only be used within the first twenty-four hours of death. However, the forensic team found evidence that he was shot point blank in the head and thrown off the cliff naked. A part of his skull discovered at the bottom of the cliff, about ten metres from where the team discovered the body. This disproved our preliminary theories that he may have been pushed, or jumped to his death. We also found evidence of the gun the fatal shot was fired from. The spent shell casing found on the scene and ballistic reports suggest it was fired from a 357 Magnum."

The DCI was proud of his officers' professionalism but when he responded all he said was, "Interesting."

"We now know from forensic evidence that something was burnt at the scene of the crime as there was some residue of ashes found at the scene," said Detective Stuart, as he displayed photographs on the table.

"Have you got a suspect?" asked the DCI, who was anxious to solve this crime. He went to his small office refrigerator and took out a carton of apple juice. He poured some into two glasses and handed one to Detective Stuart.

"Well, my prime suspect is John," said Detective Stuart.

"The solicitor?" said the DCI, looking shocked. "Why, what have you got to go on?"

"John has disappeared. I will be interviewing his secretary to see what she knew and check his appointments for the week Marcus was missing. We know that he bought a plane ticket according to his bank statement."

"I will re-assign you to Sophia's case soon, I'm waiting for a response from the commissioner on an issue to do with her father," said the DCI. "OK, carry on with your investigation and get back to me, when you have any new developments."

The next day, Detective Stuart visited John's office. John's partner was still running the business and he was still in total shock. Stuart interviewed the secretary first.

"Hi, I'm Detective Stuart," he said as he showed John's secretary his badge and pulled out his notebook. "I'm investigating the murder of Marcus Shepard. Do you know him?"

"I don't but he came here a few times," replied John's secretary.

"I need to see John's diaries—please? Here is a search warrant," said Detective Stuart, as he produced the papers.

The secretary handed the diary over. He checked it and documented the relevant details.

"Do you know his whereabouts?" asked Detective Stuart.

"I don't," answered his secretary.

"His diary states that Marcus visited him sometime ago. How much do you know about that?" he asked.

"I don't know much. Yes he came here a few weeks ago, and they left together," replied the secretary.

"Have you ever heard them fighting?" he asked.

"Not really," she replied.

"Do you think John would hurt him?" he asked.

"I don't know," she replied.

"Thank you very much for participating in this interview. Here is my card. If you hear or remember anything, or see him, please contact me. No matter how insignificant the matter is, I want to know about it," said Detective Stuart.

"OK, I will do," she replied, as he reached for the door.

The detective considered visiting John's home. He thought about getting a search warrant from the magistrate. Detective Stuart wasn't too convinced that John did it, but John was the only thing he had to go on. He drove past Martin's house and stared at it. He stopped a short time later when he saw some young people gathered. They appeared to be smoking cannabis but they hid it when he approached.

"What is that you've got in your hand?" Detective Stuart asked. He took drugs seriously as one of his cousins had died from an overdose.

"It's nothing," replied the boy.

"Let me see," said Detective Stuart but the boy dropped it through the grill of the drain. With nothing to go on, Detective Stuart gave the boys a warning and told them the next time he saw them smoking he would arrest them. The boys scattered across the estates.

CHAPTER 38

Jason had arranged to meet Tina at her house. She was hoping that this would mean something. The time they arranged to meet was perfect. Tina rose from her bed early, checking the time. She went straight to the bathroom, and soaked in the bath for an hour. Like her daughter, she had four candles around her bath. The aroma from the lavender oil bath created a calming atmosphere in the house. She hadn't hand sex in six years, so she thought this was her chance, and wanted to smell, and look her best.

Her last boyfriend was an alcoholic, so she'd dumped him after a year. She was in desperate need of a fix. She thought it was today. She started to sing, *I'm in the mood for love*. The loss of her son, and daughter, made her believe that she could try to conceive again. She thought about having a child for Jason, but shrugged it off as too early to be thinking about such things. She got out of the bath, and went into her room. The reflection of her nude body in the mirror made her feel sexier.

Tina heard a sound downstairs. She thought it was her cat but remembered she had locked it outside in the garden but realised she may not have locked the kitchen door. Tina didn't think it was anything, so she carried on, putting cream on herself. By this time, she had pulled on a black silky thong. She finished putting the cream on and decided to stay in her knickers. The plan was to trick Jason by wearing a coat as if she was going out, but then open it up and reveal herself like they did in the movies. She thought it would be best to do this without wearing her bra. But when she tried on the coat it itched her. She investigated and found the label was bothering her so she removed it. She put on black boots to match the coat and heard the sound again. This time she thought someone was in the house.

"Who is there?" she called out.

No one answered. She called out again but again there was no answer. By this time, she was scared. Tina remembered her daughter's murder, and wondered if the killer had come back for her. Her heart was pounding. She barricaded herself behind the door. Her mobile phone was downstairs so she wasn't able to call for help. It was a frightening position and she froze in fear. The landline with an extension in her room wasn't working either. She heard footsteps coming up the stairs. She was shaking. Her arms were placed on the door, trying to brace it. Pushing the table behind the door was a wise move. She struggled to move it, but got there in the end. She was about to scream, as she believed that her neighbours would come to her rescue. The sound of a car pulling up was a relief. She quickly let go of the door, and went to check from the window to see who it was. It was Jason.

She opened the window and shouted, "Jason help, someone is in my house." She opened her drawer from her bedside table and took out her keys.

Jason heard her and looked up.

She threw him the keys. She didn't hear anything after that. Jason came in the house, and spotted a man dressed in a wooded top. The man took out a knife, and pointed it at him in a threatening manner. The man had no idea who he was dealing with. Tina was still upstairs in her room, and heard the commotion. Jason had his gun on him, but he would not use it in her house, or reveal to Tina who he was. The man kept looking back as if he wanted to escape, as he realised Jason was not afraid of him. He bravely moved towards Jason and stabbed at him. Jason grabbed the hand holding the knife and kicked him in the stomach. The man tried to punch him with the other arm. He spotted the gun when Jason's jacket flopped open and dropped the knife and tried to run but Jason tripped him up and dragged him behind the kitchen door.

"Listen to me you piece of shit. If you ever come back here again, I will hunt you down and kill you, do you hear me?" whispered Jason.

Tina opened the door and made her way down the stairs. She saw Jason holding the man by the neck. He opened the front door.

"NOW GET OUT AND DON'T COME BACK," shouted Jason.

Tina rushed straight into Jason's arms, as he hugged

her and consoled her. They went to the kitchen and discovered that Tina had left her kitchen door open when she kicked out the cat. He warned her not to do this again, and she should be more careful.

"Do you think he was here to kill me?" asked Tina.

"No, he was just a burglar, but he realised you were here alone, after you called out. I found out he was going through you kitchen drawers," said Jason.

Tina forgot she was still not dressed and as the belt from her coat had loosened it revealed her naked body.

Jason spotted Tina's breasts dangling there as if she was in her twenties. It turned him on. His smile was an encouragement for Tina.

"I brought something for you," he said, as he went into his bag. He brought out an expensive perfume, and her favourite tropical juice.

"Oh thank you, you are so sweet," she said. "No one has even given me such an expensive perfume, not even Waitie."

"Really? And he is so minted," thought Jason.

She felt special and asked if he wanted a drink. He accepted and sat down at his favourite spot on her brown leather sofa.

"I have been thinking about you lately," said Jason. "You look stunning," he complimented, turned on by her earlier revelations.

Tina realised that he was beginning to find her attractive. "Thanks again for today; I don't know what I would have done. The phone was downstairs, I was just thinking to scream."

"I'm glad I was here at the right time," said Jason.

"Your time is perfect, perfect for—" said Tina.

259

"Perfect for what?" smiled Jason.

"Only one way you can find out, would you like to come upstairs?" she said, in desperation.

"I really like you, but it's way too soon, I am a gentleman and I don't take advantage of women," said Jason, as he realised that he was beginning to like her more. "Let's take this nice and slow." Jason was proud to have a woman ten years his senior falling for him.

"Sure, we can do it upstairs," she insisted.

They went upstairs. She left her coat flowing making her breasts visible whenever she walked around the room. Jason wanted her desperately but believed he should take it slow. Tina sat next to him on the bed. He looked at her breasts again and hugged her again, this time tighter as if to say I want you. She thought he was going to leave. She felt something hard pressed against her tummy near his genital area.

Tina thought it was his penis. He felt it too and realised it was his gun. He left the room and told her he was going to the car. She thought he was going to get a condom. He hid his gun in the car, and came back upstairs. The agony of seeing her looking so sexy was unbearable for him. When he came back in the room she was lying on the bed with her legs spread wide. This time she had taken her coat off and was in her knickers only. Jason sat next to her. She loosened his shirt. His hairy chest was visible. She loved hairy men so she was turned on by it. She got up, took off his shirt completely, and ran her fingers over his chest. She pulled him down on the bed on top of her and they bounced on her fluffy mattress.

They kissed passionately. Jason was turned on, but

wasn't comfortable. She went for his belt. She loosened the pin from his buckle. He didn't stop her. The sight of his opened trousers got her wet. She was about to run her hand over his pants but he stopped her. She wondered what was wrong.

"Waitie will kill me if I sleep with her," thought Jason. "But he is not with her. So why should it matter?" He got off her and lay on his back next to her. He found it difficult to reconcile sleeping with Tina.

"Is there something wrong?" she asked.

"No," he replied. "Now is not the right time."

"When is the right time?" asked Tina. "There will never be a right moment. If it happens now or later it's still the same thing. Honey, I want you so much. Don't leave me high and dry."

"You mean high, and wet," he smiled. "It won't happen today, I'm sorry. Let me think about this."

"What is there to think about? It's not a business, it's passion," pressured Tina. "Come here," she said, as she pulled him closer thinking she could convince him.

He refused, as he buckled his belt, and put his shirt back on feeling guilty. "I have to go now. The next time I come back we will discuss you daughter. I believe I have made a break through," he said as he walked out the room.

She couldn't reject that comment, however disappointed she was. She felt any resolution to her daughter's death was good news for her and better than sex. She heard the door slam. She felt like a loser.

"What is wrong with me? Why is everyone rejecting me? Am I too pushy? Am I too desperate? I will stop this now. I am a lady, and I will be my old self again. I've got

261

to be hard to get, otherwise, no one will respect me." Tina turned and looked in the mirror. She wondered what had come over her. The car started. She knew he wasn't coming back for the day. She sat and stared for a while. She then dusted herself off and continued with her daily chores.

CHAPTER 39

Martin was leading the appeal for Paul and gathered up all his paperwork. He met up with Mark at his home to discuss the procedures. Martin was aware that the BBC program *Our View* was doing a documentary on Paul. The programme contacted him to find out if he would be interested in appearing on the show. Because this could potentially free Paul, Martin was more than happy to take part. Martin also agreed to hand over the evidence given to him by the police.

"What have we got here?" asked Mark, as he examined Martin's paperwork.

"The police have handed over concrete evidence that Sophia and others had all planned to incriminate Paul. *Our View* told us that they interviewed John before he went missing. *Our View* is our only hope; this is the media, and the courts will see this as in the public interest," said Martin.

"Yeah, but wrongful conviction, is not an option. Nor was there any miscarriage of justice," warned Mark, as he continued to examine the evidence. It would be cost effective if someone who knew what they were doing that was closely connected to the case could examine it. The family felt that Mark was the correct candidate to do so. "As I have said before, your evidence has to be really strong. It is good news that the police have given you tangible evidence. It is also good that *Our View* will air this, but it is always down to the judge."

Looking through books while he analysed the paperwork, Mark found some interesting case laws that might help Paul. He compared the facts of the case with the facts of Paul's and sifted through to establish the relevant ones and read the judge's decision. One case seemed perfect and in his excitement he forgot that he had finished his drink. He only realised this when he tried to drink from his empty blue coloured glass. The case he found was from the highest court in the land; the Supreme Court.

"I know," said Martin, as if he'd just remembered something.

"Tea anyone?" asked Susan, as they sat around the table going through all the paperwork. She realised that Mark's glass was empty, which was when she decided to offer tea.

"Yes please," both replied.

"I'm going to meet with the team of the TV programme of "Our View" on Tuesday next week," said Martin.

Having figured out his next move, Mark decided how

he was going to proceed. "Moving forward, I will submit the NG form to the Crown Court with the new evidence. We will use our barrister Brian Everest again to represent the appeal. I believe he is good. If they rejected the appeal, then I will serve it directly to the High Court—the criminal division. We must wait for the program to be aired first, before we submit any appeal Although we are out of time—the 28 days to appeal elapsed a long time ago—we can still appeal under *Leave to Appeal out of Time*," said Mark, dunking biscuits Susan brought into his tea. "I will assign a new solicitor to the case, but first Paul will have to sign CDS1 and CDS2 forms," outlined Mark, as he drank his last portion of his tea. He looked for more biscuits, but he had finished the whole pack. He picked up another packet of biscuits, and opened it.

"So how much will this cost?" asked Martin.

"A lot of money," replied Mark.

Tuesday morning, two weeks later, Martin was at the studio for his interview with the team at *Our View*. He arrived early and he was told to wait in the green room. Mark was with him as well, for support. As promised, Martin handed over the evidence to the producer. The producer showed them a list of experts that had agreed to be interviewed. They asked Martin to sign a disclaimer form to protect the organisation. It was time to go into the studio.

Martin met up with their makeup team, as they wanted him to look more presentable on screen. He was taken into the makeup room. They pampered and powdered him to look the part. Martin was then taken to another room for the interview. The lights were bright and the TV crew were in position. Four cameras were lined up from different angles to capture different shots. He sat on the chair next to the flowers that gave the impression they were in a living room. Martin was told that the presenter was a nice person. Sue Pickelton lived up to her reputation.

BBC's *Our View*:

Sue: "You believe your brother was setup, and coerced by the same people that were supposed to protect him from being convicted?"

Martin: "Yes, I believe so."

Sue: "The police handed over evidence to substantiate your claim, is that also correct?"

Martin: "Yes, that is correct."

Sue: "Why do you believe that you brother did not commit the crime he was accused of? And if he didn't why did he admit to it?"

Martin: "I know he didn't because I looked after him when he was a child, and I think I know what he is capable of. Moreover, he would never lie to me. I am a man of God, and I think I would be more likely to lose my temper than he would."

Sue: "So you are telling me that he would not do such a thing?"

Martin: "That is correct."

Sue: "Tell me about the evidence the police handed over to you. How did this happen?"

Martin: "I was called by the police to report to the station, and then it was handed to me."

Sue: "How did you feel about Sophia?"

Martin: "I treated her like my daughter. I was very disappointed about what she'd done to us. But having said that, I don't think she deserved to be killed, despite her bad ways."

Sue: "Do you think that the court will accept this evidence at this stage?"

Martin: "Well, we have to try. It's all we have got—this is the only chance to free my little brother Paul."

Sue: "Do you think you have a good chance that the court will quash the conviction?"

Martin: "I hope so, I hope so."

Sue: "Martin, thank you for taking part in *Our View*."

Martin: "Thank you."

The presenter shook Martin's hand. Martin went to have another chat with the producer.

"When will this be aired on TV?" asked Martin.

"We have a few more people to interview, including the experts. As soon as we have completed our interviews, the programme will be edited, and viewed by our producers for approval. We will email you a week in advance of the date it will be aired," said the producer.

Mark waited for Martin to emerge from the studio

"How was it?" asked Mark when Martin appeared and they made their way down the stairs.

"It was OK; I answered all the questions appropriately."

"Do you think this will make a difference?" asked Mark.

"I'm sure it will. Ninety percent of journalistic investigations done by this programme have resulted in a successful outcome, either one way or the other," Martin assured him. "More often than not, it resulted in the quashing of many cases—which highlighted the miscarriage of justice. This can only be a positive thing."

They got into the car and drove off leaving all the evidence with the producer. The discussion continued in the car. Mark wanted to know if he had heard any developments on Sophia's murder. As they got towards the traffic light, Martin spotted Waitie.

"There is Chris' friend. He was there when his friend pulled a gun on Chris."

"Really?"

"You know Chris is the bravest in the family, so he stood his ground."

"Can you drop me home please?" asked Mark.

"Sure, I was planning on doing just that. It's rush hour now; you wouldn't get home on public transport until about eight tonight," smiled Martin.

Martin found a few back roads, dropped Mark home, then headed off home himself. Half way home, Martin spotted Waitie again. This time they both looked each other in the eyes.

"That's the man Chris was with the other day," thought Waitie. He believed they resembled one another and he turned and whispered something to the man he was walking with.

CHAPTER 40

Two weeks later at the police station, the DCI called Detective Stuart into his office to instruct him on how to proceed with Sophia's case.

"I called you here because I was waiting on the commissioner on a case priority issue. I can now instruct you to arrest the suspect in connection with the murder of Sophia Wait," ordered the DCI. "You and your team have done a brilliant job on this case, and we believe this arrest will be in the best interests of the public. I know CPS has given you the go ahead, but I needed clarity and I've got that now. Take all the necessary resources you need to bring the culprit to justice. I wish you good luck; off you go unless you have something to add."

"Nothing to add at this stage sir," said Detective Stuart as he turned and opened the door. Before he stepped out, he turned and said, "Thanks for all you support in this case, and I promise I have the right person," said Detective Stuart.

Detective Stuart had asked for four men, a car and a police van. Detective Stuart had one officer in his car and PC Smith was driving the police van with the other officer. Stuart valued PC Smith's experience. Ten minutes into their journey, PC Smith remembered he'd left the warrant for the arrest on his desk and went back to get it. Detective Stuart wasn't too happy as he'd asked beforehand if everything was in check.

Detective Stuart remembered that he needed to return items to the Reynolds' family but this visit would coincide with their suspect. On the way Detective Stuart received intelligence via the radio as to the whereabouts of the suspect. This didn't change their agreed route. Instead of taking the side roads, they took the motorway into South London. Their first stop was Chris' house. They turned into his road as onlookers wondered why the police were in their area. Detective Stuart drove slowly riding the road humps. As they passed, one man got off his bicycle and pulled out his mobile phone. Detective Stuart wondered if he was alerting the suspect of their arrival, but both knew why they were going to Chris first. PC Smith thought the man on the bicycle may have sent an alert for drug dealers as this was prominent in the area. Another man, on a roof top, also got on his mobile phone.

They turned onto Chris' road. The car bumped up and down over a pothole. Crowds from the community started gathering. One woman looked at the officers and asked if she could help them and why they were there.

Detective Stuart parked at Chris' flat. PC Smith

parked behind him but rode the curve. Detective Stuart got out first with a bag. PC Smith and the other man followed. Detective Stuart approached the door while onlookers watched. PC Smith and his man went to the side of the flat. Chris' door was knocked twice—there was no answer. They knocked again and there was still no answer. Detective Stuart took up his mobile phone to call him. Chris' neighbour asked if they needed help, and if something was wrong. The neighbour appeared to be an old classmate of PC Smith.

"Hi," said the neighbour, as he moved closer to his front gate. "Are you here to arrest him?" he asked.

"I can't really answer that question," said PC Smith.

"Well, he is not here. I saw him leave earlier," said the neighbour, as he played with the lock on his gate, "I think he said he was going to his sister."

"OK, thanks," said PC Smith. He informed Detective Stuart what he had learned and they went back to the cars and drove off.

The next stop on the list was Martin. He was an hour away. While they were driving past a particular neighbourhood, they spotted a fight. Two women rushed towards them waving them down. Detective Stuart slowed trying to decide whether to stop or continue. The two fighting spotted the convoy and ran. Detective Stuart radioed the local force and notified them of the situation. He realised that there wasn't a serious threat to life and limb, so he continued on his way. Martin lived in a rather posh area, so the sight of police in a convoy was strange and rare to the residents of that community. There was hardly any trouble there. Detective Stuart was aware of this, so they proceeded with caution and made out they

271

were just patrolling officers. They slowly drove past certain areas twice and waved gently at residents. When they got near Martin's house, they parked ten metres from the turn to his road and walked the rest of the way. This time, it was PC Smith that knocked but no one answered. PC Smith wanted to be sure, so he bent to have a peek through the letter box. He called out Martin's name, but there was still no answer. The neighbour that never objected to Martin playing his gospel tunes thought the other neighbour had called the police on him again. She continued to look on from her window.

As he was walking away from the house, he heard the phone ring inside the house. PC Smith went back and opened the flap on the letter box again. The phone stopped and went to message. He listened attentively. He heard Jessica's voice.

"Hi Martin, I tried you on your mobile, but you didn't pick up. We are all meeting up at mine. I cannot get through to Robert, but I will try him again later."

The message ended but it became clear why neither Martin or Chris were at home. PC Smith explained this to Detective Stuart and they returned to the car to decide their next move. PC Smith suggested they carry on to see Robert before he went to Jessica's place. Detective Stuart wasn't convinced. He believed that Jessica should be the next stop. He was in charge and had the authority to decide but PC Smith convinced him.

"If we go to Jessica before Robert, he may not be there. I think we should stick to the original plan and visit him first. Jessica said on the voicemail she wasn't able to get a hold of him. We need to go there first, as he was an important player in this investigation," said PC Smith.

"I just think he is at Jessica's given that we went to both brothers and they weren't there. Whatever we need to inform him, we could do it there," said Detective Stuart.

"I still think we should go to Robert's first," said PC Smith.

"OK, let's go then," said Detective Stuart.

They got into their vehicles, and sped off to Robert's place. Time was catching up on them, and they wanted to beat the rush hour, so they put on their sirens. But they got stuck behind an old man who wasn't paying attention to the police lights. It was too narrow to overtake him and the man's exhaust was blowing smoke, his bumper was falling off, there were cracks in his rear lights and his indicator light was also missing. PC Smith wasn't able to see ahead of him clearly, so he patiently waited until he was able to pass, and then pulled the man over. Detective Stuart wanted to get to his destination, but he couldn't resist illegal activities, so he pulled over as well. PC Smith got out of his van, and walked towards the driver.

"Have you got you licence and insurance with you?" asked PC Smith, as he looked around in the car.

"Yes," the old man said.

He handed it to him. PC Smith checked it, and gave it back to the man.

"Did you hear the siren, and see the lights flashing behind you?" asked PC Smith.

"Not really. I heard something, but I thought it was coming from the opposite direction," said the old man.

Detective Stuart wanted PC Smith to hurry up. He knew how important his mission was, and knew that time was crucial. He wanted nothing to delay his arrest.

"Hurry up," he said in his mind.

"Have you got your MOT with you?" asked PC Smith, knowing there was no way the old man could have a valid MOT with so many defects on his vehicle. He took the MOT, and as he thought, it was outdated. He looked at Detective Stuart, who indicated that he should hurry up. "You haven't got a valid MOT, you obstructed an officer on duty and this is a criminal offence which carries a one month imprisonment, or a level three fine. I will let you off this time. But if I see you again without a valid MOT, I will arrest you. Do you understand?" asked PC Smith.

"Yes sir," replied the old man.

PC Smith got in his van and drove off again. This time there was no obstruction. Both knew that it will take them three hours to get to Jessica's, but they needed to get to Robert's first. It took them ten minutes to get to Robert thanks to the siren but Detective Stuart knew it would have taken longer under normal circumstances. When they arrived they noticed his gate was locked. Normally it would be open. The fence was low, and Detective Stuart needed to get to the door, so he climbed over the fence and knocked at the door with its cast iron doorknocker. No one answered. They heard his dog barking inside. Again PC Smith opened the letter box flap. He spotted the dog coming towards him. He released it and quickly moved back.

They could hear the dog paws scratching the door and barking. Persistence was always PC Smith's motto, so he tried again; still no answer. Detective Stuart was getting a bit suspicious. He wondered whether someone had tipped off the brothers. He knew there was only one place left to go, and it was Jessica's. Detective Stuart also knew that it would take them another two hours to get there or an hour and a half if he used the siren. He didn't want to hesitate. So he got back into his car, and drove off, only this time he led the way. They got to the roundabout and had to give way. The car they gave way to was Chris'. He was heading towards Kent where Jessica lived. He spotted the police, but didn't pay any attention to them. They didn't see him either. PC Smith knew his way there, as he had been the arresting officer in Paul's case. He looked to check his petrol level. He estimated that it was enough to take him there.

CHAPTER 41

Chris' knowledge of the area was good and he was good at finding short cuts so he took the second turning after the roundabout.

"What crisis meeting is Jessica is talking about?" mumbled Chris to himself. "Oh, maybe it's *Our View* they want us to watch. I have got an hour to get there, so I better put my foot down. I hope I don't get caught along the way."

Time was of the essence, so Chris accelerated a little harder to get to his destination quickly. He then felt for the car radio and switched it on. The music was blasting in his ear, but he needed that while driving. Chris spotted someone who looked like his girlfriend, so he slowed to see if it was her. It wasn't her. He was worried about his kids. Beckton, where Kerry's mother lived, was usually a safe place to stay but he still feared for them. As he passed a convoy of lorries parked at a service station,

Chris checked his rear view mirror, and spotted a police car.

Chris checked his speed limit and noticed he was going a little bit over the limit so he eased off the accelerator. The police car wasn't the one he'd spotted earlier, as he'd checked their license plates. The car pulled closer to Chris and looked him in the eye. Chris looked back. The officer then sped off. Chris waited until he had passed the commercial area and passed the last lorry in the group, and was out of sight from the police, before stepping on it again. His tank was almost empty and he knew he would have to stop at the one down the road.

Chris pulled into the next petrol station, about five minutes from where he saw the police and the lorries. He filled his tank and picked up a bar of chocolate, and a box of juice. As he was walking out of the shop, the shop assistant shouted at him.

"Excuse me, you haven't paid for those."

"Sorry, I thought I did," replied Chris. He'd had no intention of stealing, but because he had so much on his mind, he'd forgotten to pay. He got back into the vehicle, and drove off. In his head he started to work out his next short cut. Chris decided to take the next right. This would lead him to another off road that would cut out a lot of traffic, and reduce the distance. He thought he would be the first one at Jessica's. Chris remembered something and smiled to himself. Because he was a warrior, and trained to get away by any means necessary, he knew it wouldn't be a challenge for him to get there before everyone else, even if the others had left earlier than him. As he continued, he spotted an army truck packed with soldiers. He remembered how he had once been in their shoes. Chris slowed to see if he recognised anyone. He knew this might not be possible, given that he had left the army long time ago. He saw someone that looked familiar and continued to slow. It turned out it was his former captain. Chris wound down his window and tried desperately to get his attention. Chris raised his right hand and waved, but no one saw him. A young soldier looked around, and spotted him waving. He saw Chris pointing to the captain. He alerted the captain by touching him. The captain spotted Chris, and gave him a big smile and waved back. Chris sped off and left them.

Meanwhile, Martin and Susan were heading towards Bromley. They too were going to Jessica's. Martin set off early, so he thought he was going to get there first. He had an hour to go. Martin was not a fast driver, but a careful one.

"I can't stop thinking about Sophia. She was such a nice girl so something must have happened to her. I know her father wasn't around," said Susan, as Martin concentrated on the road and nodded. "What beast would want to kill her? She did wrong to Paul, and I'm not denying that, but she didn't deserve to die."

Martin looked sad, but didn't say anything in response.

"Rumour has it that it was one of the brothers that killed her. Did you hear anything like that?" asked Susan.

"I haven't heard anything like that," replied Martin. "Wow did you see that?"

"See what?" replied Susan, as she looked to see what

Martin was talking about.

"That man just came straight out at me. If I didn't swerve, he would have run straight into me. He just came out from the crossing." They were half an hour into the journey since they had left Bromley, and Martin continued to drive at his own pace. "Why would any of us wanted to kill Sophia? That's a ridiculous assertion," he said turning left onto an adjoining road.

"Well, I heard that her father is a mad man, and he will stop at nothing until he gets the person that killed his daughter," said Susan.

Martin looked at her in fear. "I can understand, I would have done the same if I wasn't a changed man. Oh no," said Martin, as he tried to pull over when he heard police sirens.

"What is it?" asked Susan.

"I cannot pull over to let the cops through, because the road is too narrow. There's a gap up ahead. I'll pull over there as they seem like they are in a rush. Usually, when they drive like that, and in a convoy, it means they are going to arrest someone."

"Really, how do you know that?"

"I just know," said Martin.

"I hope they find the killer for her murder if those are the cops looking for Sophia's killer," she said.

"Me too. What is causing this traffic?" he asked as he slowed down to about 20 MPH.

"We are going to get there late, it seems," replied Susan.

As they drove past the traffic block, Martin spotted a police van on the opposite side of the road blocking traffic with Detective Stuart at the wheel on his radio. He also saw a policeman directing traffic. It was the same van he'd pulled over for on the narrow road.

Detective Stuart was calling for back up or an extra vehicle. He didn't see Martin drive past.

"What happened to them?" asked Susan.

"It looks like a tyre blew out on the police van. They will be fine, they are the government," assured Martin.

Further back were Robert and Mark. They had set off late. Robert had to pick up Mark from his first intern as a trainee solicitor. He knew that Mark's next step was a trainee contract so he wanted to support him as much as possible.

"We are going to get there late," said Mark.

"Don't worry, Jessica won't start without us," he assured him, while checking for his camera on the back seat.

"Focus on what you are doing Dad. What is it? Tell me and let me get it for you."

Robert indicated the camera and Mark stretched over to pick it up.

"Why did you take your camcorder?" asked Mark, while he examined how to operate it. "This is a new one isn't it? I have never seen this one before."

"It is. I want to film the discussion. I'm getting a bad feeling that something is about to happen.".

"What could possibly go wrong tonight? Come on Dad, you are always superstitious," said Mark. Mark dived around in his bag to see if he had anything to eat, as he was hungry. He searched and found nothing. His tummy was rumbling, loud enough for his dad to hear. He picked up his dad's bag. He opened it to look for food but there was nothing in it except for a plan titled "East London plan B." Robert was concentrating on the road and didn't know what Mark was doing. In the plan was a map leading towards Strawberry Road where Sophia lived. Mark didn't think anything of it at first and he didn't want to search his dad's things so he zipped up the bag and started to focus on the road again.

"I'm hungry Dad, can we stop somewhere and grab something to eat?" he asked.

"Sure, when we get to the next set of shops," replied Robert.

The hunger was becoming unbearable, so Mark took his bottle of water to neutralise the hydrochloric acid in his stomach. That helped for a short while, just in time to get to the shops. As Robert pulled over, Mark opened the door and jumped out of the moving vehicle.

"Dad do you want anything?" asked Mark, as he closed the door.

"I'm not in the mood to eat now son, especially when I'm driving," he replied.

Mark made his way into the shop. As he slammed the door the bells attached to it rang and the shopkeeper emerged from the back. Mark went to see if they had what he wanted. He picked up a packet of crisps, a drink and a muffin. He thought this would be enough to hold him until he got to his aunt's house where there would be dinner.

He paid for his snacks, and hopped back into the car. He started to munch on the crisps. The crunchy sound of the crisps pissed his dad off.

"Hurry up and eat that thing boy, I don't like the sound of it," said Robert.

"OK Dad," said Mark with his mouth full. He smiled. "Dad, I'm sure this meeting will be about Sophia."

"It will also be about Paul as well," said Robert.

"OK. Are going to watch the programme on TV as well?" asked Mark.

"I think so. I'm sure I heard Martin saying that it will be aired tonight."

"After this, I think we have enough evidence to win the appeal," said Mark.

"What makes you so sure?" asked Robert.

"With this overwhelming evidence and the TV programme there's no way a judge wouldn't overturn the decision, despite him pleading guilty. But it is always down to the judge."

As they approached a junction, they saw the traffic ahead. It was getting dark. Mark spotted a police vehicle. He also spotted a police tow truck. The flashing of the police lights blinded Robert as he approached.

"Dad I think the tyre blew out on this one. But it has a dent in the side as well," said Mark.

As Robert got to the scene, one of the officers directing the traffic stopped him. He looked him in the eye and then told him to go. Robert continued on his journey. He decided to put his foot down. He sped off shortly after passing the police. Mark wondered if it was the right thing to do so soon after they had passed police and thought the police in the unaffected car might give chase. But Robert was lucky. He was clocking about 80 MPH on the motorway because he realised they were late and didn't want everyone to be kept waiting. Mark was getting a bit frightened as his father continued to speed. Mark spotted another police vehicle and shouted at his dad to slow down. One thing he didn't want was the police to stop them.

"If anything goes wrong tonight, please promise you will continue you career," said Robert.

"Dad, come on now. You are freaking me out. What are you on about?" asked Mark. "Is there something you are not telling me?"

"No son, but I just have a funny feeling," he replied.

"About Paul?"

"Well, everything."

"Everything like what?"

"Son. I don't know," replied Robert. "Chris didn't look too happy the other day. And Martin looked distant recently. The only person that looked calm, since the rumour about the family involvement in Sophia's death was Jessica. Well I suppose I should be positive. It's not worth it. I have complete faith in this family, and no one would be so stupid. We all love Paul, but he wouldn't want us to do anything so stupid."

Despite the reassurance, Mark thought his dad knew something, or was hiding something about Sophia's murder.

CHAPTER 42

Chris was the first one to get to Jessica's. Taking the side roads had worked out. Jessica lived in a quiet area with lot of trees leading up to her semi-detached five bedroom house. Her green hedges were properly trimmed and groomed to perfection. Her jealous neighbours always commented on how she kept the garden so well. The road leading to the house curved into the entrance of the house, passing big white metal gates that arched in the middle with pegs on the top for security. Driving up her slightly sloped driveway towards her house, there was a grassy space where two cars could park parallel to the house. On the left towards the back of the house there was another huge space for parking.

Chris got out of his black Jeep and opened the gate. He got back in and drove up the driveway and parked on the grass towards the left, parallel to the house. Jessica heard the sound of the engine and came towards the door to greet him. Chris eased out of the driving seat, looked at the vehicle, and slammed the door shut. As he was walking towards the house, he turned and pressed the button on his remote key fob which locked the doors.

"Hi Chris," said Jessica as she hugged him. "Thanks for coming, let's go inside. "How was your journey? I heard there was traffic on the road."

"I don't know. I took sides roads," smiled Chris.

"That's why you got here first," smiled Jessica, as they walked into the house.

Chris handed her some snacks he'd bought on the way. "Where is Jade?" he asked.

"She is upstairs resting," she replied. "Can I get you something to drink?"

"Scotch," said Chris.

"You must be joking," smiled Jessica, as she went in the kitchen and got him a beer, and brought it back to the sitting room.

"Not too long now to go with Jade " said Chris.

"Yes, not too long," she replied, finalising her tidying up to welcome the family. She fixed the cushion on the far right corner of her sofa for the third time.

"I thought I heard Chris' voice," said Jade, making her way down the stairs walking like a duck with one hand on her tummy and the other holding on the staircase. "Hi Chris, how are you?" she asked as she hugged and kissed him.

"I'm fine," said Chris hugging her with a smile.

"I haven't seen you since the last time you were here when that strange man asked me those questions. Did you find out who it was?" asked Jade.

"Yeah, a friend of an old friend. Don't worry about

285

it," he assured her, taking a sip of his beer. "How is my nephew?" asked Chris, as he felt her tummy, smiling.

"How do you know it's a nephew?" smiled Jade, as she'd forgotten she'd broken the news to him after the scan. "You may get a surprise."

"I don't care, once it's healthy, then that's all that matters. Unless the scan is lying," replied Chris.

Jessica checked her watch and watched the door, looking to see if the others were coming. "Where are the others? The programme will start in exactly an hour," she warned.

Meanwhile, Martin had just pulled up with Susan and spotted Chris' Jeep.

"Damn, he got here before me," smiled Martin.

"With the way you were driving, anyone would have gotten here before you," remarked Susan.

"Please get the bag in the back seat with the package for Jessica," said Martin, as he gave her a look, and checked his tyres. They looked flat, so he got out his pump hoping they weren't punctured. Susan made her way up the driveway with the bags and to the front door thinking she had to walk all the way up the slope with the bags. Martin got back into his car and parked it next to Chris' Jeep. Jessica heard them and came to the door. By this time, Martin was standing next to Susan.

"Hi to you both," said Jessica, as she hugged and kissed them. "Is this for me?" she asked as Susan handed her a package. "Thanks very much."

They made their way into the house. Martin sat at the

far end of the sofa next to the cushion Jessica had struggled to fix next to the computer desk, while Susan sat in the middle, between him and Chris.

"Hi Martin, Susan. How are you?" asked Jade, as she walked closer towards them opening her arms to hug them.

"We are OK," replied Martin.

"How is my nephew coming on?" asked Martin, as he examined her tummy, checking for movement.

"What is with you guys? It's a girl," joked Jade, although she tried to look serious.

"It's a boy, I can tell. Paul would be proud," Martin said, twisting his body to the right to see her properly.

"Well, you all will be surprised," smiled Jade.

Jessica brought orange juice for Susan, and the same for Martin.

"Oh, hi Chris," said Martin, while he stretched out his hand to shake his.

"Hi Chris, how have you been?" asked Susan.

"Hi you two, I'm fine," replied Chris, as he emerged from the toilet, and stood at the entrance to the sitting room.

"Jade, can you help me in the kitchen please?" asked Jessica.

"Sure," she replied.

"I will join you guys," suggested Susan, as she slowly rose from her seat, and stood next to Martin touching him on his head, before joining the girls in the kitchen.

"This suspicion about one of us murdering Sophia is beginning to make me feel nervous," said Chris.

"Why? We are innocent," replied Martin, surprised to hear Chris saying he felt nervous. "The focus tonight is to

287

free Paul. So let's watch the programme and then work out what action we take."

"I agree with you, but we cannot ignore what people are saying, and we must not be complacent. If her father finds out, or even has any inkling, there will be war between me and him," said Chris, opening up a little for the first time to Martin.

"War?" asked Martin, as he finished the last bit of his orange juice. "No way. None of us had anything to do with it."

"Don't worry about it, I don't want to get you guys involved," said Chris. "There are certain things you guys don't know about me, and I would rather keep it that way."

"We know everything about you, for start, you are a secretive man," joked Martin. "You have been like this since you were a child."

Chris didn't find it funny and looked at him seriously. He knew the object was to protect them, especially Paul. Chris was trying to prepare them for what may come. He knew that the confrontation between him and Waitie was inevitable, and was just a matter of time. The room went quiet, as Chris moved towards the window looking outside into space. Martin knew something was troubling him, and couldn't work out what it was.

Robert finally arrived. "Mark, can you get the drinks in the back for me please?"

"Where?" asked Mark, as he turned his head around to look over his shoulder for bags in the back seat.

"Sorry they are in the boot of the car," he replied.

"Dad, you are not concentrating. Wait until you are parked near the house so I don't have to walk up the hill with a heavy box," suggested Mark.

"Lazy," thought Robert as he stood holding on to the car door, but instead he said, "Good idea," and drove towards the back of the house for the available parking space there, as Chris and Martin's vehicles had taken the available spaces at the front. As he turned towards the back of the house, the motion lights came on. This was helpful, as he was able to see clearly while reversing. The girls could hear the vehicle from the kitchen, as it was situated at the back of the house.

Chris got up and opened the door. All the ladies came to the living room to greet them.

"Hi," said Robert to everyone.

"Hello," they all responded.

Jessica as always walked towards Robert to greet him formally.

"Hi everyone," said Mark, emerging from behind his dad, when everyone was about to ask where he was.

Hi Mark," they chorused.

Jessica hugged and kissed them both, while the others followed suit.

"How is my nephew?" asked Robert to Jade, as he rubbed her tummy.

"IT'S NOT A BOY," laughed everyone remembering what Chris and Martin had said earlier.

"You see, we all know it's a boy," said Chris, letting the cat out of the bag and smiling.

"OK, it's a boy everyone," said Jade.

They all hugged her and congratulated her again, and

formally welcomed her into the family.

CHAPTER 43

Dinner was ready, and everyone sat around the table as a happy family, except for Paul, whose absence was felt by everyone. Jessica had roasted chicken, potatoes and Yorkshire pudding. Carrots, broccoli and cauliflower had also been prepared. Jade had set the table. Martin sat at the head of the table with Chris opposite him. Robert and Mark sat side by side on Martin's right with Susan and Jessica opposite them. Jade was squeezed next to Chris on a spare chair that was usually located in the kitchen as it was only a six seater table. Chris offered his space to Jade, but she refused knowing that she wasn't going to stick around for too long for what she thought was a family affair. Chris stretched and served himself more than the rest, as everyone knew he was the greediest of the brothers. Robert took the least.

"This chicken tastes really good. Who cooked it?" asked Chris, as he took a big bite from a leg of chicken.

"It was Jade," replied Jessica, as she poured gravy on her rice and vegetables while Martin waited patiently for it.

"So who in the family is the best cook?" asked Mark, as he smiled looking at Susan's glass of cranberry juice—it surprised him as he knew she loved her orange juice. "I think it's me."

"No, I think it's Jessica," said Robert.

"I think it's Susan," said Martin.

Everyone knew it was Susan, but Jessica had always wanted to compete with her.

"Well, I agree it's Susan," admitted Jessica.

"I'm going to be honest, I think it's Susan," interjected Chris, while Martin looked proudly at her.

Jessica changed the subject. "I'm not comfortable with what I have been hearing recently. The talk of the town is that one of us killed Sophia. I know it's not me."

Susan took a sip of her cranberry juice. Martin's head was down fixing his sock and he appearing to be hiding. The bottle of wine on the table was still sealed. Chris was looking at it as if he wanted to pop the cork.

"You went to East London that night," joked Chris, as he took his eyes off the bottle, and looked at Jessica.

"So did you as I understand it," hit back Jessica.

"Why are we having this conversation? We need to focus on Paul's release—that is why we are here," said Martin.

"Yeah, but I'm still uncomfortable about what I am hearing," continued Jessica. "I'm going to put the question to you one by one, and I need an honest answer."

Everyone had finished their meal. Chris decided to

clear up, avoiding the question. Robert also decided to help. They took the plates and glasses into the kitchen. Martin, Mark and Susan stayed at the table. Jessica could not ask what she wanted to ask, as everyone was not settled.

"I don't think there is any point asking, because none of us would do such a thing," said Mark.

"I agree with you," said Martin.

Jessica looked uncomfortable and unhappy with what she was hearing, as she quivered in her seat with anger. Despite part of her wanting to believe, she thought there was something someone was not telling her. Mark remembered seeing what he saw in his dad's bag. He was never going to revealing anything to the family. He didn't believe that his dad had anything to do with it, but he thought he was hiding, or shielding someone. Whatever it was, he was never going to say a word.

Everyone except Jade sat down on the sofa. It was almost time for the programme to begin.

"Were anyone of you involved in Sophia's murder?" Jessica asked one more time looking each of them in the eye in turn.

Chris looked nervous and drank a lot of wine. He'd opened it when everyone had been distracted tidying up. Martin looked the coolest of the group. On the chair next to the TV was Mark, looking shocked. Jessica sat looking at Robert as they got along very well. Susan was now having tea. Jade was in Jessica's room as she decided that it was a family matter and the stress was not good for her and the baby. This was the perfect time for then to open up as Jade was not there.

Everyone looked at Robert, as he had a plan B. No-one believed anyone in the family had anything to do with it except for Jessica, but a feeling of suspicion was flowing through the air. Breaking the ice was Martin.

"Listen, none of us liked what she did to Paul, but none of us would want her dead, OK."

"Well, I did," said Susan, joking.

"This is not a joking matter, this is serious," said Chris.

"Yes, it is," added Martin.

"My plan was for her to incriminate herself hence why I hired the private detective," said Robert. He wondered if Paul had friends on the outside that would do such a thing.

"We went to the funeral to pay our respects, but we were ignored by the family, that's all we could do. But something is just not right here. Why did everyone look guilty?" asked Jessica.

"Do you think Jade would have anything to do with it?" whispered Robert.

"Don't be silly," defended Chris, still looking uncomfortable.

Meanwhile, Detective Stuart, and PC Smith had received the replacement van to carry on with their journey. The setbacks hadn't dissuade them from their mission. Detective Stuart was determined to get his killer. They had forty-five minutes to get to the house. The build-up of traffic slowed them down and there was no point using the siren as the road was too narrow to pass safely.

It was slow going; slow enough for Detective Stuart to grab at passing branches while his window was down. PC Smith on the other hand was viewing the hillside. The officer next to him was playing games on his mobile. The sound of thunder frightened the other officer next to Detective Stuart who was also playing games on his phone. "Coward," though Detective Stuart, as he turned his head and looked at him.

The rain started to come down. Detective Stuart pulled in his arm and wound up his window. The squeaky noise of the wiper on the windscreen aggravated him and he wondered why it hadn't been fixed. The rain came down heavily. Rain droplets pelted on the top of the vehicle and affected his visibility.

Detective Stuart's map indicated that the one way road he was on would continue for another two miles. He wondered superstitiously if all the bad luck they'd had meant they shouldn't go after the suspect. Everything seemed to have gone wrong so far.

"Are you there yet?" asked the DCI over the radio, as it cracked with interference.

"Not yet sir. I had a lot of setbacks, but we are still on the trail," said Detective Stuart.

"I'm sure control would have told you what the situation was," said Detective Stuart.

"You must be calling me from home?"

"Yes, I am. I left the office at six today. But as you know I have a police radio here as well," replied the DCI.

Detective Stuart turned the button and adjusted the channel frequencies knob on the top of his radio. It improved quality a little bit while they continued the conversation.

Meanwhile, PC Smith on the contrary, was not affected by the thunderstorm. In fact, he liked the sound of rain drops pelting on the roof of his police van. His wiper was functioning properly. The navigation system on PC Smith's dashboard however was playing up. He'd hit it twice earlier and it appeared to have worked. Concerned about Detective Stuart, he decided to radio him to see how he was doing.

"Are you OK, sir?" asked PC Smith, over the radio, while steering with one hand towards an upcoming bend in the road.

"I'm fine. But this old vehicle is getting on my nerves," he replied.

"I know you said the wiper wasn't working properly. Didn't you ask for it to be fixed?" asked PC Smith, as he straightened after the bend.

"I sent it to the garage recently, and the mechanic said he had repaired it, but it is still making that funny noise," replied Detective Stuart, glancing at a woman with her dog.

"We've had a lot of setbacks today," said PC Smith.

"Yes, but I'm determined to see this through. The culprit must be caught, and I will make sure of that," replied Detective Stuart.

Road signs indicated that they had another thirty minutes to drive.

"My wife thinks I'm too dedicated to the job, and not so much to them," thought Detective Stuart. "She doesn't understand that this is what pays the mortgage, and the bills."

Since leaving the station, Detective Stuart had not

eaten. The other officer heard his tummy rumble and they both looked at each other and smiled. Without saying a word, the officer handed him a chocolate. He took it and started unwrapping it. He bit off the top bit and the first taste of food brought him instant relief. He held it with both hands with his wrists resting on the steering wheel. Realising that it was risky driving like that, he handed it to the officer to complete the unwrapping. It lasted barely a minute; a clear demonstration of how hungry he was. He felt energised after having it. Coming towards a junction, he slowed to let a man on a bicycle cross. They then continued on their journey.

CHAPTER 44

It was time for *Our View*. Everyone gathered on the sofa ready and focused on the TV. Robert started his own personal documentary with his video camera.

"Did you setup the recorder?" asked Martin.

"Yes. Everything's ready," replied Jessica.

Cakes and biscuits were set out on the table between the TV and the sofa. A pack of beer was also there on ice next to the orange juice. Jessica had found some hidden behind a case of yoghurt in the refrigerator. Susan sat next to Martin with her head on his shoulder. Jessica sat on a single chair adjacent to her computer desk. Chris sat by himself on a two seater sofa, while Mark sat next to Susan. He was picking his teeth with a toothpick to get out chicken residue from dinner. Robert wanted to stand and walked around to get the best focal point for his filming. The clock struck 9 P.M. and the programme started. Jessica increased the volume on the TV, and adjusted the surround sound speakers. Everyone went quiet. Jessica's cat came in the room, while Jessica quickly ushered her out.

BBC's *Our View*:

"Welcome to Our View, I'm Sue Pickelton. Why was an innocent man sent to prison? Paul Reynolds was in loved with his girlfriend Sophia. The relationship had broken down, and he subsequently left her. She later accused him of rape; something which he has denied up until today, despite pleading guilty for the crime. Was this a miscarriage of justice, or a deliberate plan to incriminate him? Our View is mindful of the fact that Sophia has been murdered. We are aware this is very sensitive for both families and sought permission from them to be interviewed. Some of the scenes may be disturbing, and may affect family, relatives and friends. But Our View does not intend to cause any hurt to the families involved, and has received assurances from them to go-ahead with tonight's broadcast, as they both expressed their wish for the truth to come out.

We met up with Martin one of Paul's brothers to hear his views on the issue. This is what he had to say:

Martin: *'I know he didn't because I looked after him when he was a child, and I think I know what he is capable of. Moreover, he would never lie to me. I am a man of God, and I think I would be more likely to lose my temper than he would. My brother doesn't deserve this, nor did Sophia. We will fight with every penny we have to clear his name.'*

Martin believed in his brother so much that he was not surprised to receive evidence from police that seems to clear Paul's name. We asked the police why they handed it over to the family. This is what Detective Stuart had to say:

Detective Stuart: *'As a crime fighter, I believe in solving crimes. If a crime has been committed, and the wrong person sent to jail, not only will this affect the force's credibility but, it will promote the miscarriage of justice. It would be wrong for the police to withhold evidence that may assist in the freedom of others. I believe to withhold such evidence is illegal. We contacted our lawyers, and they advised us to hand it over.'*

Sue: *'But there were vital signs missed by the police before prosecuting Paul, was this followed up by the prosecuting team?'*

Stuart: *'The defence did not contest the evidence presented to them and instead Paul pleaded guilty. This cannot be the fault of the police.'*

Detective Stuart said he was not the main officer working on the case at the time. PC Smith was the arresting officer, and this was what he had to say:

PC Smith: *'The police have a job to do. We put the evidence to the suspect's lawyers, and they didn't challenge it in court—the police are not to be blamed for the incompetence of the accused's lawyers.'*

Our View believe the police stories corroborate with each other. Our View accepts that it was up to the defence to challenge the evidence. Detective Stuart distanced himself from the issue and failed as a senior officer to regulate his officers' conduct. We understand that PC Smith, when arresting Paul, went into the house uninvited. We believe Paul was not even given an arrest warrant.

Our View uncovered a cunning plot of deception by the deceased, Sophia Wait, and her co-conspirators. Evidence in her diary shows how strategic the plan was. Our View obtained information by the Freedom of Information Act that the police had no evidence to proceed with the case. The hand written notes gathered from the police suggest that there was disquiet between the officers over the arrest.

We understand that the alleged incident took place a long time ago. There was no forensic evidence to link the suspect to the crime. We put this to a leading criminologist, Professor Wilkie, and this is what he had to say:

Professor Wilkie: *'An allegation was made for a crime that took place a few years ago. There was no evidence to proceed with the case, therefore this should not have gone this far. The police also have a responsibility to the victims. They need to let them know how serious the crime is, and what support is available to them. They also need to know that a case with no evidence will be vigorously defended. On the contrary, this was not done by the defence lawyers. It was open for the police to assess the case. This would also mean to ascertain whether the victim was telling the truth after such a long time.'*

So we now know that the police didn't really have a case, but pursued it anyway. One of our leading criminal barristers told us that the defence had a very good case. There was no way a jury would convict, without tangible evidence.

[Mark held his face in his hands at this point, as the programme demonstrated how strong Paul's case was].

Armed with this evidence, is it possible it will be enough for the conviction to be quashed? We put this question to our leading barrister, and this is what he had to say:

Professor Jackson: *'Sure, this is in the public interest, and therefore the courts have an obligation under circumstances like this to look again at new evidence. It may have to go to the Supreme Court, as lower courts may struggle with overturning a precedent set by higher courts. The courts are also reluctant to overturn convictions where someone has pleaded guilty. There is an argument for this, I believe. They believe this could open the flood gate for anyone who pleads guilty or who may want to change their plea after being in prison. Serious evidence would have to come forward, and it takes years for the courts to hear these cases.'*

So our findings suggest that there is still a chance for Paul. It's now down to the family to source a good barrister and the courts.

The conspirators we understand in the plot to frame Paul were Marcus Shepard—recently found murdered—and a well-known solicitor, John Sunderland. Unconfirmed information received from the family, suggests that they were involved. We tracked down Mr. Sunderland, who agreed to speak to us, and put this to him:

Sue: *'We heard that you had something to do with the implication of Paul Reynolds, it that correct?'*

Mr. Sunderland: *'Yes. I know Sophia's friend Marcus, who threatened to kill me if I didn't go ahead with the plan.'*

["That is a lie," said Chris while twisting and turning on the sofa feeling uncomfortable].

'I realised that the crown had no evidence to convict Paul, something which I initially communicated to him.'

Sue: *'So what changed you mind? Did it not occur to you that an innocent man would go to prison?'*

Mr. Sunderland: *'Yes, that is why I'm doing this programme now. I cannot live with myself. I'm planning on telling her mother, and I hope she will find it in her heart to forgive us.'*

Sue: *'This is a serious matter. You could find yourself in some serious trouble with the Solicitors Regulation Authority, or The Law Society (SRA). What was you role in the matter?'*

Mr. Sunderland: *'I was told to encourage him to plead guilty. The plan was to paint the situation in a bad light and there was no way out but to plead guilty for a lesser sentence. I now regret that move, and I hope the family will find it in their hearts to forgive me.*

Sue: *'If Sophia was not murdered, would you have come clean?'*

Mr. Sunderland: *'I think I would. I wasn't happy with their suggestion at first, but because Marcus and Sophia were known to me, and I thought Marcus was a friend, until he threatened me, I thought I was helping Sophia, as their stories were touching, and I felt for her.'*

We now know from John's testimony that he was forced to go ahead with the plans. The question is, is he telling the truth?

["No he is not—he was in this from the beginning. They all cooked it up and deliberately went after my uncle," said an angry Mark flipping through his solicitor's rules book.]

We decided to put our findings to an ex solicitor's regulator, Mark

Samuels.

Sue: *'Like the medical council, can a solicitor be struck off the register?'*

Mr. Samuels: *'The family could make a complaint to the SRA, who then would carry out their investigation, and come up with a remedy. But I believe the family, or the SRA could take it further to the Solicitors Disciplinary Tribunal. They have the power to fine, or suspend the persons involved, or both. A solicitor could be suspended for five years for professional misconduct.'*

Sue: *'He said he was threatened to be part of the deception; could that be an excuse to let him off?'*

Mr. Samuels: *'I don't think so. This is not a good reason to professionally misbehave. If you were under duress to do something, unless his threat was imminent, he could have gone to the police. I believe the tribunal would not buy that story. He is a professional, and he should have acted in his professional capacity.'*

We now know from Sophia's diary that her account flatly contradicts John's story. Page twelve of her diary reads: 'John was approached late, but he was happy to go ahead with the plans, and he knew what he was getting into. In fact, he came up with the idea to plead guilty. He was always contradicting Marcus, and never afraid to confront him.'

Her account suggests that he was totally in on the plan, and his account about a threat, appears to be a lie.

["We told you it was a lie," said Mark.]

So what is the truth? If we go by the diary, then John is not telling the truth. We cannot interview her, or Marcus, because they are both dead. Besides, why would Sophia cook all of this up, when her diary proved consistently to document of unrelated engagements that were proved to be true? Our View found Sophia's account to be credible. Her diary continued to state that her mum was not fully aware of her plans. She kept all of this from her mum because she did not want her to be caught up in all of this, or to be angry with her. She wrote about her fears of people following her. She thought someone might get her at some point. Page fourteen of her diary states that Marcus wanted her to be his girlfriend: 'He would do anything for me, but I don't love him. He knew that Paul would trust him to find a solicitor, so he was the perfect candidate for the job. He means well, but he goes overboard sometimes. He can be over protective.'

We put this to his flatmate to find out a little more about Marcus. I must say at this point that whatever we report would not jeopardise the police investigation. His flatmate confirmed all that was said in her diary. The flatmate, who we cannot name for legal reasons, said Marcus was obsessed with her. He also confirmed that he was overprotective. So from the facts we have, it appears that he was the ring leader in this plan.

Evidence obtained in the diary, suggests that she regretted what she had done, albeit in despair. At one point she contemplated visiting him in prison. Page fifteen states: 'I feel sorry for him. I would love to visit him, but I cannot bring myself to do so. I hope he will find it in his heart to forgive me. I think he deserves someone better than me.'

["You got that right; Jade," said Chris.]

It is now clear to us from the evidence we have obtained that Paul

305

Reynolds was not guilty of rape. He was persuaded to plead guilty for a crime he did not commit. Marcus appeared to be the ring leader and John lied to save his skin. There is a chance for an innocent man to walk free. The question is, will the courts listen? Next week we will be examining who could have wanted Sophia dead.

The music from the program was playing as everyone sighed in relief at the chance their brother could be freed. Mark knew what he had to do and rushed over to the computer to research on the net. Chris went outside for some fresh air, while Martin looked a bit uneasy for the first time, as he paced up and down the passage. Susan sat still looking at the TV as she read the credits. Robert's face was anxious but Mark thought it was probably due to the filming. But he asked his dad what was wrong and the anxious look disappeared shortly afterwards.

"Can you stop pacing up and down please?" asked Susan.

He turned around and looked at her, as if he was asking what was her problem. No one could read Robert's mind as he continued to film everyone and what they were doing. He focused his lens on Martin pacing up and down, and almost tripped over the hoover that had been left in a corner of the kitchen. He then went outside and pointed his camera at Chris who had another glass of wine in his hand. When he saw Robert he pretended to examine his car.

"Get that thing out of my face," said Chris.

Robert spun the camera on to the road as he walked down the hill towards the gate. The gate was still open so he locked it with one hand while still holding the camera.

He then walked back to the house speaking into his camera.

Susan spotted Robert coming, and went upstairs to check on Jade. She was embarrassed about being filmed so she thought the perfect excuse was to go upstairs. She was smiling as she made her way up the stairs, thinking that he was going to follow her.

CHAPTER 45

The family gathered again to discuss the programme. They were winding Martin up by laughing at his make up on camera.

"No on a serious note, he looked nervous," said Jessica.

"Leave my husband alone," said Susan, hugging him and smiling at the same time to wind him up more.

Jade came down to make herself a cup of tea in her nightgown. "Tea anyone?"

"Yes with one sugar," replied Chris sitting still.

"No sugar for me," said Robert still filming. He was starting to annoy everyone, especially his son.

"What about you Mark?" asked Jade.

Mark's head was still buried into the computer and did not hear a word anyone said.

"MARK?" shouted Jade again. "Do you want tea?"

"Yes," he grumbled.

Jade went into the kitchen. The kettle was broken, so she had to boil the water in a pan. It took a long time so Chris decided to check on her. He spotted the water on the stove. He walked back out of the kitchen and shouted, "TAKE SOME BISCUITS WITH YOU AS WELL PLEASE, JADE."

"What is our next move?" asked Jessica, while looking at Martin, the oldest brother.

Martin looked back at her and said, "Ask the lawyer."

Mark heard them and smiled. "I will be with you in a sec," he said as he wrapped up his research. "We will obtain the tape from the programme and use it in the appeal. We have everything ready; it's now down to me to submit the form to the trial court."

"I have something to tell you," said Robert, while he struggled to find the button to switch off the camera. He managed to switch it off a few seconds later, and was about to say something, when Mark looked at him.

"Dad, you've had too much to drink, I think you need to relax," he said as he tried to protect his father. Although he didn't know what his dad was going to say, his suspicion were enough that he didn't want to hear what he had to say. Mark thought that his dad had something to do with Sophia's death.

It was 10 P.M. and the news headlines contained a piece about the *Our View* programme. The volume on the TV was very low, but Chris spotted the broadcast and increased the sound so everyone could hear. Everyone gathered again, while Jade stood before them with four cups of tea on a tray. They saw through her, until Chris spotted her and ask her to leave it on the table. She left it on the table for everyone to take what they ordered, and went straight back into the kitchen. Jade came back and stumbled on the same hoover that had tripped Robert earlier. Chris rushed to her aid. He grabbed her arm with his left hand, and the tray with the right. Chris then thought how serious it would be if she had fallen given that she was pregnant. He helped her to the table. On the tray were a litre of orange juice and two packs of biscuits. She had also brought out some peanuts for Martin. When he spotted them he grabbed the packet before Robert could. They both loved peanuts.

"Can I have some please? You know I love peanuts," said Robert.

"No, you can't," joked Martin, as he tried desperately to hide them by twisting his arm behind his back.

"OK. How about we swap? I give you a spin of my car, and you give me some," suggested Robert, who knew that Martin had always wanted a spin of his posh car.

"Clever idea, but this is ridiculous to play games over peanuts," thought Susan as she watched the brothers acting like kids.

"OK, deal," said Martin as they shook hands. He handed over the peanuts to Robert to share, who then handed over his keys.

Jessica and Susan watched what was going on between the two and whispered to each other. They smiled as they had bet with each other what would make Martin give up his precious peanuts. Susan won the bet as she knew her husband better than anyone else.

Jade was walking like a duck again with her big tummy and became the centre of the conversation. Jessica started to wind up the comments, but Chris wasn't having any of it. He interjected by shielding her and then went down on his knees listening to her baby.

"Leave her alone," he said and jumped back when the baby kicked.

"Good," everyone said laughing.

"Can't you see she is pregnant with Paul's son. Let it go," said Jessica.

"Yes, let it go," said Robert for the first time, chewing his peanuts.

They laughed at him, thinking that the peanuts had gone to his head to the point he had traded his car for some. He wanted a boy too, so they were surprised by the comment. He filled his palm with more peanuts from the pack, while Martin snatched the rest from him.

"I'm going outside. Are you coming Jade?" asked Chris.

"Yes."

"What is up with Chris?" asked Jessica as she pondered about this connection with Jade.

"They are jealous ," thought Chris, as he made his way to the door.

"I don't know," said Martin.

Outside it was cool and bright. Jade didn't need a jacket, as her jumper was warm enough. She could hear the music from the party next door and began to sway in time with it.

"Not my type of tune," Chris thought, but rocked a little to say he was enjoying it too. "I haven't had a chance to catch up with you about that promise I made to you. It is still on. I will make sure you get all of what you want for both you and the baby."

"OK. But where would you get money from? I don't

see you working," she asked.

They heard loud voices from inside the house and when they looked through the window it was obvious a heated debate was going on in there. Jade turned back towards Chris waiting for his answer.

"I work at nights, sometimes; agency work and special projects and contracts. I get big money for my jobs," he replied, clinching his fist with courage as he remembered how he had almost killed her. "I made a promise, and I will keep it."

He walked towards his Jeep, and she followed him there. Chris inspected his tyres, and checked around the vehicle for any scratches. He examined a scratch on the left hand side, wondering if he had bought it like that. Chris' phone rang as he moved towards one side of the vehicle. It was his daughter. He did not know what Jade knew about him and his family, so he moved away even further.

Jade could not hear what he said but she saw his face and realised whoever was on the phone meant a lot to him. She pressed the door button on his key fob which opened the Jeep. She looked around his vehicle and spotted a picture of him and Paul when they were young. Snooping around Jade checked his car glove box looking for CDs to play, while she waited for him. The music next door was not enough it seemed. She spotted a police car pass the house with lights flashing. She looked through the right hand window and saw Chris was still on the phone. He was about to finish the conversation and she heard him saying goodbye in a soft voice.

"Goodbye, love you. Remember what I told you, you won't be seeing me for a long time."

Chris walked towards the vehicle while Jade quickly closed his glove box, as she didn't want him to know she was prying.

"As I was saying, I'm a working man. I work harder than you lot put together but my job is risky and dangerous."

From what he said Jade thought he worked at nights on a construction site. She knew that they paid well, and that the job was hard and risky.

"Are you happy that Paul will be coming home soon?" he asked while he bent over tying his shoes. He got up slowly hanging on to the opened Jeep door on the driver's side. "I have worked hard on this to make it happen. Without me, none of this would have been possible."

"What do you mean?" she asked.

"I'm not telling you yet, it's a surprise. You will know when Paul is out."

"Why are you not telling me now?" asked Jade, as she spotted Martin looking out the front door, wondering where they were. It didn't appear that he had seen them, as Chris' Jeep was parked next to a big tree. "Martin just came to the door and checked for us," said Jade with one feet outside the Jeep.

"I know, they must be wondering how, umm, me and you are so close. Umm, errh, I just think Paul made a good decision. I also think you are a nice person," said Chris, as he complimented her. "You fit well into the family, umm and you are very humble. Let's go back inside."

They walked back towards the house, while Chris turned and pointed his remote key fob at the Jeep and locked the doors. They went back in the house where everyone was happily chatting and making fun of each other. The argument was clearly over now.

Meanwhile, Detective Stuart and PC Smith had lost their way.

"I told you we've passed the house," said PC Smith. "I have been here before, so I should know."

"So where are we now?" asked Detective Stuart looking at his map.

"We are about half a mile away from the house," said PC Smith.

"Really? Let's go back then."

PC Smith spun the van around so quickly it kicked up dust, limiting the visibility for Detective Stuart, who was following him. They put on their sirens and sped off in the direction they had just come from. They were going so fast a man on a motorcycle swerved and ran off the road to get out of the way. PC Smith narrowly missed his rear wheel.

Everyone apart from Mark, who was upstairs, was celebrating the potential breakthrough for Paul. No-one knew or thought that anything would interrupt their celebrations. Loud music continued to be heard from the party next door. Jessica had been invited to the party by the Fowlers' family who were celebrating the birthday of their second son. Jessica had known him since he was two, and used to take him out to the parks, and the town centre. Although she hadn't wanted to miss his sixteenth birthday, she preferred to celebrate with her family. Chris put on Jessica's stereo system and Robert, an ex DJ, helped him sift through the selection. Jessica came over and asked for some of her favourite soul tunes which she pointed out on the top of the CD rack. Mark came downstairs again but he wasn't celebrating. He was happy, but had things on his mind. He knew he had work to do, and preferred to celebrate when it was done.

The sound of police sirens interrupted their revelry. Chris looked uneasy. Chris knew he was clean and had no weapons on him—he had left them at his usual hiding place as he never took them with him unless he believed he could encounter trouble. Jade remembered the police flying past earlier when she had been outside with Chris. She looked outside and saw the same police vehicles stop next door and knock.

Chris asked for the keys for the back door. He then went to the front room window to see what was going on outside and saw the police heading towards them. Chris alerted everyone in a whisper and Martin advised everyone to stay calm. Robert got into a panic, but was reassured by the sight of his son Mark, who took a writing pad off Jessica's desk and a pen from the shelf. They heard the door knock and Mark opened it.

"Good evening," said Detective Stuart with PC Smith and the other officers standing behind him.

"Good evening, how can I help, sir?" replied Mark.

Detective Stuart recognised him straight away, and thought he would not be a challenge on this occasion. He didn't hear him say "sir" as the neighbour's music was too loud. Detective Stuart asked if he could come in. Mark invited Detective Stuart and his officers joined the family in the living room.

"I need to speak to...drowned out by the music next door, Reynolds, please?" Stuart said looking around the room.

"Yes," said Mark, and called him over.

The officer looked at him while the other officers moved behind their suspect.

"You are under arrest for the murder of Sophia Wait," Detective Stuart said. "You do not have to say anything, but it may harm your defence if you do not mention when questioned something which you later rely on in court. Anything you do say may be given in evidence." Detective Stuart had to shout to be heard above the music. No one clearly heard what he was saying except Mark and the brother he was arresting.

The officers handcuffed him, and led him away in the police van. The family remained in place looking shocked and distraught...

TO BE CONTINUED.

Deadly Contemplation

Made in the USA
Charleston, SC
31 August 2014